S0-AXR-291

Drinking with the Enemy

"That's strange," Buck said. "I'm feeling peculiar myself." He took another sip of coffee. "Even my mouth is tingling."

"Maybe you are coming down with something," Ezriah said. He scratched his chest and slid his hand under his shirt, still scratching.

"I feel fine," Fox said. He glanced at Buck, and at the cup in Buck's hand, and then at Granger, and at the cup on the table in front of him, and said, "Son of a bitch."

"Too bad you didn't drink some, too," Ezriah said. He brought his hand out from under his shirt. In it was a Cloveland House pocket revolver in .41 caliber. He cocked it and pointed it at Fox.

"What is this?" Buck said in alarm.

Ezriah shot Fox. The slug cored Fox's forehead and snapped his head back. He tried to speak, but all that came out was a grunt. A red drop trickled down his brow as he slowly folded and his body slid off the chair to the floor. He twitched a few times and was still.

Both Buck and Granger went to reach for their rifles. Both only raised their hands a few inches and then looked at their arms in dismay and disbelief.

"What the hell is happening?" Buck said. "I can't hardly move."

"Me either."

Ezriah Harkey held the smoking pistol level. "It's the poison. Pretty soon you won't be able to move at all."

Buck and Granger said together, "Poison?"

"Woman's doing," Ezriah said, with a jerk of his thumb at his wife. "She's good with potions and herbs and"—he grinned a wicked grin—"poisons."

BLOOD FEUD

DAVID ROBBINS

A SIGNET BOOK

SIGNET
Published by New American Library, a division of
Penguin Group (USA) Inc., 375 Hudson Street,
New York, New York 10014, USA
Penguin Group (Canada), 90 Eglinton Avenue East, Suite 700, Toronto,
Ontario M4P 2Y3, Canada (a division of Pearson Penguin Canada Inc.)
Penguin Books Ltd., 80 Strand, London WC2R 0RL, England
Penguin Ireland, 25 St. Stephen's Green, Dublin 2,
Ireland (a division of Penguin Books Ltd.)
Penguin Group (Australia), 250 Camberwell Road, Camberwell, Victoria 3124,
Australia (a division of Pearson Australia Group Pty. Ltd.)
Penguin Books India Pvt. Ltd., 11 Community Centre, Panchsheel Park,
New Delhi - 110 017, India
Penguin Group (NZ), 67 Apollo Drive, Rosedale, North Shore 0632,
New Zealand (a division of Pearson New Zealand Ltd.)
Penguin Books (South Africa) (Pty.) Ltd., 24 Sturdee Avenue,
Rosebank, Johannesburg 2196, South Africa

Penguin Books Ltd., Registered Offices:
80 Strand, London WC2R 0RL, England

First published by Signet, an imprint of New American Library,
a division of Penguin Group (USA) Inc.

First Printing, October 2010
10   9   8   7   6   5   4   3   2   1

Copyright © David Robbins, 2010
All rights reserved

Ⓟ REGISTERED TRADEMARK—MARCA REGISTRADA

Printed in the United States of America

Without limiting the rights under copyright reserved above, no part of this pub-
lication may be reproduced, stored in or introduced into a retrieval system, or
transmitted, in any form, or by any means (electronic, mechanical, photocopying,
recording, or otherwise), without the prior written permission of both the copyright owner and the above publisher of this book.

PUBLISHER'S NOTE
This is a work of fiction. Names, characters, places, and incidents either are the
product of the author's imagination or are used fictitiously, and any resemblance
to actual persons, living or dead, business establishments, events, or locales is
entirely coincidental.
    The publisher does not have any control over and does not assume any re-
sponsibility for author or third-party Web sites or their content.

If you purchased this book without a cover you should be aware that this book is
stolen property. It was reported as "unsold and destroyed" to the publisher and
neither the author nor the publisher has received any payment for this "stripped
book."

The scanning, uploading, and distribution of this book via the Internet or via any
other means without the permission of the publisher is illegal and punishable by
law. Please purchase only authorized electronic editions, and do not participate
in or encourage electronic piracy of copyrighted materials. Your support of the
author's rights is appreciated.

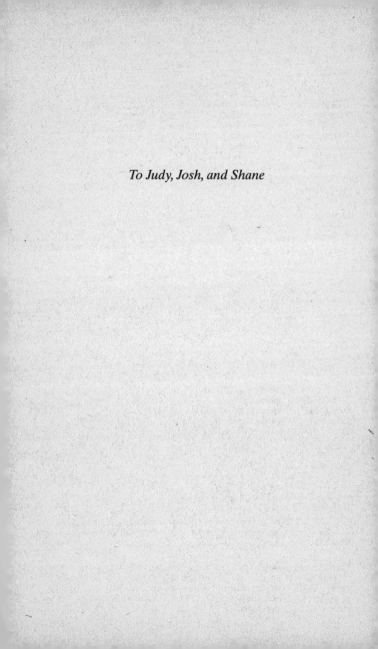

To Judy, Josh, and Shane

1

---·---

Summer green clothed the rugged slopes and deep valleys of the Ozark Mountains. Bears and cougars prowled, coyotes yipped and coons ran, and a wealth of birds warbled and sang. It was a beautiful land, and it was a beautiful girl who came to Harkey Hollow.

The girl was all of eighteen. Tawny of skin, with corn silk hair, she moved with agile grace. She wore a plain homespun dress, green like the world around her, and nothing else. Her feet were bare. They had never known shoes.

Scarlet Shannon was her name, and she was where she should not have been.

Scarlet knew better than to come to Harkey Hollow, but she was fond of blackberries and they grew thick and delicious. She was wary but sure of herself, ready to flee should there be cause. She pricked her ears, and her eyes darted like a doe's on the lookout for wolves.

The vegetation thinned. Scarlet hunkered behind a sugarberry tree and surveyed the hollow. The blackberry bushes were as thick as ever and hung heavy with plump berries.

Save for a few bees and a swallowtail butterfly, nothing moved. The only sound was the tweet of a wren.

Scarlet moved into the open. She hefted the old wooden pail she'd brought and scooted to the nearest blackberry bush. She plucked a ripe berry and plopped it into her mouth. Closing her eyes, she chewed slowly, swallowed, and grinned. She commenced to pick berries as fast as her fingers could fly. Every so often she glanced about her.

The sun's golden glow splashed the hollow and the surrounding woodland, lending the illusion that all was well.

Scarlet went on picking. For every two she put in the pail, she helped herself to another. She plucked and ate, plucked and ate, moving deeper into the patch as she went. Once she looked up and saw how far she had gone and took a step as if to turn back but shook her head and continued plucking.

The cicadas stopped buzzing.

Somewhere a squirrel chattered as though it was angry and a blue jay screeched noisily.

Scarlet's pail was half full. She came to a bush with some of the biggest blackberries yet and put two in her mouth. She bent to get at those near the bottom and heard the blue jay do more screeching. Belatedly, she realized what it might mean. Her fingers froze midway to a berry.

Just then the forest became completely still.

Scarcely breathing, Scarlet rose high enough to peer over the bushes. She scanned the woods. A goldfinch and its mate took wing and she studied the shadows where the birds had come out of the trees. Her whole body went rigid with dread.

Some of the shadows were moving.

Crouching, Scarlet moved deeper into the patch. She held the pail with one hand and the handle with the other so the handle wouldn't squeak. Rounding a bend, she flattened on her belly as close to the bushes as she could without being pricked by thorns. She folded her arms and rested her chin on her wrist. Time crawled. So did a large black ant, practically under her chin. The temperature climbed. She closed her eyes and fought the tension inside her. The crunch of a twig brought her out of herself.

Harsh laughter pealed and a voice like the rasp of a file on a corn cutter hollered, "You might as well show yourself, girl. We know you're in there."

Scarlet bit her lower lip and felt the blood drain from her face.

"You hear me? We were coming for berries and seen you."

Quietly, Scarlet rose but stayed stooped over. By small fractions she unfurled to where she could see over the bushes.

"We got you surrounded. You ain't going to get past us nohow. Make it easy. Come on out. You don't, you're liable to make us mad."

Scarlet counted seven heads. She dipped low and moved along the path, seeking another way out. But it appeared to be the *only* path, and meandered helter-skelter. Worse, it was taking her deeper into the hollow.

"We know you ain't a Harkey," the voice went on. "That means you're one of *them*. You got grit coming here, girl, but it was awful stupid. What, there ain't no blackberries on your side of the ridge?"

Some of the others thought that was funny. Scarlet

almost went past a gap in the bushes. An animal trail, not as wide as she was, but it was better than being cornered. Flattening and holding the pail in front of her, she crawled. Brambles snatched at her dress and scratched her arms.

"I'm patient, missy, but I won't wait forever," the voice warned. "Either you show yourself or we're coming in. And if you make us do it the hard way, there will be hell to pay. We'll take it out of your hide."

Scarlet wasn't overly scared yet. She had confidence in her ability to outrun them if she could find her way out without being spotted. She wriggled along, wincing when she was scratched, until she came to the thicket's edge. A shadow moved across the opening. One of her enemies was out there, pacing back and forth.

"Come on, girl," the voice urged. "Don't be this way. You don't stand a snowball's chance in hell of getting away. Come out and I'll treat you nice. You have my word."

As careful as she could, Scarlet stuck her head out. A stocky block of muscle with no shirt and no shoes had his back to her. She drew her head back before he turned.

"Which one are you?" the voice called. "I don't know all of you by sight. Those I've laid eyes on over to Wareagle won't hardly ever give me the time of day."

Scarlet had a sharp retort on the tip of her tongue, but she swallowed it. She slid the pail to the opening and deliberately moved the handle so it squeaked. Dirty feet appeared and a freckled face lowered and fingers as thick as railroad spikes reached down.

"Rabon! I done found her pail!"

Scarlet exploded into motion. She was out of the gap

like a fox-chased cottontail out of a hollow log. Some girls would have scratched or pushed, but she punched him flush on the jaw. He fell onto his backside and grunted, more surprised than anything. It gained her the seconds she needed to wheel and flee into the forest. Her pail and the blackberries were forgotten. She had something more important to think of.

Scarlet flew. Shouts and the thud of pounding feet told her they were after her. She glanced back and her confidence climbed. She had a good lead. There wasn't a boy anywhere who could catch her when she had a good lead. She flew, and she laughed. Her legs were tireless. She had taken part in footraces since she was knee-high to a calf, and could go forever. She needed that stamina now to make it over the crest before they caught her. Once she was on the other side, she was in Shannon territory. They didn't dare follow.

Scarlet's dress whipped about her. Her long legs flashed. The soles of her feet slapped the ground in rhythmic beat. She glanced back again and laughed louder. She had increased her lead by a good ten yards. She vaulted a log and avoided a boulder and came to a leaf-covered slope where the footing was treacherous. She slipped but recovered and churned higher. Something moved in the leaves, a snake, and she bounded aside.

A rock missed her ear by a whisker.

Startled, Scarlet ran faster. She hadn't thought they would resort to rocks. But then they *were* Harkeys, and as her pa liked to say, the Harkeys were worthless no-accounts. She concentrated on running and only running. A flat clear stretch gave her a chance to put more distance between them. She was almost to a stand of maples when pain flared in her left leg and it buckled under her and the next thing she knew she was tumbling cattywampus. She hit so hard, the breath was knocked from her lungs. She lay dazed, her ears ringing, her vision blurred, struggling against an inner tide of darkness.

Voices and a poke in the ribs brought her back to the here and now.

Scarlet blinked and looked up and felt the way a raccoon must feel when it was ringed by dogs. The seven of them were puffing and sweaty from the chase. Only four wore shirts, and the shirts they wore were little more than rags with buttons. The biggest had a shock of black hair that fell in bangs over bushy brows. His dark eyes regarded her as her little brother used to regard the hard candy in the general store at Wareagle.

"Well, well, well. Ain't you a looker?"

Scarlet realized her dress had hiked halfway to her hips. She sat up and smoothed it and stood straight and tall. Her left leg still hurt and when she put pressure on it, she winced. "Who threw that rock?"

"The one that hit you?" the big one said, and chortled. "That would be me. Good aim, huh?"

Scarlet hit him. She punched him on the jaw as she had punched the other one, but where the other one went down, the big one didn't. His head rocked and he put his hand to his chin and did the last thing she expected; he laughed.

"Not bad. I've been hit harder but only by them that was larger than me, which ain't many."

"What do you want? Who are you, anyhow?"

"As if you don't know. We're Harkeys, all of us. I'm Rabon Harkey and these here are my brothers and my cousins."

"You're a Shannon, ain't you?" one of the others said. "You look like a Shannon with that yellow hair and those blue eyes."

"She's a Shannon," Rabon said. "She can deny it but we know better and now she's in a fix."

Scarlet put her hands on her hips. "I was picking berries. You had no right to come after me like you done."

"You're on Harkey land," Rabon said. "That's all the right we need." He took a step and poked her, hard, in the shoulder. "What, you reckoned that since you're a girl we'd go easy on you? That you could sneak in and steal our berries and if we caught you we'd let you go?"

"They're not *your* blackberries," Scarlet said. "They're there for anyone who is of a mind to pick them."

Rabon shook his head. "Not if they're on Harkey land. Harkey blackberries are for Harkeys and no one else." He crossed his thick arms across his broad chest. "The question is, what do we do with you?"

"You let me go or there will be trouble," Scarlet warned. "My pa won't take kindly to you mistreating me. I won't tell him if you let me be. I give you my word."

"Is that supposed to scare us?" Rabon snorted, and gestured at the one Scarlet had punched down at the thicket. "Are you scared, Woot?"

"I surely am not, brother," Woot replied. "It'll be a cold day in hell before I'm afeared of a Shannon."

"What do we do with her?" the smallest and the youngest of them asked.

"We can't beat her like we would a feller."

"Why not, Jimbo?" Woot said. "It makes no difference to me. If they're a Shannon they have it coming."

Jimbo turned to Rabon. "It wouldn't be right hitting a female. My ma wouldn't like it. Your ma, neither."

"You ever cut free of those apron strings, you might be a man, cousin," Rabon said. "But you're right. Pa is always saying as how we need to be nice to ladies. So we'll be nice to this one if she's nice to us."

New fear clutched at Scarlet. "How do you mean?"

Rabon stood so they were almost touching. His breath smelled of onions and his teeth were yellow. "You're more than old enough. I bet you have already, plenty of times. A few more won't hardly matter."

"No," Scarlet said.

"It ain't like I'm giving you a choice. It'll be me first and as many of the rest as want, and you can be on your way."

"No," Scarlet said, more forcefully. She went to step around him, but he pushed her back.

"I'm not kidding, neither," Rabon said. "Here or in the shade yonder. I'll let you decide that much."

Scarlet looked at each of them. She saw no pity, no mercy, only resentment of who she was or, rather, *what* she was. The only exception was the young one.

Jimbo; he was troubled. She appealed to him, saying, "Your ma wouldn't like this. It's not decent."

"No, it's not," Jimbo agreed, and turned to Rabon. "All she wanted was some blackberries. You do this, everyone in the hills will be against us."

"She won't ever tell," Rabon said, and took hold of Scarlet's arm. "Will you, girl?"

Before she could respond Jimbo grabbed Rabon's wrist and pulled his big hand off her. "No. I won't stand for it. You hear? She's free to go."

Rabon's features twisted in amazement and then fury. Yet he smiled and patted his much smaller cousin on the head and said, "We'll talk about this later. Right now, the only reason I don't stomp you into the dirt is because you're kin. Remember that when you wake up."

"But I am awake," Jimbo said.

"You were," Rabon said, and punched him. Rabon's knuckles were the size of walnuts, his fist as large as a sledge. His blow lifted Jimbo onto his heels and sent him sprawling in a heap. Rabon rubbed his fist and regarded the rest. "Anyone else object?"

No one did.

Scarlet rammed her shoulder against Woot and drove him back. She was through the ring in a single leap and had taken several more strides when iron fingers locked in her hair and she was jerked off balance and slammed to the ground.

She fought but they were too many and too strong. Her arms and legs were pinned and spread and Rabon reared above her.

"Truth is, girl, I don't care if your kin find out. I'm tired of the stupid truce. My pa and his stories, he had a lot more fun than me. Now I aim to have me some, thanks to you."

And Rabon laughed.

2

Mulberry Creek was the heart of Shannon country. The valley it drained was the longest and widest and, as the Shannons liked to boast, the most fertile in the Ozarks. A third of their clan lived along its banks and farmed the adjacent land. One of the largest of those farms, the fields as well maintained as a Quaker's, was that of Buck Shannon.

Buck was the second oldest of four brothers. Three were farmers like him. The fourth worked in the mine at Haversaw and only got home at Thanksgiving and Christmas and on special occasions, such as weddings or deaths or when someone broke in a new still.

Buck's farm was a hoot and a holler west of Wareagle. To the east of the settlement, over a high ridge, was Harkey country.

On this particular morning Buck had hitched the team to the wagon and was on his way into Wareagle to buy a bonnet for his wife. He thought it would make a dandy birthday gift. He whistled the tune to "Dixie" as the wagon clattered along. The two mules had made the trip so many times, he didn't have to do anything but sit back and enjoy the ride.

In the wagon bed were his two youngest. Chace and Cassie were twins, Chace the older by seven minutes. Now sixteen, both had the Shannon yellow hair and the Shannon blue eyes. Both had the Shannon high foreheads and were uncommonly good-looking. Chace wore a shirt his mother had made—the only shirt he owned—and britches but no shoes or belt. Cassie wore a dress the same color as her eyes. He was leaning against the right side, she the left. A breeze stirred her fine long hair.

"It sure is nice of you, Pa, going to all this trouble for Ma's sake," Cassie remarked.

Buck took his corncob pipe from one pocket and his tobacco pouch from another. "She's stuck by me all these years—it's the least a man can do." He shifted and winked at his son. "Take heed, boy. Your turn at being hitched will come one day."

"No, Pa," Chace said. "I ain't ever getting married."

"So you think now," Buck said. "But you'll change your mind. A gal will come along and turn your head to where you can't breathe without her, and you'll be doomed."

Cassie giggled. "Oh, Pa. You better not let Ma hear you say something like that." She nudged her brother with her toe. "And you. What makes you think you're never taking a wife?"

Chace shrugged. "I know, is all."

"Can't none of us predict the future."

"That's a fact, boy," Buck agreed. "Human nature is human nature. We all like to think we're different, but we're not. You'll get married and you'll have kids and

one day you'll be riding in a wagon just like this one."
He tapped the bowl of his pipe against the seat. "There's
nothing new under the sun."

Chace raised his blue eyes to the sky. His weren't the
same shade as his sister's; they were paler, so light a blue
that some folks mistook them for gray.

They had a quality about them that was beyond his
years, as if they were the eyes of someone much older. "I
know what I know."

Buck tamped tobacco into the bowl. He twisted
around and placed his arm across the back of the seat.
"You sure are a stubborn cuss. Sort of like me when I
was your age."

"I'm nothing like you, Pa," Chace said matter-of-
factly.

Buck and Cassie swapped glances and Cassie said,
"There you go again. Always staying strange things like
that. You're a lot like Pa. You have his hair, his chin."

"Inside I'm not."

"What makes you say that?"

"Because I'm not. He's happy being a farmer. I could
never be. He's happy living in a cabin. I could never be.
He's happy being *here.*" And Chace motioned to include
the whole of the long valley. "I could never be."

"You worry me, boy, when you talk like that," Buck
said. "There's nothing wrong with farming."

"Except it's boring."

Buck had taken out a match and wagged it at Chace.
"Here, now. I won't have my livelihood insulted. Farming is good, decent work."

"For those as are interested in good and decent."

"Are you saying you're not?"

Chace shrugged.

"Answer me." Buck had been worried for some time now about his one and only son. The boy kept too much to himself. Worse, Chace would never open up about his feelings or what he was thinking unless he was pressed and even then it was like pulling teeth.

Chace turned his pale blue eyes on his father. "I'm saying your notion of good might not be my notion of good."

"That makes no kind of sense," Buck said. "Good is good. Bad is bad. Either you live a good life or you live a bad life."

"What else can there be?" Cassie asked, watching her brother closely.

"Explain it to me."

"There's what people say is good and what people say is bad. But just because people say it don't make it so. Maybe my notion of good ain't the same as theirs. Maybe my idea of good is their notion of bad."

"God Almighty," Buck blurted. "How do thoughts like that get in your head? Didn't you pay attention in church all these years? Haven't you ever listened to the preacher?"

"I paid a heap of attention," Chace said. "It's why I know what I know and I'm not shy about saying so."

Buck shook his head and turned around. He didn't know what to say about talk like that. He truly didn't. Sometimes he wondered if maybe his boy was addle-pated. At other times he wondered if maybe his boy was smarter than the rest of them combined. Frowning in annoyance, he struck the match and stuck the lit end in the bowl. He heard whispering behind him but paid it no mind. The twins had been whispering since they were old enough to talk.

Cassie leaned toward Chace. "You better be careful saying things like that. If Ma found out she'd throw a fit."

"It's her fit," Chace said.

"There you go again." Cassie glanced at their pa's broad back. "You ever expect we'll burn in hell? For the bad things, I mean."

"Bad according to who? The parson?"

"Bad according to me."

Chace pressed the sole of his right foot against the sole of her left. "You think like that, you'll end up just like Ma."

"I can't help it."

"Yes, you can." Chace pressed the sole of his left foot to the sole of her right.

He wriggled his toes and she wriggled hers, and she grinned. "We don't have to follow in their footsteps. We can make our own life."

"I wish I had your confidence," Cassie admitted.

"You're my twin," Chace said.

"Not in that."

"You are where it counts, in here." Chace touched his chest over his heart.

"Two as one. For as long as we live."

Cassie tilted her head back and closed her eyes. "You make it sound so easy. But it's not."

"It's up to us and no one else," Chace said. "We don't have to live like them. We don't have to live like anyone."

"I'm not as free-minded as you. I'm sorry. I wish I was but there it is. We're twins but we don't always think alike. There are times when I think no one thinks like you do."

"You're getting too serious," Chace said, and wriggled his toes some more. "No, we're not always alike." Reaching across, he tenderly touched her chin. "Anyone can tell how different we are. Your nose is longer." He laughed and scrunched up his own nose.

Cassie loved his laugh. It lit up his face and his eyes and reached her, deep inside. She laughed, too, and cast a quick glance at her father, hoping he didn't suspect what they were talking about. It would upset him terribly. He was a good man, even if his idea of good wasn't the same as Chace's.

The wagon clattered on and presently the cluster of buildings that constituted Wareagle sprouted where the flatland lay at the base of the high ridge. The settlement was smack in the middle between Shannon country and Harkey country and considered neutral ground. Anyone from either clan could go there anytime. Old resentments were set aside. Old hatreds were smothered. On the surface, at least.

Wareagle wasn't much, by Yankee standards. It had a general store and a saloon and tavern, both, and a stable and a blacksmith and a feed and grain and that was pretty much it except for the cabins and houses of the fifty or so folks who lived there.

"Are you excited?" Cassie asked her brother.

"About going into Wareagle? I might as well get excited about watching grass grow."

"There are people," Cassie said. She loved to socialize. To see what the women were wearing and what everyone was up to.

"I'm not as fond of them as you are."

"I have never understood that about you," Cassie confessed. "How you can be so cold toward everyone."

"That's the parson talking."

"No, it is me," Cassie said. "I like to mingle with other folks. I like to talk and dance and eat and have a good time. You'd rather be off in the woods with the bears and the squirrels."

"It's not that I don't like them as much as I don't trust them," Chace explained, adding, "Everyone except kinfolk."

"Strangers don't always mean us harm."

"Harkeys do."

Cassie frowned. "You're never going to let that go, are you?"

"No."

"You were little. You didn't know. Those boys caught you and beat you, but it wasn't like you were close to dying or anything."

"The beating was enough," Chace said.

Cassie dropped it.

Buck stirred and looked back at him, his pipe clamped in a corner of his mouth. "We're almost there. Remember, I want you young'uns to stick close. I don't want to have to come looking for you when it's time to go."

"Yes, Pa," Cassie said.

"Chace?"

"I'll kill a horse and boil some glue and glue myself to your backside. Will that do?"

"You worry me, boy. You truly do." Buck clucked to the mules.

The road was Wareagle's main street. On the one side was the saloon. Buck looked at it and smacked his lips. On the other side was the general store. Buck sighed and brought the wagon to a stop in front. He hopped down and offered his hands to Cassie and swung her lightly to the boardwalk. "Remember what I told you two," he said, and went in.

Chace lithely leaped down and leaned against a post, his arms across his chest. "Yes, sir," he said, and chuckled. "If this place was any more lively, it would make a fine cemetery."

The heat of the day had driven most indoors. The street was empty except for a dog sniffing at a pile of who-knew-what, and a pig and her piglets rooting around a stump. Horses were tied to hitch rails and one was drinking from a trough.

"Let's go in," Cassie prompted.

"What for?"

"I want to look at the catalogue."

"You always want to look at the catalogue."

"Please," Cassie said, and took his hand. She pulled and he came with her.

"You must have it memorized by now."

"So?" To Cassie, the Sears, Roebuck and Company catalogue was a slice of heaven on earth. Three hundred pages of everything there was in the world worth having: dresses, gowns, skirts, corsets, hats, bonnets, coats, jackets, shoes, china, silverware, brushes, combs, ostrich feathers, plus all that stuff men liked to look at.

She saw her father at the counter with Mr. Steever and she smiled at Mr. Steever and went to the far end and there it was. Eagerly, she opened it and thumbed the pages. She couldn't read well, but thanks to her ma she could wrestle with words fair enough, and besides, the catalogue had pictures of nearly everything. She turned to one of her favorite sections, Girls' and Misses' Cloth Dresses. "Look at how pretty these are," she said, and turned, but Chace was over by the glass cabinet that held the revolvers. He always liked to admire them.

Cassie touched a picture of a girl wearing a dress. The girl who wore it was blond, like her. She bent over the page, her mouth moving as she read, "Girl's dress, made of the newest plaid material, in the newest shades, large collar extending from front to back, trimmed with lace." She stopped reading. "Oh my," she said to herself, imagining how she would look. She bent to the page again. "Pointed yoke in front, made of cashmere to match and trimmed with silk gimp. Two rows of silk gimp around sleeve." She stopped and said, "Oh my, oh my." She ran her finger to the price. "One dollar and ninety-eight cents." It might as well have been ten. She had forty-seven cents to her name and it had taken her a year and a half to save that much. There was fine print under the price and she read it out loud, "If by mail, postage extra. Thirty-two cents."

"Like that one, do you?"

Cassie nearly jumped. Her father was at her side, looking over her shoulder.

"I like it the most of everything."

"I heard you reading," Buck said. "Wish I could read but I ain't never had the time to learn. Thank goodness your ma does." He showed her the bonnet he had just bought. "Do you really think she'll like this?"

Cassie had helped him pick it out. In the catalogue it was called a Lady's Gingham Sun Bonnet. It was made of the best gingham and had a shirred hood and a cape and bow strings. It cost twenty-five cents. "She'll love it, Pa."

Just then the bell over the front door tinkled and in

came old Doc Witherspoon. Usually he was cheerful and smiling, but now he was scowling and he saw Buck and came straight down the aisle, saying, "My wife told me she saw you come into town. Here I was, ready to send someone to fetch you."

"What?" Buck said. "What for?"

"It's your oldest," Doc Witherspoon said.

"Scarlet? What about her?"

"You'd best come quick."

3

The Witherspoons lived in one of the few frame houses in Wareagle. It had a gabled roof and a picket fence and a flower bed that Mrs. Witherspoon watered twice daily in the summer. Their parlor was spacious and cool after the heat of the outdoors.

Cassie had only ever been there twice. Once when she had the croup and again when she broke her wrist and her pa didn't set it right and her arm healed crooked, so they had to bring her to Doc Witherspoon and he broke it again and set it so her arm was straight. She loved the parlor with its grandfather clock and polished settee and the rug that tickled her feet. "I hope I have me a fine house like this someday," she said to her pa, but he wasn't paying attention.

"Where's Scarlet?" Buck demanded of Witherspoon.

The physician motioned and led them down a narrow hall to the examination room. Cabinets lined one wall; a desk was by the other. In the center was a flat table and on the table lay Scarlet. She turned her head as the door opened and tears filled her eyes. "Pa," she said simply.

Buck Shannon stopped in his tracks. "My God," he blurted.

Cassie recoiled in horror. She pressed her hands to her mouth and shook her head and said, "It can't be."

Scarlet's face was black-and-blue. Not just in a few spots but all over. Her left eye was swollen shut. Her lower lip was twice its normal size. Her hair was in a tangle and bits of grass were caught in it. Her arms were covered with bruises. Her legs were worse. Her dress had been ripped and torn nearly to tatters and she self-consciously covered her bosom with her left arm. "I'm sorry, Pa."

Buck stared, his face as white as the sheet that covered the table.

Cassie whimpered.

Chace came around them and took Scarlet's hand. "Tell me who did this and I'll take care of it."

"No," Scarlet said. "You'll have the law after you."

"Out of my way," Buck said, and shouldered his son aside. He clasped her same hand in both of his and ran his eyes down to her feet and said, "How could anyone do this?"

Doc Witherspoon cleared his throat. "I cleaned her up as best I could. No bones are broken and she doesn't appear to be bleeding inside, which is good. I recommend you take her home and keep her in bed for as long as she needs to recover from the other."

"The other?" Buck said, and his face became whiter. He turned to Scarlet. "They didn't?"

Scarlet nodded.

"How did you get here?"

Doc Witherspoon answered. "She dragged herself

through my front door about an hour ago. That's one tough young lady you've raised."

Buck said, "Cassie, I want you and your brother to go in the other room. I need to talk to your sister alone."

"It's all right," Scarlet said.

"I'd rather they did," Buck insisted. "It's not something they need to hear."

"I'm staying, Pa," Chace said.

"Not if I say you're not."

"Yes, I am."

Buck started to turn, but Scarlet held on to his hand and said quietly, "They can hear, Pa. It makes no never mind to me." She smiled weakly at her sister. "And it might be good, Cassie knowing how they are, so it won't happen to her."

Buck nodded at Witherspoon. "What about him? Does he know the particulars?"

The physician nodded. "She had to tell me so I could gauge the extent of her injuries."

"I reckon she did," Buck said. He touched Scarlet's cheek and his Adam's apple bobbed. "All of it. The who and the why but especially the who."

"There were seven of them, but only six took part in . . ." Scarlet stopped and tears trickled from the corners of her eyes. "They caught me picking berries in Harkey Hollow."

"God in heaven, girl," Buck said. "What were you thinking?"

"I know."

"We have our own patch right out back of the spring-house."

"I know." Scarlet sniffled.

"Go on."

Scarlet rubbed her arm across her nose. "I tried to run. They got hold of me and tried to force me. I fought them, Pa. Honest I did. But they held me down and took turns." She bowed her head and tears trickled down her cheeks. "I kicked the big one where it hurts the most and he got so mad, he beat on me, him and his brother. The others hit me but not as much." She sniffled some more. "One didn't. He was against it and the big one hit him."

"Names, girl," Buck said. "There are over a hundred Harkeys. I need the names."

"The big one was called Rabon and his brother was Woot. They never said the other names."

Chace asked, "What about the one who was against it? Did you get his name?"

"What does he matter?" Buck said.

"Jimbo," Scarlet answered. "His name was Jimbo. He stood up for me. He was the only one who did."

"I'll find out the rest," Chace said.

Buck jabbed a finger at him. "You'll do no such thing, boy. This is for grown-ups to handle. Me and my brothers will take care of this."

Scarlet rose on her elbows. "What will you do, Pa?"

Buck patted her hand and smiled. "Don't worry your pretty head over it. We'll do what has to be done, is all. They can't get away with it. Not this, they can't."

"There will be blood," Chace said.

Buck let go of Scarlet and glared at his son. "Didn't you hear me? You're not to get involved. I'm her pa. It's for me to do."

"I'm her brother."

"I said no and that's final." Buck fished in his pocket. "How much do we owe you, Doc?"

"Not a cent," Witherspoon said. "Not for this."

Buck stopped fishing, and nodded. "That's decent of you. I'm grateful." He looked down at Scarlet and trembled. "About the other thing. Did they hurt her there, too?"

"There's no bleeding, if that's what you mean," Doc Witherspoon said. "The thing to watch out for is if she misses her monthly."

"Oh God. I didn't think of that." Buck swallowed and averted his face for a few moments. When he turned back his features were as hard as flint. "Chace, you go bring the wagon. Your sister can't walk down the street looking like she does."

"I'll go with him," Cassie offered, and followed her brother out. As they emerged into the glare of the afternoon sun, she snatched at his arm. "You're not going to listen to Pa, are you?"

"No."

"You hadn't oughta. It's his to do."

"She's my sister."

Cassie held him so he couldn't walk. "I want your word. I want you to promise me you'll let Pa take care of it."

Chace pinched his lips together and exhaled through his nose. "Why are you making such a fuss?"

"You're my twin."

"That's no answer." Chace tried to move, but she still held on. "You're the only one in the world I'd let do this to me."

"Please."

Chace stared at the doctor's door and then at the sky and then at the ground and then at her. "I'll let Pa handle it."

"You will?"

"I just said so, didn't I?"

Cassie beamed and clapped her hands and hugged him. "Thank you. You are the best brother ever."

"But," Chace said.

"There's a 'but'?"

Chace nodded. "I'll stay out of it so long as Pa and his brothers get it done, but if they can't or they won't, then I'll put the quietus on the Harkeys who hurt Scarlet myself."

"Pa hasn't said anything about killing."

"He should." Chace made for the wagon and she fell into step beside him.

"I don't much like him treating me like I'm a kid. I stopped being a boy when I was eleven." He glanced meaningfully at her. "You were there."

"Pa doesn't know about that," Cassie said. "No one does but me. When they found his body they thought he fell. If they knew you had pushed him . . ." She gazed down the street at the stable and didn't finish.

"He had it coming," Chace said. "Him wanting you to sit in his lap."

"He was drunk. He didn't know any better."

"He knew exactly what he was about. You never should have gone up in the loft."

"He said he had licorice."

"Enough about him." Chace stood aside and she climbed onto the seat and he did the same. He let loose the brake lever and raised the reins and flicked them. The mules were sluggish in the heat. He flicked again and brought the wagon to the gate in the picket fence.

The front door opened and out came Buck carrying Scarlet. A blanket had been thrown over her and covered her to her neck. She averted her face from a pass-

erby as Buck carefully lowered her over. "You can climb
in the back with Scarlet," he said to Chace, and when
Chace complied, Buck climbed up and gripped the reins
in his callused hands.

Doc Witherspoon stood at the gate. "I don't suppose
it would do any good to caution you not to do anything
foolish?"

"If by foolish you mean kill them, I haven't decided
yet," Buck said. "First I mean to beat them half to
death."

"Just so you don't end up in prison." Doc Witherspoon tapped his fingers on the top rail of the picket
fence. "You could put them behind bars, you know. Go
to the sheriff and file a complaint. Have Scarlet testify
in a court of law."

"No," Buck said.

"No," Scarlet echoed.

"Dare I ask why you won't even consider it?"

"How long have you been practicing medicine in Wareagle now, Doc?" Buck rejoined.

"Twenty-one years. I came from Ohio. You know
that."

"You were born an outsider but you've lived among
us long enough that our ways are no secret. We don't run
to the law, ever. We don't hold with courts, neither. This
ain't the North. We tree our own coons and we skin our
own bears."

"Why not talk to Ezriah Harkey, at least?" Doc Witherspoon suggested. "He'll have no truck with what those
boys did, I guarantee. Could be he'll punish them himself. Then the truce holds."

"They broke it when they hurt Scarlet," Buck said.

"The last time there were fourteen dead before the

two sides came to their senses. How many have to die this time?"

"Keep your nose out of it, Doc." Buck yelled at the mules to get along and turned the wagon back up the street. A man came out of the saloon and waved in greeting, but Buck didn't wave back.

"Pa?" Cassie said. When he didn't reply she touched his arm. "Pa? Are you all right?"

"I may never be all right again," Buck said. He patted a pocket and then another. "Have you seen my pipe? I don't recollect putting it out, but I must have."

"The last I saw was when you took it out of your mouth at the doc's," Cassie told him.

Buck checked his back pocket and sighed in relief. "Here it is. I'd hate to lose it. Takes forever to break in a new one." He pulled the pipe out and set it in his lap and produced his tobacco pouch.

"Let me," Cassie said. "You don't want to run over anybody." She switched the pipe and pouch to her own lap.

"I'm obliged."

Behind them, Scarlet curled on her side with her arm for a pillow. "Pretty stupid of me, huh, little brother?"

"It was more stupid of them to do what they done," Chace said.

"You stay out of it—you hear? Leave this to Pa."

"You sound like Cassie."

The wagon hit a bump and Scarlet winced. "I care for you. We're not as close as you and Cassie, but then hardly anyone is, short of being married. Comes of being twins, I guess."

Chace didn't say anything.

"You two have always been like two peas in a pod,"

Scarlet went on. "I remember how when you were little you went everywhere together and did everything together. Pa used to joke that you were joined at the hip."

"We have been on occasion," Chace said.

"Ask me, you still are." Scarlet stuck her arm out from under the blanket and held her hand for him to take. "This is my fault. I brought it down on us by being so dumb. Pa wants revenge and then the Harkeys are liable to want revenge for what he does and then our side will want revenge for what they do, and on it will go for years. Just like the last time."

"No."

"No what?" Scarlet asked.

"It won't go on for years. It won't go on for months."

"Is that so? And what's different about this time from the last?"

"Me," Chace said.

4

Jedediah Shannon showed up at Buck's farm shortly after sunrise two days later. His lanky frame was clothed in buckskins nearly as old as he was. Curly gray hair framed a face with as many wrinkles as Methuselah's. His armament consisted of an old Sharps rifle and a bowie knife. A large leather bag and a bandoleer crisscrossed his chest.

Buck answered the knock on the cabin door. He blinked and said, "Pa?"

"Unless it's my ghost, and I ain't dead yet," Jed said. "Are you going to stand there with your jaw on the floor or welcome me in?"

Buck sheepishly moved and gestured. "You're always welcome. You know that. It's a surprise, is all."

"It shouldn't be. You're my son." Jed entered and looked around. "Erna keeps this place as cozy as ever, I see."

Buck closed the door. "It's been full near a year. Now you show up out of the blue."

"You know what brought me."

"How did you find out? Doc Witherspoon is the only

other one who knows. I sent for Granger and Fox but didn't say why I needed them."

"A catbird told me. He landed on my pillow and whispered in my ear and here I am." Jed strode to the table and sat, the Sharps cradled in his arms.

"Friendly as ever, I see," Buck drily remarked.

"Where's your family? The day's begun and I don't see them up and about," Jed said.

"Scarlet is in bed like the doc told her. Erna just took her some grits. The twins went out to the chicken coop for eggs. Would you like to join us for breakfast?"

"Don't mind if I do." Jed stretched out his long legs and propped them on the table. "But first, why in hell didn't you send word to me? Why did the head of our clan have to hear it from an outsider who's worried sick blood will be spilled?"

"I knew it was Witherspoon." Buck sighed and claimed another chair. "He's a good doctor but he likes to meddle where he shouldn't."

"You haven't answered my question."

Buck ran a hand through his hair and reached into his pocket for his corncob pipe. He took out his tobacco pouch and loosened the drawstring and pinched tobacco and tamped it in the bowl.

"You're stalling," Jed said.

Buck ignored him and spent all of a minute lighting his pipe. Then he sat back and contentedly puffed.

"And you're not too old for me to wallop."

Buck took the pipe from his mouth. "Here, now. I won't have talk like that. Not in my own house. You come down out of the hills acting high and mighty. Why don't you ever come just to visit? Why do you only show your face when there's trouble?"

"I come when I'm needed. Otherwise I leave you be. If I was invited I would, but you never invite me."

Buck was about to stick the pipe back in his mouth but jabbed it at his father instead. "Damn it, Pa. You're welcome here anytime. You know that. And hell, you haven't called the clan together in pretty near two years. You'd think it would be more often."

"Quit your cussing," Jed said. "I never cussed out of respect for your ma and I taught you the same."

A door at the back opened and out came a woman in her middle years. She wore homespun and had her hair in a bun and a sad expression until she saw their visitor. Then she smiled and came over, and Jed rose and she warmly embraced him. "Jedediah. I knew you'd come."

"You did but my own son didn't. Tells me a lot right there." Jed kissed her on the cheek. "It warms my cockles to see you again, Erna."

Erna sniffed and said, "You're even sober. I'm honored."

Jed colored slightly and sat back down. "I haven't had a drop since I heard about Scarlet. About rode my horse to death getting here."

"Why exactly did you come?" Buck asked.

"On a list of stupid questions, that's at the top," Jed replied. "My granddaughter has been violated. The Harkeys are to blame. I'm here to decide what to do about it."

"I've already decided," Buck said. "Me and Granger and Fox are going to pay Ezriah Harkey a visit and demand he turn those who abused my daughter over to us."

"That's your plan?" Jed leaned the Sharps against

his chair and folded his hand on the table. "I figured it would be something foolish like that."

"Jed, please," Erna said.

"What's foolish about it?" Buck demanded.

"He'll be expecting you, for one thing. He's their patriarch and, like me, the man to go to when there's a dispute. For another thing, by now those who did it have bragged. The whole Harkey clan is likely to know. Put those two together and if you go in you might not come back out."

"Ezriah wouldn't have me killed when they're in the wrong."

"Wrong, son. That's exactly why he *would*. He might not want to, but he will to protect his kin. Plus, that wife of his will egg him on. She's the most bloodthirsty bitch there ever was." Jed glanced at Erna. "Sorry. I forgot a lady is present."

The front door opened and in walked Chace and Cassie. She was carrying a pail full of eggs. "Grandpa!" she squealed in delight. Shoving the pail at Chace, she ran to the table and threw herself into Jed's arms as he was rising.

"Cassie girl," Jed said huskily. "How's my favorite person in all the world?"

"Fine, Gramps." Cassie kissed him on both cheeks. "I've missed you something awful. You don't visit nearly often enough."

"I told him the same thing," Buck said.

Erna took the pail from Chace and announced, "I'll have breakfast ready in two shakes of a lamb's tail."

Jed sat and Cassie sat next to him and held out her hand to Chace, who stood next to her chair. Chace looked at Jed, and Jed looked at him and said, "Been to the stable today, boy?"

Chace glanced at Cassie.

"I have a barn," Buck said. "You can call it a stable if you want. But why would you ask him that?"

"He knows," Jed said.

"Well, it makes no sense to me." Buck puffed a few times. "And I don't know as you should be bringing stables up, anyway. Don't you remember that drunk over to Wareagle? The one who fell out of the hayloft in the stable and broke his fool neck? It was Chace and Cassie who found the body."

Erna, about to place a skillet on the cast-iron stove, remarked, "That was awful. They were so young. It must have been terrible for them."

"It was, Ma," Cassie said quickly.

"It must have been terrible for the drunk, too," Jed commented. He was looking at Chace when he said it.

"Enough of this talk of death," Erna said. "Our hearts are heavy enough over Scarlet."

They made small talk about the weather and the crops and kinfolk and Jed informed them that a cougar had killed a calf over to their cousin Rufus's place. The cabin filled with the aromas of cooking food.

Erna brought a steaming cup of coffee to Jed and gave him sugar and cream.

"I haven't had any in so long, I've about forgot how it tastes," Jed said.

"Maybe you'd like for me to break out a jug instead?" Buck asked. "I bet you haven't forgotten how shine tastes."

"Bucklyn," Erna said.

"That's all right." Jed sipped and smacked his lips. "I don't pay him no mind."

"Can I ask you something, Grandpa?" Cassie said. "It's something I've been meaning to."

"Child, you can ask me anything."

"Good." Cassie leaned on her elbows and gazed at him affectionately. "Why do you live so far back in the woods like you do? All alone? Why don't you live closer so we can see you more?"

Buck said, "I'd like to hear that answer myself."

Jed swallowed and set the cup on the saucer. "I never made a secret of it, Cassie girl. I like the wilds. I was born and bred in a cabin half this size on Slate Mountain, which didn't have a name back then. I spent every day of my early years in the woods and it got in my blood. Some would say I'm a hermit, but I'm no such thing. I like to be alone but only because people are an aggravation."

"Us, too?"

"Thunderation, child. Never in a thousand years. Kin is special. You ever hear of me not being there when a Shannon was in need?"

"No, Grandpa," Cassie said. "Everyone says you lead the clan as good as anyone." She patted his hand. "It was you who arranged the truce with Ezriah Harkey, wasn't it?"

"That it was," Jed confirmed. He sat back. "It was twenty years ago, or thereabouts. The killing had gone on for so long, no one could recollect what started it. It might have gone on except I ran into Ezriah in Wareagle." He grinned wryly. "The settlement is as much to thank for the truce as me or Ezriah."

"How's that?" Buck asked.

"Wareagle wasn't there when I was Cassie's age. It sprung up later. Us Shannons and the Harkeys would sneak in and sneak out, never knowing when the other might take a potshot. One day I went to the general store and over to the pickle barrel, and who should be there but Ezriah Harkey getting a pickle. He looked at me and I looked at him and I said, 'We'd be laughingstocks if we died over pickles. How about we hold off shooting each other while we eat?' So we sat on stools and talked while we ate and it turned out he was as sick of the killings as I was. We agreed the bloodletting should stop and called a truce."

"And now the Harkeys have broke it," Buck said.

"That's what I'm here to talk about."

Erna carried a stack of plates and spoons and forks to the table and began setting them out. "The talk can wait. The food is ready and you'll eat it while it's hot."

"Yes, ma'am," Jed said, and patted his belly. "Bring on the feed. I ain't ate since I left and my stomach is sticking to my backbone."

"You won't be disappointed," Erna promised.

Chace stepped around the table and sat across from his sister. He picked up his fork and rubbed it on his sleeve.

"You hungry, boy?" Jed asked.

"For Harkey blood."

"Here, now," Erna said. "There will none of that. Save the blood talk for after breakfast. Cassie, you help me serve."

There was a pot of Arbuckle's coffee for the men and mint tea in a kettle for the ladies. The food consisted of beaten biscuits, bacon and collard greens, buckwheat cakes, and eggs. A jar of apple butter was set out to smear on the biscuits. Erna even offered molasses for the buckwheat cakes, a treat since molasses was pricey.

The family ate in silence save for "pass me this" or "pass me that."

Jedediah heaped his plate high. He was particularly fond of the buckwheat cakes and helped himself to half a dozen. He ate with enthusiasm and complimented Erna on her fine cooking.

"I'm no great shakes but I thank you."

Jed nodded at Buck. "The smartest thing you ever did was to marry this gal. She reminds me a lot of your mother." Some of the joy went out of his face. "God rest her soul."

"I wish I'd gotten to know her," Cassie said. "What did she die of, anyhow? I don't think anyone's ever said."

"Pneumonia, they call it," Jed said. "A fancy word for the shakes and shivers. There wasn't a sawbones within a hundred miles back then or I'd have taken her. I did all I could but it wasn't enough." Jed stopped chewing and set down his fork. "I miss her more than anything. I should have come down with it and died with her."

"I'm glad you didn't," Cassie said.

Erna stood up. "I made dessert. Brown Betty. Who wants some?"

"For *breakfast*?" Buck said.

"It's a special occasion, your pa being here. I made it last night for supper today, but we can have it now."

"Now I've heard everything," Buck grumbled.

Cassie rubbed her hands in glee. Brown Betty was her favorite pudding. When it was warm, the apples and bread crumbs melted in her mouth.

"I have died and gone to heaven," Jed said when he

was given his portion. He winked at Erna. "Times like this I almost regret not taking another wife."

"Why didn't you?" Cassie asked.

"Your grandma was the only woman for me. We were meant for each other. She knew it and I knew it."

"How did you know?"

"Cassie," Erna said. "You shouldn't pester the man."

"I don't mind," Jed said, and patted his granddaughter's hand. "We were sweet on each other when we were your age. Her pa didn't take to me, though, and wouldn't let her marry me. She refused to marry anyone else and after four or five years he gave in just so she wouldn't be an old maid." He paused. "You asked me how we knew?" Jed touched a finger to his chest. "Love is of the heart, girl. You feel it in all you are. One day it will hit you like a thunderclap and there won't be nothing you can do."

Cassie glanced at Chace.

"But enough about that." Jed stared down the table at Buck. "Let's talk about the Harkeys."

5

___

Deep in the shadowed woods of the Ozarks rode three men. They sat their saddles quiet and alert, their rifles in their hands. Two were on mules, the last astride a clay-bank. Around them the shortleaf pines and hardwoods teemed with wildlife. Occasionally they skirted meadows where yellow jasmine grew. Once, as they climbed a steep slope, quail were startled into flight. They saw mockingbirds, a cardinal, a robin.

Buck Shannon was in the lead. He sat stiffly, holding his Winchester by the barrel, the stock on his thigh. He passed through a stand of ash and drew rein at the base of a bluff with a lightning-scarred tree partway up. He studied the tree. "That must be the one."

His brothers came to a stop on either side of his mule.

Granger was younger by two years but looked older. He had the Shannon eyes and the Shannon hair but less of the latter than either of them. He had started balding at an early age and now had no hair on top and precious little on the sides. He was heavier than Buck by twenty pounds. A farmer, his features were deeply tanned and his hands thickly callused.

Fox was a farmer, as well. He was the youngest and not nearly as big. He did have all his hair. His rifle was a Henry. It had cost him most of the money from last year's corn crop, but he considered it worth it. As the saying went, you could load a Henry on Sunday and shoot it all week. He wasn't much of a shot, but the Henry could shoot a lot. No other Shannon owned one. No Harkeys, either, from what he'd gathered.

"So far Pa's landmarks have been right where he said they'd be," Granger said.

"So far," Buck replied. "But I wouldn't put it past him to trick us. You wait. Farther in, the landmarks won't match and we'll have no choice but to turn back for home."

"Pa wouldn't do that to us," Fox said.

"Where were you when he was giving us a piece of his mind? He doesn't want us to do this. He says no good will come of it. That if we were smart we'd bring him and let him dicker."

"Maybe we should have," Granger said. "He knows these woods better than any of us and he's friendly with Ezriah."

"Friendly ain't exactly the word I'd use," Buck quibbled. "They shook hands once, is all." He gigged the mule and reined to go around the bluff rather than tempt fate on the slope.

"I'd still feel better if Pa was here," Granger said.

"There's nothing he can do that we can't," Buck said irritably.

"That may be," Fox said, "but he does it a lot better."

"I don't want to hear any more about him—you hear? Not another peep, by God."

"Simmer down," Granger cautioned.

Sunlight streamed through the forest canopy in sparkling shafts. A carpet of leaves and needles dulled the thud of hooves. A woodpecker *rat-a-tat-tatted* high in an oak, and finches chirped and flitted from tree to tree. Farther on they flushed a young buck with its antlers in velvet; the buck bounded off in graceful leaps, its tail erect. A monarch butterfly flew past Buck's mule, so close its wing pretty near brushed the mule's eye.

In due course they came to a tableland. The trees included more evergreens. They took advantage of a long, winding gully to stay hidden until they were half a mile along. Beyond were a series of grassy mounds.

Jed had told them that the Indians believed the mounds were the burial grounds of a race of giants from long ago. Buck had little truck with the red race and no belief at all in their superstitions.

The mounds ended at thick woods. Here, human feet had rarely trod. The shadows darkened.

"We're getting close," Fox whispered.

Buck nodded. *If* Jed had remembered right and *if* the landmarks were as Jed said and *if* the gent they were going to such lengths to see still lived where he had lived when he invited Jed over twenty years ago, then yes, they were getting close.

They rode at a walk. They stopped often to listen. Twice Jed snapped his Winchester to his shoulders, but it was only a trick of the light that made him think figures had appeared from behind trees. Inwardly, he swore. He was jumpy and he hated it.

The thick woods ended where they were supposed to, on the crest of a small valley nestled deep in Harkey country. The brothers drew rein well below the rim and went up on foot, crouching so they weren't silhouetted against the sky. A few yards from the brink they fell onto their bellies and crawled.

Buck was the first to poke his head over. "Well, I'll be," he said.

"Pa did it," Granger said.

"No, we did it. Pa only told us how."

"We couldn't have done it without him remembering."

"I could have set up a meet on my own. Don't make him out to be of more help than he was."

Fox said testily, "Will you two cut it out? Granger, you're right. We couldn't have done it without Pa. And, Buck, what the hell is the matter with you? You never give Pa credit for anything."

"Him and me haven't always seen eye to eye," Buck said sullenly.

"That may be, but now's not the time and this sure ain't the place to squabble about it."

Buck grunted.

The valley was a quarter of a mile long and half that wide. A ribbon of blue was bordered by grass. At the far end stood the dwelling they had taken great risk to find. From its chimney curled wisps of smoke. Horses dozed in a corral. There was an outhouse and a shed, and that was all.

"I don't see anyone," Granger said.

"It's close to noon. Maybe they're sitting down to eat," Fox guessed. "That would explain the smoke."

"We can either sneak in or ride up," Buck said. "I say

riding is best. Show we're peaceable by staying out in the open."

"I vote we sneak," Granger disagreed. "Wait for someone to come out and take them prisoner."

"That will sure put us in their good graces."

"I'd rather be breathing than friendly."

Fox made a sound reminiscent of a goose having its neck strangled. "There you two go again. I swear. You act no older than when you were twelve and ten."

"What's your vote?" Buck asked.

"Were it up to me, we wouldn't even be here," Fox answered. "We'd find out where the boys who did your daughter wrong live and bushwhack them some night and that would be that."

"And start the feud up all over again." Buck shook his head. "I'm trying to avoid that. I thought you understood."

"I do. Which is why I vote that we ride in to prove we're friendly and hope to heaven they're as friendly as we are."

Granger muttered, then said, "We're making a mistake, but if it's what you both want, then I'll go along."

"Decent of you," Buck said.

They stood and climbed on their mounts and Buck led down the slope to the valley floor and along the gurgling stream. He had his Winchester across his saddle so he could raise it fast if he had to.

A dog came from behind the shed and commenced to bark. A black mongrel, he was large enough that if he tangled with a bear the issue would be in doubt.

"Yapping cur," Granger said.

"Strange no one has come out," Buck remarked.

"Strange house," Fox said.

The dwelling wasn't exactly a house and it wasn't exactly a cabin. It was an odd mix of both. Logs and boards had been used in its construction and put together unevenly and the gaps filled with mud. A rock foundation, likewise filled, framed the bottom. The chimney was lopsided and one side of the house was slightly higher than the other.

"Looks like it was built by a drunk," Fox said.

"A dumb drunk," Granger added.

Buck came within a stone's toss and drew rein. He didn't raise his Winchester. He held his right hand up with the palm out and hollered, "Ezriah Harkey! You in there? This is Buck Shannon. Me and my brothers have come to have words with you."

The door creaked on leather hinges. The man who came out was a lot like his house: bulky, slovenly, uneven. The moment he emerged the dog stopped barking. His overalls bore a dozen or more patches. His shirt was open to the waist and flab oozed out. He had tufts of brown hair sticking from above his ears and wisps on the top. He wasn't armed. Dark, close-set eyes raked them, and he said, "To have words, you say?"

"That's right," Buck replied. "We came in peace."

"So you claim."

"If I'd wanted to I could have laid up on the rise yonder and picked you off with my rifle, but I didn't. I came in open and friendly."

"So you did," Ezriah Harkey said.

"I reckon you know why I'm here."

"I do. And I reckon I know how you found me. Your pa must have told you. He's the only one of your clan who's ever been here."

Buck nodded. "He wanted to come himself but I

asked him not to. I wanted this between us. Man to man. It was my daughter who was wronged."

"For what it is worth I am sorry about that," Ezriah said. "I don't hold with them that hurt womenfolk."

Just then someone else appeared. A female about the same age as the patriarch. Her dress was black, her shoes black, her hair gray. She had ferret eyes and a pointed chin and no lips to speak of. Around her neck was a string of small bones. On each wrist were more bones. Around her waist was a belt made of what appeared to be human hair. She looked at the three of them and tittered as if she found them funny.

"This is my missus," Ezriah introduced her.

"How do you do, ma'am?" Buck said. "What might your name be?"

In a voice that cracked with every syllable, she responded, "A name is power and I'll not give you any. Not a Shannon, I won't."

"Power?" Buck said.

"Her mother was from New Orleans," Ezriah said, as if that explained it. "She answers to Woman and likes it that way. You know her real name, she figures you could cast a spell on her."

"A witchy woman, by God," Fox declared.

"No one told us his wife was a witch," Granger said.

"No one outside the Harkeys knows she's special," Ezriah said. "She heals and reads signs and can put a hex on folks if I ask her to."

"How do you do, ma'am?" Buck said again.

Woman tittered and shook her wrists so that the bones rattled. "I do right fine, Shannon man. I do better than you."

"Don't," Ezriah said to her. "We'll do this my way, you hear? Go in and set coffee out."

She glanced at him sharply. "You're inviting them into our house? Them as is our enemies?"

"You heard him. He came in peace. The least I can do is hear him out." Ezriah motioned. "Coffee. Now."

Woman hissed like a kicked snake and stalked indoors.

"Climb down," Ezriah said to the brothers. "You can put your animals in the corral if you want. There's feed and a trough."

"Don't mind if we do," Buck said. Dismounting, he led his around.

Three mules and a horse were already there.

Ezriah Harkey came with them. "You must be Granger and you must be Fox."

Fox's eyebrows arched. "How did you know? We've never set eyes on you until today."

"I make it a point to learn all I can about you Shannons," Ezriah told him. "Who is born to who and how many and what you look like. Doesn't your pa do the same?"

"Not that we know of," Granger answered. "He keeps to himself off in the woods, just like you do."

"Us oldsters like our breathing space." Ezriah scratched himself and looked at each of their weapons. "Nice rifles." He pointed a thick finger. "That's a Henry you have, ain't it?"

Fox patted the brass receiver. "Sure is."

"First I've ever laid eyes on but I've heard about them." Ezriah gazed down the valley and then at the woods that bordered the back of the corral. He nodded and looked at Buck and said, "Yes, sir. I'm glad you came. Even if it wasn't your doing."

"What do you mean?"

"Woman did a conjure. She brought you here. Don't get mad at her, though. She did it for me."

"You're saying she put some kind of spell on us?" Buck laughed. "I don't believe in hexes."

Ezriah shrugged. "Believe or not believe, they still work. She has the gift. And this makes things a lot easier. Saves me the trouble of having to look you up and maybe it will spare our families some misery."

"That's why I'm here."

"You're an honorable man, Buck Shannon. I'd expect no less from the son of my old enemy, Jedediah."

"I'm hoping there is honor on both sides. I'm hoping you'll do the right thing by me and my daughter."

"I always do the right thing," Ezriah said. "Come along. We'll talk inside." He added with finality, "When we're done, this will be settled."

6

Chace took his rifle down from the pegs on the wall. He sat on the bed and worked the lever to feed a cartridge into the chamber.

"Why do you keep it up there?" Cassie asked. She was leaning against the jamb, watching him.

"So I can get it quick in the night if I need to."

"Did you see Uncle Fox's Henry?"

"I have eyes."

"What did you think of it?"

"Just like him to pick a pretty gun. I'll stick with this." Chace wagged his Spencer.

"It's as old as you are."

"Old don't mean useless." Chace took down the special belt he'd made from rawhide; it held twenty .50-caliber cartridges. He wrapped it around his waist and buckled it. Hunkering, he reached under his bed and pulled out an Arkansas toothpick in a leather sheath. He slid the sheath under his belt behind his back and moved to go.

Cassie blocked his way. "I want to come."

"No."

"I'll bring my rifle. We'll hunt together."

"No, I said."

"Please."

Chace brushed past her and crossed the family room to the front door. He stepped out into the bright afternoon sun, and squinted. He went to close the door but Cassie was in the doorway.

"You're worried about him, aren't you?" Cassie asked.

"He's our pa."

"Ma is worried, too. I think that's why Grandpa offered to take her into Wareagle. To take her mind off it. Well, off that and Scarlet. She's sound asleep, by the way. I checked a bit ago."

"You should have gone with them."

Cassie put her hand on his shoulder. "I wanted to stay with you. When I'm away from you I don't feel whole."

"Must come from being twins."

"Or something." Cassie gave his shoulder a playful shake. "What do you say? I promise not to make noise. I'll be so quiet you won't even know I'm there."

"You're female."

"What does that mean?"

"I'll know you're there." Chace turned and took a couple of steps and stopped and looked back. "Consarn you, anyhow."

"You'll let me?"

"When have I ever denied you? Fetch your gun. We'll go back of the apple orchard and see about something for the supper pot."

Cassie grinned and raced in and was back out in half a minute with her own rifle. It was a single-shot Ballard in .32 caliber. She also had a small doeskin pouch in which she carried her ammunition. "Ready," she said.

The sun was hot; the breeze barely stirred the leaves. They passed the barn and went along a cornfield to the orchard. Beyond was a finger of woodland that separated the wheat field from the barley and beyond that the forest.

"I like how you walk," Cassie said.

Chace looked at her.

"You're like a puma, all tanned and tawny. When you move, it's just like a cat."

"Cut it out."

"I'm serious."

"That makes it worse. I ain't no damn cat."

"Try to give some folks a compliment," Cassie said.

The shade did little to lessen the heat. Chace hardly made a sound. Cassie tried to imitate him and wasn't entirely successful. When she accidentally stepped on a twig that crunched, he glanced at her as if she should be kicked.

"You promised to be quiet."

"We can't all be Apaches," Cassie said.

"I'd like to meet some one day."

"Apaches? Are you loco? They'd slit your throat as soon as look at you. I hear they kill every white they come across."

"Can't hardly blame them. The government is trying to put them on a reservation. If I were an Apache, I'd kill every white, too."

"Don't let Pa hear you say that. You know how he is about redskins."

Chace raised a hand for silence. He peered into the foliage and then extended his left hand and pointed.

A gray squirrel scampered along a high limb. It stopped and rose on its hind legs and rubbed its chin with its paws and then resumed scampering.

"It's yours," Chace whispered.

Cassie took a step for a better view. She pressed her rifle to her shoulder and aligned the rear sight with the front sight and centered the front sight on the squirrel. It was perched in a fork and gazing about, unaware they were there. She remembered to aim at the head. Squirrels didn't have a lot of meat and a slug through the body ruined a lot of what there was. She held her breath to steady her aim, counted to three in her head, and fired. She missed. The squirrel moved just as she shot and at the boom it spun and raced along a branch and vaulted to another tree and disappeared.

Chace looked at her.

"It wasn't my fault."

Chace went on looking.

"You saw what it did. You'd have missed, too."

"I'd have waited until it was still."

"I ain't perfect like you," Cassie said.

"You can always go back." Chace shifted his Spencer to the crook of his elbow and walked on.

"You're not getting rid of me that easy," Cassie declared, and quickly caught up. "You can be so mean."

"Hush. We're hunting."

"I want to know something."

"Figured you did, the way you were staring at me back at the cabin." Chace stopped and faced her. "Let's hear it."

"Mind if I sit?" Cassie went to a willow and curled her legs under her. She leaned the Ballard against the trunk and folded her hands in her lap. "I want the truth out of you."

Chace placed the Spencer's stock on the grass and leaned on the barrel. "You can say that? When you know you're the one person in the world I would never, ever lie to?"

"What do you plan to do about the Harkeys?"

"It's not up to me. Pa is taking care of that. If this is all you wanted, you're wasting our time."

Cassie plucked a blade of grass and stuck the stem between her teeth and spit it out. "Let's say Pa gets what he wants. Let's say the Harkeys agree to punish those who hurt Scarlet. Will that satisfy you?"

"It will if Pa says it has to."

"You won't go after them? You won't hunt them down and do what I know you secretly want to do?"

Chace bent and plucked a blade of grass and stuck it between his teeth but he didn't spit it out. "They should suffer as Scarlet suffered."

"An eye for an eye."

"A hurt for a hurt." Chace raised the Spencer. "Let's go. And this time I'll do the shooting."

Frowning, Cassie stood and grabbed her rifle and followed. "You're awful contrary today."

Chace studied the ground as they went. Twice he stopped and knelt and ran his hand over some prints.

Cassie was good at tracking but not as good as he was. The tracks were made by a deer but she couldn't say how long ago. She found out when they came to a circle of flattened grass.

"He bedded down here last night."

"How do you know it's a him?"

Chace indicated a spot where the grass was discolored. "Do you know what that is?"

"I'm not a simpleton," Cassie said indignantly. "It's pee." She had an idea and brightened. "I get it. Bucks lift their legs when they pee and does squat."

"Bucks don't always lift," Chace corrected her. "Look closer."

Cassie squatted and cocked her head from side to side but for the life of her she couldn't tell anything and said so.

"I thought I explained this to you once." Chace hunkered beside her. "Is the mark between the hind tracks or where?"

"It's in front and almost to one side."

"There you have it."

"Have what?"

Chace looked at her again. Cassie glanced at the hind prints and at the pee spots and at him and back down. "Oh," she said, and laughed. "He would have to spray to the front, wouldn't he?"

"Sometimes they spray straight down, but it's still not the same as when a doe squats." Chace rose and resumed tracking. "You'd have remembered if you gave a hoot."

"I admit it," Cassie said. "I don't care as much about tracking as you do, and I don't care at all about how deer pee. But then, as you say, I'm a girl."

"Girls have to fill their bellies the same as boys. It might do your family good someday that you know how to track."

"I'm never getting married, the same as you."

"You'll meet a man one day and crave him for your own. You'll throw a loop for him to step into and when he does you'll have kids just like Ma had us."

"Would you step into my loop?"

"I'm your brother. What would folks think?"

"Then I'll live my days as a spinster."

Chace stopped unexpectedly and she almost walked into him. "I don't like to hear that."

"It's my life."

"It's not right you live alone on account of me."

Cassie reacted as if he had slapped her. "I never really expected to. Or is all your talk just wind?"

"We have to grow up sometime," Chace said gently. He reached for her hand, but she pulled away.

"It's not about growing up. It's about *us*. It's about being twins, about us having—what did Ma call it? A special bond. I could no more live without you than I could without breathing."

"I knew it was a mistake." Chace went to go on, but she snagged his wrist.

"Being twins makes us different."

"Other folks can't see that."

"We can. We think alike about a lot of things. We *feel* alike. All I have to do is look at you and I know what is in your head." Cassie touched his chest and then she touched hers. "And what is in your heart."

"You make more of it than there is."

"Tell me I'm wrong. Look me in the eye and say you've never felt it. Tell me that when we're apart you don't feel like part of you is missing."

"Dang it, Cassie."

"Don't worry. I'll keep it to myself. But if you ever leave, I'm going with you. Whatever you do, I want to be at your side."

"You act like you're my wife."

"I'm better. I'm your twin."

Chace shook his head and pulled loose and walked on. Cassie said his name but he ignored her. She tried a few more times and finally subsided into a sulk.

She didn't care that she stepped on twigs or dry leaves.

Chace stayed glued to the tracks. Eventually they came to a thicket that covered half an acre. He stopped, showed her a trail into the thicket, and whispered, "He's bedded down in there."

"Good for him," Cassie said loudly.

"Spook him and we won't have venison for supper."

"That was cruel of you. Sixteen years we've been two sides of the same coin and now you say it never meant anything."

"You're putting words in my mouth." Chace bore to the left, rising every few steps onto his toes. When he had gone a short way he turned and selected an oak. Thrusting his Spencer at Cassie, he jumped and caught a low limb. He swung up, straddled the limb, and lowered his hand for her to give him the rifle. His other hand against the bole, he stood and surveyed the length and breadth of the thicket.

Cassie folded her arms and tapped her foot.

Careful not to drop the Spencer, Chace climbed higher until the branches were almost too thin to bear his weight. Shielding his eyes, he scoured the thicket again. Slight movement drew his gaze. He eased lower, wrapped his legs around a branch, and braced his back against the trunk. Tucking the Spencer to his shoulder, he fixed a bead on a particular spot, put his cheek to the rifle, and uttered a shrill whistle.

Fifty feet away the buck rose, head and antlers in profile.

Chace stroked the trigger. The shot was as perfect as a shot could be; it drilled the buck's brain and burst out the other side of its head. It was dead before it crumbled. He worked the lever, then descended. On the bottom limb he lowered the rifle for Cassie to take, but she didn't take it. "Suit yourself," he said, and jumped, alighting on the balls of his feet. "It doesn't help when you act this way."

"You could at least say you're sorry."

"I never apologize when I'm right."

Cassie stamped her foot. "Do you know what I am thinking? I'm thinking you're the worst brother ever."

"I know," Chace Shannon said.

7

Buck and Fox and Granger sat at an oak table in Ezriah Harkey's cabin with their rifles leaning against their legs. Buck was at one end of the table, Ezriah at the other. Over at a stove, Woman filled cups with coffee.

Buck looked about them. All four walls were hung thick with animal heads. Deer, bear, cougar, even rabbits and a possum and two raccoons. In a corner stood an entire stuffed black bear. On a small stand was a stuffed eagle. Mixed in with the mounted heads were bare skulls, and in another corner was a pile of skulls nearly as high as Buck's waist.

Ezriah noticed where he was staring, and smiled. "That's Woman's collection. She uses them in her spells and when she casts the future."

Granger said, "You don't really believe she can do that?"

"She does. And I've learned not to dispute her." Ezriah shrugged. "How she does the things she does, I can't say."

Woman went to a cupboard. Inside were dozens of

jars, none with labels. She sorted through them and took down a small jar and brought it to the stove. Opening it, she took a pinch of the contents and put it in one of the cups and did the same with the next.

"What's that she's doing?" Buck asked.

"Brown sugar," Ezriah said. "You're guests, so she's treating you. We don't use it much ourselves."

Fox motioned at the front door. "Why did you leave that open?"

"To let air in," Ezriah said. "It's hot out, in case you ain't noticed." He chuckled. "You boys sure are suspicious. You relax. You're guests in my home. Nothing will happen to you here. Besides, there's the truce."

"Which some of your clan broke when they raped my girl," Buck said bluntly.

Ezriah frowned and slid a hand inside his open shirt and scratched himself. "If I could, I'd shoot them my own self for what they done. But the blame isn't all theirs, is it?"

"How do you mean?"

"Your girl was on Harkey land. She should have known better."

"She did," Buck admitted. "But the young don't always listen. And with the truce and all, she probably figured she'd be safe."

Granger said, "There were seven boys who did her. Or six, 'cause one of them tried to stop them."

"Do you know who they are?" Fox asked.

Ezriah nodded. "There were two brothers, Rabon and Woot, and four of their cousins, Darnell, Ardley, Preston, and Calvert. Oh, and Jimbo, the one who got hit for trying to talk them out of it."

"I don't care about Jimbo," Buck said. "The others must be punished. I could kill them and be within my rights."

"That you could," Ezriah agreed, and fell silent as his wife came over bearing a tray with the four cups of coffee. She set down a cup in front of each of them and placed the empty tray on the table and stepped behind Ezriah's chair and stood with her hand on the chair.

Granger reached for his cup, and stopped. "She just going to stand there like that?"

"She can listen if she wants," Ezriah said.

"What I want to know," Buck said, picking up his cup, "is what you intend to do about it." He sipped, then blew on the hot coffee and took another sip. "Sort of bitter."

"Woman never could cook worth a lick," Ezriah said. "If you think that is bitter, you should taste her tea."

"About them boys?" Buck prompted.

"In the old days I'd have had them whipped. Tie them to posts and use a bullwhip on their backs to teach them a lesson. But these ain't the old days."

"What do you aim to do, then?"

"They can't be allowed to get away with it," Fox said.

"No man should do to a woman what they did," Ezriah agreed. "But the situation is delicate."

"We're not talking eggshells," Granger said.

Ezriah laced his fingers and gazed out the door. "Rabon and Woot aren't just any old Harkeys. They're my grandsons," he said sadly.

"Hell," Buck said.

"Yes. I know." Ezriah shrunk a little in his chair. "My own blood doing that. I wouldn't have thought they had it in them but blood don't always tell. Now they've stained the Harkey name. Once word gets out . . ." He paused and looked at Buck. "How many people know?"

"We've kept it quiet," Buck informed him. "Doc Witherspoon, since he treated Scarlet. My pa and my family and my brothers here."

"That's all?"

"No one else."

"Really?" Ezriah sounded genuinely surprised. "I didn't expect that. No, sir. I didn't expect that at all."

"What difference does it make how many know?" Granger gruffly asked.

"It makes a big difference to me," Ezriah replied. "The less who hear of it, the better for my clan. The easier the problem is to solve. Doc Witherspoon won't say anything. He knows better. That leaves your family."

Buck drank half his cup in several swallows and set the cup down. "We're getting off the trail. I want to hear about the punishment."

"What would you have me do? What do you think is fair?"

"That whipping sounds good. Or a beating with a switch until their backs are raw."

"I did mention they're my grandsons?"

"That's not what's important."

Granger drained his cup. He ran his sleeve over his brow and said, "It sure is hot in here."

"Would you like more?" Ezriah asked.

"No, thanks."

Ezriah turned to his wife and said, "How long?"

"No more than five minutes," she replied.

"How long what?" Buck inquired.

"She has a pie in the oven. It was for supper tonight but I don't mind sharing with you boys."

Fox sniffed a few times. "I don't smell no pie."

Ezriah bobbed his chin at Fox's coffee cup. "I notice you didn't touch yours. After Woman made it special, too."

"I'm not much of a coffee drinker," Fox said.

"Can she get you something else? Tea? Water? Hell, how about some liquor?"

"Nothing. I'm not thirsty."

"That's too bad." Ezriah reached inside his shirt and scratched again. "As for this other, you have to look at it from my side. From the Harkey point of view. Your girl came on Harkey land knowing she shouldn't. She was the one in the wrong. She was the one broke the truce. She was—"

Buck held up a hand. "Wait a second. You're not blaming all of this on her?"

"Not all, no. But most. If she hadn't been so foolish, we wouldn't be sitting here and I wouldn't have to do what I have to do. It's a shame. The truce was good while it lasted."

"The truce can go on once the wrong had been righted."

"No, it can't. Once a truce is broken, it's broken for good. Here, today, is the end of it."

"That's crazy talk," Buck said. "We can patch things up. All you have to do is punish those boys."

"So you keep saying. But it's not that simple. I'm the head of my clan. I have to do what's best for the Harkeys, and what's best for the Harkeys might not be what's best for you Shannons."

"What are you saying?"

"That my clan comes first. It always comes first. I do whatever it takes to protect them even if it means doing something I might not like to do, something I wouldn't do if it wasn't forced on me. Take now, for instance. You show up on my doorstep and demand I punish the boys who did your girl wrong. Deep down I agree with you. They *did* do wrong and they *should* be punished. Hell, if it was a Harkey girl who got raped by a bunch of Shannon, I'd want their peckers cut off."

"Then we see eye to eye," Buck said.

Ezriah sighed. "No, we don't. You're not listening. I can't punish a Harkey. I can't hurt a member of my own clan. I sure as hell can't hurt my own grandsons. I'm sorry but that's how it is."

"But you said you want to settle this."

"I do."

Granger placed his hands on the table, palms up, and moved them back and forth, then looked down at his legs and moved them, too.

"What on earth are you doing?" Fox asked.

"I feel funny," Granger replied. "My arms and legs are tingly and my stomach is trying to crawl up my throat."

"That's strange," Buck said. "I'm feeling peculiar myself." He took another sip of coffee. "Even my mouth is tingling."

"Maybe you are coming down with something," Ezriah said. He scratched his chest and slid his hand under his shirt, still scratching.

"I feel fine," Fox said. He glanced at Buck, and at the cup in Buck's hand, and then at Granger, and at the cup on the table in front of him, and said, "Son of a bitch."

"Too bad you didn't drink some, too," Ezriah said. He brought his hand out from under his shirt. In it was a Cloveland House pocket revolver in .41 caliber. He cocked it and pointed it at Fox.

"What this?" Buck said in alarm.

Ezriah shot Fox. The slug cored Fox's forehead and snapped his head back. He tried to speak, but all that came out was a grunt. A red drop trickled down his brow as he slowly folded and his body slid off the chair to the floor. He twitched a few times and was still.

Both Buck and Granger went to reach for their rifles. Both raised their hands a few inches and then looked at their arms in dismay and disbelief.

"What the hell is happening?" Buck said. "I can't hardly move."

"Me, either."

Ezriah Harkey held the smoking pistol level. "It's the poison. Pretty soon you won't be able to move at all."

Buck and Granger said together, "Poison?"

"Woman's doing," Ezriah said, with a jerk of his thumb at his wife. "She's good with potions and herbs and"—he grinned a wicked grin—"poisons."

"That wasn't brown sugar she put in our coffee," Buck said.

"It was not."

"And that's why the coffee tasted bitter."

"It was." Ezriah sighed. "If you don't mind my saying, you boys sure are dumb. Your pa would never have let himself be taken this away. When he came to visit me that time, he wouldn't drink nor eat. Truce or no truce, he knew better. I'm surprised you don't take after him more."

Buck again tried to lift his arms, and couldn't. He tried to stand but stayed on the chair. The tingling had spread from his limbs to his belly and was slowly creeping up his chest. "This can't be."

"It is."

Granger strained mightily. His face grew red and the veins in his neck stood out and he rose several inches, swayed, and abruptly sat back down so hard his chair nearly fell over. "You bastard. You miserable yellow bastard."

"Here, now," Ezriah said. "Yellow has nothing to do with it. I ain't no coward. I could have just shot you. This way is less messy, and I have a few things I want to say before we get to it."

"Oh God," Buck said.

"What Woman used on you is toad poison. She collects it herself. Everything in you freezes up so your muscles won't work. Pretty soon you won't be able to talk. But you'll still be alive. You'll see and hear."

"Goddamn you," Granger snarled.

"The three of you are going to disappear. I'll bury the bodies where no one will ever find them and take your horses off a ways and strip them and shoot them and leave them for the scavengers to eat. If the sheriff or any of your kin come around asking if you showed up, I'll say I never saw you."

"Not this way," Buck said.

"It's the only way," Ezriah said. "Your wife and pa might suspect but they won't have proof and without proof your pa won't break the truce. Life will go on as it was."

"Please."

"Don't beg. It's not manly." Ezriah let down the hammer of his pocket pistol and slipped it under his shirt. "I reckon I won't need this." He turned to his wife. "Fetch me the ax handle from out of the shed. The one that broke. It makes a good club."

Woman chuckled and went out.

Buck found it increasingly hard to talk. The tingling had risen to his throat. "Please, mister. I have a wife and family."

"I have my clan."

Growling like a wild beast, Granger attempted to heave to his feet. Instead, his legs gave out and he and his chair crashed to the floor.

"You're wasting yourself," Ezriah told him. He rose and came around the table. Sliding his hands under Buck's arms, he lifted and eased Buck to the floor next to Granger. "Any last words?"

"You won't get away with this," Buck said. Panic filled him. He willed his arms and legs to move but they wouldn't.

"Dumb to the last," Ezriah responded. He walked to the counter and filled a glass with water from a pitcher and leaned against the counter and drank. "You might want to make your peace with your Maker."

Woman returned carrying the ax handle. She brought it over and gave it to Ezriah. "I want to watch."

"It will be a sight." Ezriah hefted the ax handle and went and stood over Buck. "Can you still talk?"

Buck lay motionless save for his eyes, which grew wide with fear.

"Reckon not." Ezriah raised the ax handle and brought it down with all his force on Buck Shannon's mouth. Teeth crunched and blood splattered and Buck made mewing sounds. "I told you," Ezriah said, not without a trace of pity. "My clan comes first." He swung again and again and again.

8

---◆-◆---

A week passed. On the seventh evening Jed Shannon sat down to supper with Erna, Chace, and Cassie. Scarlet was still in bed. She'd wanted to join them, but Erna told her it would be a while yet before she was permitted to be up and about.

Cassie gave thanks.

Erna helped herself to a slice of corn pone and handed the bread to her son. "Pass this around."

"It's been too long," Jed said. "They should have been here yesterday at the latest."

"They'll show," Erna said. "My Buck knows what he's doing. He wouldn't let anything happen."

Jed pursed his lips. He heaped hog and hominy on his plate and stabbed a piece of pork with his fork. "Buck was wrong not to want me along. I should have been with them."

"Please," Erna said. "Let's not bring it up at the table. After, if you insist. But let us eat in peace."

"Whatever you want."

Cassie could tell her grandpa would rather talk about it; he only gave in to be polite. She wanted to talk about it, too. She was worried near to sick over her pa and uncles. The past few nights she'd hardly slept. She tossed and turned and when she did doze, she had bad dreams that woke her. She looked at her brother. Chace was as calm as you please, quietly eating, his face showing no more emotion than a wall. She had asked him earlier how he was sleeping and he had replied, "Just fine."

In addition to the hog and hominy and corn pone, there was succotash. Cassie ladled some out and ate, with no real appetite. She was glad when everyone was done. She sat back and waited for her grandfather to say something but it was her brother who broke the silence.

"I'm going after Pa."

Erna was refilling her glass with milk. She stopped pouring and said, "No, you are not."

"You don't have a say," Chace said.

"I beg your pardon? I'm your mother. I do so have a say. We'll wait two or three days and if they haven't shown we'll go to the sheriff."

"Wonderful," Jed said.

"Something the matter?"

"You know as well as I do, Erna, that Sheriff Wyler has been in office so long, the only thing that matters to him is *staying* in office. He won't do anything to rustle Harkey feathers. Not when half the voters in the county are Harkeys."

"He might send one of his deputies."

"Do you think the Harkeys will come right out and admit it if they've done my sons harm?" Jed said. "Hell, no. Ezriah ain't stupid. He'll hide the bodies so they won't ever be found and act as innocent as a newborn."

"You talk as if my Buck is already dead."

"Odds are he is."

"No. Him and me have been together nigh on thirty year. I would know if he was dead."

"Hell," Jed said.

"I'll thank you not to cuss." Erna turned to Chace. "We're agreed, then, that you won't go looking for your pa?"

"We are no such thing." Chace pushed back his chair and stood. "I'm leaving at first light." He went to the front door. His rifle was propped next to it, and he took hold of the barrel and went out and closed the door after him.

"The gall," Erna said.

"I'll go talk to him for you," Jed offered.

A blazing orange sun hung on the cusp of creation. Cows grazed in the pasture while others rested and chewed their cud. In the hog pen the sow was nursing her brood and chickens pecked in the dust near the coop. A flock of pigeons winged in and landed on the barn.

Chace was making for the corral. He stopped when his grandfather called his name. "If she sent you to stop me, you're wasting your breath."

"Stop you?" Jed said, and laughed. "Tarnation, boy. Don't you know me better than that? I'm going with you."

"No," Chace said, "you're not."

"I can if I want."

"No."

Chace continued on and Jed caught up and walked beside him.

"Now listen here, boy. Not only am I the head of this clan but I'm your grandpa. It's bad enough your pa saw fit to go without me. I'll be hornswoggled if my grandson will treat me with the same disrespect."

"It's not about you, Grandpa," Chace said. "It's about Pa. He ain't coming back. If he was he'd've been here by now. You said so yourself."

"That don't give you call to go off and get yourself killed. You need me. I know the way, and unless you know the landmarks, you won't find Ezriah's place in a million years."

"I was listening when you told Pa." Chace opened the gate and went over to the blackest of the mules and patted its neck. It was fifteen hands high and had a white muzzle. "This here is Enoch. He's mine."

"After the Bible Enoch?"

"Ma named him. She's fond of Bible names for our critters. The cow she likes most is Esther. She calls our rooster Beelzebub." Chace rubbed Enoch and scratched under the mule's jaw. "He's as surefooted as can be."

"Explain to me why you don't want me along."

"I can't have witnesses. Not even you. I won't have it come back to plague me later."

"Won't have what?" Jed asked. When Chace didn't answer he asked it again, adding, "What exactly do you have in mind?"

"Pa handled this wrong." Chace turned from Enoch. "He went to the Harkeys to talk when he should have gone with fifty Shannons at his back and strung up the ones who did Scarlet wrong. She's still lying in bed with bruises all over her and her spirit crushed. She'll never be the same girl she was."

"Listen to you. You'd break the truce just like that?" Jed snapped his fingers.

Chace didn't answer until they were out the gate and he had closed it. "There never should have been a truce in the first place."

"It was my idea, you might recall."

"A bad idea." Chace motioned at the animals in the corral. "A mule is a mule and not a dog."

"That makes no kind of sense."

"Doesn't it, Grandpa?" Chace said. "Then let me make it plain. A thing is what it is and not something else. A person is who they are and not somebody else." His eyes lit with a fierce light. "And an enemy is an enemy and not a friend. You did our clan no favors when you and the head of their clan agreed to a truce. All you did was put off the day of reckoning."

"Why, you ..." Jed caught himself. "You weren't there, boy. You weren't even born. Shannons were dying. Good men. Men I knew. Men I cared for. You didn't have to comfort their grieving widows. You didn't have to listen to their kids bawl. I did what I did to save lives."

"You did what you did because you weren't strong enough to do what really needed doing."

"And what was that, you and your smart mouth?"

"To kill every Harkey there is."

Jed shook his head in amazement. "Listen to you. What do you know about killing, boy? What do you know about anything?" He paused. "Oh. I forgot the drunk in the hayloft."

Chace stared at his grandfather. Finally he said, almost to himself, "I always suspected she told you."

"She needed to tell someone and she sure as hell couldn't tell your ma or your pa. So, yes, she came to me."

"Why didn't you go to the law?"

Jed's lips became a thin slit and he clenched his fists. "Anyone but family said that to me, I'd pound them. That was an insult, boy. A pure-as-sin insult."

"About the law?" Chace nodded. "Yes, I reckon it was. I'm sorry. I shouldn't have said it."

"And no, I never told them nor anyone else. Why would I? You did what was right. Benton was the town drunk. He was always getting into fights and making a nuisance of himself. He'd be rude to women on the street. It doesn't surprise me a bit that he tricked your sister into climbing up into the hayloft or that he—" Jed stopped. "I only thank God you were there. I thank God you saved her before he could get her clothes off. Although I still don't know how you could have done it. Benton was big. Bigger than me. And you were eleven."

"He didn't see me or hear me come up the ladder," Chace said. "They were over by the loft door. He had her down and was doing things and she was trying to fight him, but like you say, he was big."

"So how did you?" Jed asked.

"I snuck up behind him. He was on his knees and I hit him in the side of the neck. When he turned, I hit him in the throat. He fell onto his hands and was trying to get his breath. His head was next to the loft door. I pushed it open and ran behind him and shoved." Chace stopped. "It wasn't nearly as hard as I thought it would be. He went out that door like a greased pig down a chute. Never screamed or cursed or nothing. When I looked out, he was lying there in the street, his head bent so that I knew his neck was broke."

"I'll be damned."

"I got Cassie down and we went out the back and on around. Then people were there. They took the body to the undertaker's."

"And the sheriff decided Benton was so drunk, he fell

out and broke his own fool neck." Jed was filled with wonderment. "You killed a man, and you were only eleven."

"What does age have to do with it?"

"Nothing, I suppose."

"It had to be done. Just as *this* has to be done." Chace turned and walked into the barn. He went to the table where they kept the tack and picked up a bridle and examined it.

Jed stayed with him. "None of that gives you the right to tell me I can't go. I'm your grandfather, goddamn it, and you listen to me, I don't listen to you."

Chace put down the bridle. When he spoke he did so quietly, gently, without a trace of anger or resentment. "In this you do. If something happens to me, Ma and Cassie and Scarlet will need you. One of us has to stay and you'd be better at looking after them than I would, so it has to be you."

"That's why you don't want me to go?"

"We have to think of them."

"Damn," Jed said. He placed his hands on the table and leaned on them. "I had you pegged wrong, boy. You're older than your years."

"Not really. I just do what needs doing and I try to do it smart."

Jed looked at him. "They'll be expecting someone to come."

"They'll expect a lot of Shannon men. They won't expect what you and everyone else keeps calling a boy."

"They might try to kill you."

"Whether they do or they don't, they have to answer for Pa and for Scarlet and for my uncles."

"That they do," Jed agreed, and sighed. "The feud will

start up again, sure as shooting. The truce will be over for good and forever."

"Good riddance."

"Old Ezriah will be disappointed."

"Old Ezriah won't be around."

"Him, too?"

"Him first."

Jed studied Chace as if seeing him for the first time. "You *are* beyond your years. But you be careful. Ezriah isn't like Benton. He won't be drunk, and he's clever as a fox. That you're young won't stop him from planting you."

"My age will get me close," Chace said.

"You could pick him off with that rifle of yours. I hear you're as good a shot as Daniel Boone."

"I want to look into his eyes when I do it."

"You're beginning to scare me, boy."

Erna was drying dishes at the counter when they came back in. She draped the towel over her shoulder. "Did you talk sense into him?" she asked.

"He talked sense into me."

"How so?"

It was Chace who answered. "I'm still leaving at first light. I'd be obliged if you'd spare some food for me to take on the trail."

"As if I wouldn't," Erna said, and put her hands on her hips. "I'm dead set against this. What if I flat-out say you can't go? Will you still go anyway?"

"I have to, Ma."

Erna bowed her head. "Oh God," she said softly.

"I'll be all right."

"Don't do that," Erna said.

"Don't do what?"

"Don't patronize me."

Chace stepped over and hugged her. "Ma, I don't rightly know what that means. I don't want you to worry, is all."

"How can I not? I'm your mother." Erna pushed away and went to the counter.

Just then Cassie came out of her bedroom and stood with her arms folded, staring hard at her twin.

"What?"

"You know."

Chace turned to Jed and said half jokingly, "Is it me, or are the women in this house ready to thump me with canes?"

"It's not you, grandson," Jedediah Shannon said. "They know death is in the air."

9

Chace was up before the rooster crowed. Slipping out of his nightshirt, he pulled on his britches and shrugged into his shirt. He strapped on the cartridge belt and stuck the sheath and toothpick at the small of his back. Taking the Spencer down from the pegs, he patted it. The night before, he had thrown things he'd need into a burlap sack and left it next to the bed, and now he hefted the bag over his shoulder and walked out of his bedroom.

All three were waiting for him. Erna was at the counter, filling a pouch.

Jedediah was at the table, tapping his fingers. Cassie was over by the front door wearing a pall of gloom on her usually sunny face.

"You're all up early." Chace went to the table and set the sack down. "Say what you have to say and I'll be on my way."

Jed bent toward him. "Any chance you've changed your mind about me tagging along?"

"I thought we had that worked out."

Jed glanced at Erna, who chose that moment to come

over carrying the pouch. "I fixed you some eats. Jerky, mainly. Plus some bread and a few cans of beans."

Chace slung the pouch crosswise over his chest so that it hung on his left hip. "I'm obliged."

Erna's lower lip quivered and suddenly she threw her arms around him and held him close. "Oh God," she said. "I wish you wouldn't. I don't want to lose you, too."

"I have it to do," Chace said. Wet drops trickled down his neck. He ran a hand over her hair. "Quit your fussing. I'll be fine. I'm not Pa."

Erna drew back, her eyes flashing. "That's a terrible thing to say, and him maybe dead."

"No maybe about it," Chace replied. "He'd have been back by now if he was still breathing."

"Oh . . . you!" Erna exclaimed, and covering her face with her hands, she burst out bawling.

Jed came around the table and enfolded her in his arms, saying, "There, there." Over her shoulder he gave Chace a hard look. "See what you've done, boy?"

Chace picked up the sack and stepped to the door. He went out without glancing back and didn't say anything to the shadow he acquired until after he had gone into the barn for the bridle and then around to the corral. "You're not coming, if that's what is on your mind."

"I want to see you off," Cassie said, "and to tell you something."

Chace waited with his hand on the gate.

"I know I can't talk you out of it. No one can. Once you take a notion into your head you're more stubborn than a mule." Cassie touched a finger to his cheek. "Don't let anything happen to you. I couldn't stand it. If you die I won't want to live."

"That's silly."

Cassie gripped his chin almost fiercely. "Don't interrupt. We're twins. Two made as one, as you put it once. And that's true. I feel closer to you than to any human being on God's green earth. We're joined in our hearts and our minds now and forever."

Chace went to open the gate, but she held on to him.

"So don't tell me I'm being silly when I say that if you die, I'll take my own life rather than go on without you."

"Cassie, damn it," Chace said.

"I can't help my feelings. We are what we are. Other folks might laugh. Normal folks might think it strange, us being so close. But they're not us. They don't have a twin. They have no idea what it's like."

"I'll be back. I promise."

Cassie's eyes were misting. She let go.

Enoch came when Chace whistled. Chace slipped the bridle on and brought the mule around to the front of the barn, where he draped a worn saddle blanket over the mule's back and swung his old saddle up and over. He tied the sack to the saddle horn and started to lift his leg to the stirrup.

"Don't I at least get a hug?"

Chace slowly lowered his leg and turned. He opened his arms and Cassie stepped into them and clung to him as if she were drowning and he was a log.

"I hate this," she whispered, and smothered a sob. "I hate us being apart."

"In a week I'll be back and we can get on with our lives."

"That long?"

"Maybe longer."

"Oh God."

Chace pried her fingers off and gently pushed her back. "I can't stand around hugging you all day." He forked leather and lifted the reins. "Take care of Scarlet. She'll be up and around soon and she'll need someone to take her mind off things."

"She should look after herself," Cassie said sullenly. "This is her fault. Traipsing off to Harkey Hollow thataway."

"She's powerful fond of blackberries," Chace said. He leaned down and put his hand on Cassie's head. "Just as I'm powerful fond of you." He smiled and jabbed his heels. She called his name but he didn't look back. He rode down the lane and came to the fork that would take travelers to Wareagle to the east or to Siloam Spring to the west. Chace took neither. He went straight across the road and into the woods. For a quarter of an hour he made steadily north. A willow with a wide trunk caught his eye. He rode under a low branch and drew rein. Dawing his legs up under him, he looped an arm over the branch and in another moment was straddling it. Enoch stayed where he was.

Chace gripped a higher limb to steady himself. He leaned against the trunk, the Spencer in his lap, and let his leg dangle. Time crawled to the buzz of a cicada. A cardinal alighted and took quick wing when it noticed him. A mockingbird sang. Chace was watching a fuzzy caterpillar when the dull thud of hooves intruded.

A saddle creaked, and Chace said, "Up here."

A study in consternation, Jedediah had reined up next to Enoch and was scouring the forest. He slapped his leg and swore. "I should have guessed. But your mule was standing here so long, I thought . . ." He didn't say what he thought.

Chace swung from the limb to the saddle and slipped his bare feet into the stirrups. "I'm disappointed."

"It's your ma's doing," Jed said. "Last night she made me promise. I am to follow you and lend a hand if you need it."

"We've been all through this. Go back. Tell her I shook you off. Stay with them until I come back."

Jed frowned and twisted and slid his hand into a saddlebag. He groped inside and pulled out a silver flask. Opening it, he took a long swig. "Ahhhh. I needed that." He smiled contentedly.

"What's that?" Chace asked.

"What does it look like?" Jed wagged the flask. "My affliction. I've held off as long as I can. Any longer and I'll come down with the shakes."

"I'd never have guessed."

"I hide it real well, don't I?" Jed chuckled and treated himself to another swallow. "I've always liked liquor but a lot more so since your grandmother died. Some days all I do is drink. It helps numb the pain." He took a long pull at the flask, his throat bobbing.

"You shouldn't drink around the women."

Jed made a show of peering into the woods. "You see any hereabouts?" He chortled. "Don't worry. I'll sneak off and do it in private like I usually do." He drank more and held the flask out to Chace. "How about you, boy? To fortify you for what you've got to do."

"I don't need no fortification."

"No. Of course you don't. At your age you think you don't need anyone or anything. But you're wrong. We're none of us hard as iron as much as we might like to make believe we are."

"I don't do make believe, neither."

Jed sipped and squinted at him. "No. That's right. Come to think of it, you never were one for playing and acting the fool. From as far back as I can recollect you've been serious as hell." He swallowed and smacked his lips. "You need to learn to savor life."

"Is that what you're doing?"

Jed held the flask so it caught the rays of the sun and gleamed like spun silver. "Now that you ask, yes. Some folks would accuse me of getting drunk just to get drunk. But I *like* getting drunk. I like the burning when I swallow and the warmth in my belly and how light-headed I get. But most of all I like how for a short while I can forget."

"Forget what?"

"The hurt of losing your grandmother." Jed raised the flask on high. "To the sweetest and best gal who ever drew breath, my wonderful Mary."

"Was she a whiskey funnel, too?"

Jed lowered his arm so fast he smacked it against his saddle. "If you weren't my kin I'd shoot you for that. But no, she wasn't. Oh, she'd take a nip now and again, but only to please me."

"Then she wouldn't like what you've become."

"Watch yourself, boy," Jed warned. "I've barely had half this flask. You've no call to accuse me of being worse than I am."

"You're swaying," Chace said.

"I'm what?"

Chace pointed. "You're swaying in your saddle, Grandpa. Any more of that red-eye and you're liable to fall and break your bones."

"Ridiculous," Jed said with ripe scorn. "After a bottle or two maybe I get tipsy but not on no half a flask." He looked down at the ground and his eyebrows pinched. "Damn. Then again, maybe you're right. Either the ground's moving or I am."

"I have no more time for this." Chace reined to the east and said over his shoulder, "Don't follow me again. Next time I'll shoot your horse out from under you."

"Don't you dare talk to me like that," Jed hollered.

There was more but Chace didn't listen. He brought the mule to a trot for half a mile and then stopped and watched his back trail for a good twenty minutes.

Satisfied his grandfather wasn't trailing him, he made a beeline for the distant high ridge that separated Shannon country from Harkey territory. By sunset he was halfway to the crest. Instead of making camp he pushed on until along about ten, when he reached the top. In all directions stretched a sea of ink broken by scattered points of light. A cluster to the south was Wareagle.

Chace made a cold camp. He sat with his back to his saddle and the Spencer across his legs and munched on jerky. Above him a host of stars sparkled. Twice shooting stars cleaved the firmament with streaks of fire. Now and again coyotes yipped. A wolf wailed a lupine lament. Owls hooted and crickets chirped.

The woods were alive with the cries of predators and prey.

"I reckon I like this more than just about anything," Chace said to Enoch. The mule went on dozing.

Soon Chace joined him.

A pink streak marked the impending dawn when Chace was again under way. He rode slower than the day before and stopped regularly to rise in the stirrups and scan the countryside. Toward the middle of the morning he was threading through a stand of saplings when voices brought him to a halt. Dismounting, he wrapped the reins around a tree and advanced on foot.

Two men had shot a doe and were butchering her. Both had the Harkey dark hair and dark beards and dark eyes, and wore clothes that had seen better days. They had set down their rifles to cut the doe up.

The biggest held up the heart, which was dripping with blood. "You want first bite, cousin?"

"You go ahead," said the other.

The big one sank his teeth into the ripe flesh and hungrily bit off a piece. Chewing lustily, he said with his mouth full, "Nothing beats deer hearts unless it's bear hearts."

"I like hog hearts myself," the cousin said. "They don't taste much like ham, though, like you figure they would."

Chace set down the Spencer. He drew the Arkansas toothpick, held it against his pant leg, and started to rise. Then he sank back down. He looked at the toothpick and at the backs of the men and he frowned and slid the toothpick back into its sheath. Soundlessly, he crept to Enoch.

The sun was straight overhead when Chace stopped to rest the mule. He sat on a small boulder with the Spencer across his legs and gazed at the blue vault overhead. "We need to talk, you and me."

A bluebird flew past, chirping.

"My ma believes. My pa did, too, some anyway, more because of her than because of you. The parson sure believes. He goes on and on about you every single Sunday. Those like him and my ma say we shouldn't do what I'm about to do on account of it don't sit right with you.

But I've been thinking and thinking, and I want you to hear me out."

Several turkey vultures were soaring circles high in the air, their red heads bright in the sun.

"The question I have is, why?" Chace said to the sky. "Why did you let them do to Scarlet what they done? Why didn't you stop my pa from going off and getting himself killed? Why did you let that damn drunk paw my sister? If you're up there, and you're as the parson says you are, then it makes no sense. Either he's lying or you're not at all like everyone thinks you are or you're not there at all."

The vultures wheeled over the clearing, and him.

Chace raised the Spencer and took a bead on one but only grinned and lowered the rifle again.

"You can't love us and let a girl be raped. You can't love us and let my pa and his brothers be killed for doing what was right. Or how about my aunt's infant, taken in the night and they don't know what killed it? So much of that goes on."

Chace ran his gaze from one end of the blue to the other. "Is that your notion of love? The parson says so. Me, I think if you're up there, you don't care. I think you look down on us and don't give a good damn if we die bloody or screaming or puking our guts out. But here's your chance to prove me wrong. Give me a sign. Show me I shouldn't do to the Harkeys as they've done to us. Anything will do. Have one of those buzzards fall dead at my feet. Make the ground shake. Send a dove like you did with Noah. Anything. Anything at all."

Chace stared at the sky until eventually he sighed and said, "I didn't think so."

10

Chace was deep in Harkey land. In most respects it was no different from Shannon country: rolling mountains, thick woods laced by gurgling streams, and plenty of wildlife.

Another landmark—a mountain with a notch at the top—rose to the north and Chace reined to the northeast.

The valley was exactly as Jedediah had described: narrow, with a small creek and a cabin made of stone and logs. Chace didn't try to hide. He made straight to the homestead as calmly and as casually as if it were his own.

A big dog came out of the shadows and commenced to bark. A woman appeared, wiping her hands on an apron. She wasn't armed, but she showed no fear as Chace came to a stop.

He smiled a bright smile. "Nice place you have here, ma'am."

"Who might you be, boy, and what do you want?" she demanded.

"I'm Chace Shannon. I'm looking for my pa, Buck Shannon. This Ezriah Harkey's home?"

"That it is," the woman said, "but he ain't here. He went off yesterday morning and won't be back until the day after tomorrow. I'm his wife."

"What might your name be, ma'am?" Chace asked, still smiling.

"Woman."

"I beg your pardon?"

"Folks call me Woman 'cause I want them to."

"How peculiar."

"There's a lot of strange things in this world, boy. You're too young to have seen them yet."

"I'm a fast learner, ma'am," Chace said, and gazed about him, his smile a fixture. "Was my pa here, then?"

"He was, boy," Woman said. "Him and his brothers. They visited and talked with my Ezriah and then they went off to home. That's the last I saw of them."

"They never got there. They should have been back long ago."

Woman shrugged. "Maybe they stopped over to Wareagle. Maybe they got drunk and got themselves whores. Men do that."

"Not my pa," Chace said. "He's not a whore man. He loves my ma too much to touch another female."

"So you may think, boy. But when a man can, he will. Men have no control over their peckers. It's the first thing a female learns."

Chace's smile widened. "Why, ma'am, you are a delight of frank talk. I've never heard a lady say 'pecker' before."

"So young and so innocent." Woman smiled and beckoned. "Tell you what. Why don't you climb down and come on in? You must be tuckered out after your long ride. I'll fix you a bite to eat, and my special tea. How would that be?"

"I'd be grateful, ma'am." Chace alighted and arched his back and held the Spencer at his side. He took a step and the big dog growled.

"Quiet," Woman snapped. "Go lie down."

With a hostile glance at Chace, the dog obeyed.

"He sure is a big one, ma'am."

"We keep him around to ward off bears and such," Woman said. "When he gets old we'll get another and I'll cut him up and use him in my medicine." Woman stepped to the doorway.

"You're a healer, ma'am?"

"I'm many things, boy. After you."

"No, ma'am," Chace said sweetly. "My ma raised me to always be polite. Ladies first."

Woman tittered and went in, saying, "You Shannons aren't as I figured. To most Harkeys you are downright evil."

"I guess the Shannons feel the same about you Harkeys." Chace stopped just inside and let his eyes adjust. He swept the place, his gaze lingering on a pair of rifles propped in a corner. He walked to the table, leaned his Spencer against it, and sank into a chair. "Nice place you have here."

Woman was at a cupboard. She took down a jar. "I like it. I'm a simple woman with simple needs." She opened the jar. "How about the tea first and then some vittles?"

"That sounds fine, ma'am."

Woman stepped to the stove and touched a kettle and frowned. "Damn. It's cold. I'll have to heat the water."

"I'm in no hurry, ma'am," Chace said. "Take as long as you like."

Woman tittered again. "Yes, sir. Polite as hell. And so handsome, too. You're about the good-lookingest boy I ever did see."

"Why, thank you, ma'am. That's awful kind. But I reckon I'm no better-looking than most."

She appraised him in earnest. "No, boy. I've seen more of the world and I'm telling you true. You're handsome as hell. Any chance you'd like to poke me while we wait for the tea?"

"Poke you, ma'am?"

"You have poked, haven't you? A handsome boy like you?"

"A gentleman never tells, ma'am. And what about your husband?"

"He has his secret pokes he thinks I don't know about. I don't mind 'cause I know how men are. Plus, it's less he has to poke me and when he does he about bores me half to death."

"How can poking be boring, ma'am?" Chace asked.

"Trust me, boy. When a man does it the same way, year in and year out, you could sleep while he's doing it and not hardly notice."

Chace laughed. "You sure are sassy, ma'am."

Woman removed the top from the kettle and filled it with water from a bucket on the counter and set the kettle on the stove. She rekindled the fire and took off her apron and put it on the counter and came over and stood beside him. Leaning against the table, she ran a hand down her black dress. "What do you say to my offer?"

"About what, ma'am?" Chace leaned back in his chair, his right hand on the seat.

"About that poke, silly boy."

"You were serious?"

"I never joke about pokes." Woman touched his hair and fingered it. "Fine as silk, yet curly some. Topaz eyes, too. Were you to grow up, you'd be a lady-killer for sure."

"I'm counting on growing up," Chace said.

"We all do. But we never know but when our time has come." Woman traced her finger across his temple and down his cheek and along his lower lip. "You ain't answered me yet. Don't let my hair fool you. I'm gray on top, but my body is right fine. I won't disappoint."

"I couldn't, ma'am."

"Why the hell not? Are you shy? Or is it you haven't ever done it before? Is that it? I'd be your first?"

"There's been one other," Chace admitted.

"Who?"

"I can't say." With his left hand Chace reached up and gave her arm a light squeeze. "I thank you, though. The thing is, when I said I couldn't, I meant we won't be able to because you won't be breathing." He brought his right hand around and up, quick as a striking cottonmouth, and sank the double-edge blade to the hilt in her belly. Woman went rigid with shock. Still smiling, Chace twisted the blade. "One of those rifles yonder belonged to my pa, the other to my uncle. You shouldn't ought to have left them out in the open."

Woman came to life. Screeching like a bobcat, she pushed Chace so violently that he and the chair rocked back and he lost his grip on the toothpick. She bounded to one side and yanked the knife out and screeched louder. Blood poured as she flew at Chace in a rage and swung the red blade at his neck. Chace dived from the chair. He landed on his shoulder and rolled up into a crouch and tried to level the Spencer but she was on him before he could take aim. The toothpick sheared at his head. Barely in time, he thrust the rifle up. Metal rang on metal. Straightening, Chace backpedaled. Woman hissed through her clenched teeth and rushed him, spearing the blade at his ribs. Chace dodged and she came after him, swinging furiously. He skipped back and collided with a wall. Woman, her eyes aglow with bloodlust, lanced the toothpick at his belly. Chace twisted sideways. The knife sliced his shirt and his skin, but not deep. He drove the Spencer's stock at her face, felt her nose give and a spray of wet on his fingers. Woman howled and staggered back. He struck again, smashing the stock against her arm, and the toothpick clattered to the floorboards. He drew the stock back to strike at her face, but she grabbed it and screeched and sought to tear the rifle from his grasp. Struggling fiercely, they went round and round. The lower half of Woman's dress was soaked with blood and the lower half of her face was a scarlet smear. Chace crashed into a rocking chair and it toppled. Woman shrieked and wrenched on the Spencer, and Chace let go. Off balance, she staggered. Chace was on her before she could recover. He punched her in the throat, once, twice, three times, and she went to one knee. He tore the rifle free, reversed his grip so he was holding it by the barrel, and raised it on high.

Woman had both hands to her throat and was sucking in breath in ragged heaves. She looked up.

Chace smiled. "For my pa," he said, and brought the rifle down. The stock caught her above the ear and she folded like a poled cow. He stood over her, breathing heavily, and said, "Damn."

Backing against the table, Chace leaned on it. He set the Spencer down.

His side stung and he examined the cut and the trickle of drops.

Woman groaned.

Chace straightened and picked up the toothpick. He wiped it clean on her dress, then cut a strip from the hem. He tied her wrists behind her back. He cut another strip and tied her ankles. Sheathing the toothpick, he went to the stove and touched the kettle. It was warm, not hot. He carried it over and upended the spout over her face.

Woman sputtered and swallowed and cried out and opened her eyes. She glared and said, "You rotten little bastard."

"How did he die?"

"Go to hell."

"What are the names of the Harkeys who raped my sister?"

"Go to hell."

"Where do they live?"

"Go to hell, I say."

Chace squatted and set the kettle on the floor. He palmed the toothpick. "Before I'm done you'll tell me."

"That's what you think," Woman said, and laughed. "In a minute I won't be able to tell you a thing. And it's your doing."

"What are you talking about?"

Woman nodded at the teakettle. "I was fixing to poison you, same as I did your pa and his brothers. It doesn't kill. It makes it so you can't move or speak. Yet you can still feel. You're still aware of what goes on around you."

"It doesn't kill? Then how did you do him in? Did your husband shoot them?"

"I ain't saying." Woman looked down at herself. "The tingling has started. Won't be long now, it will reach my neck and my brain and then you are out of luck."

"One of us is," Chace said. He held the knife so the tip was close to her eyes. "You can still feel, you say?"

"You wouldn't."

"I have nothing better to do until your husband shows up."

"You're forgetting you stuck me." Woman's head sagged and she rested her cheek on the floor. "I'm not long for this world."

"A few minutes or half an hour, it will seem a lot longer," Chace said. He pricked her shoulder and she flinched. "Your poison is taking its sweet time. Maybe you didn't swallow enough."

"Don't do this, boy. You won't ever be the same, you do a thing like this. Hate me. Kill me. But don't make a game of it."

"A game?" Chace repeated, and shook his head. "This isn't fun for me. It's pleasure."

"What?"

"You helped kill my pa. Your kin hurt my sister. What I do to you will be like eating a slice of my ma's apple pie. It will be sweet and delicious and make me feel good."

"God, what *are* you? You can't compare killing to eating."

"I just did." Chace reached behind her and took hold of a finger. "How about if I start with these and then do your toes?"

"Rufus!" Woman screamed. "Kill, boy! Kill!"

Chace spun. He hadn't closed the door when he came

in, and the big black dog was in the doorway. Chace
lunged at the table and the Spencer, but he didn't quite
have it in his hands when the dog rammed into him, a
four-legged monster that weighed almost as much as he
did. Together they went down, Chace with his free hand
locked in the dog's throat, the mongrel snapping and
struggling. Chace stabbed it in the body and it went into
a frenzy, tearing from his grasp. He slashed at its eyes but
it was too fast for him and skittered aside. He rose onto
his elbows and the dog was on him. Fangs gnashed at his
jugular. He cut it, stabbed it. Teeth opened his shoulder.
Then he was on his back with the dog on top and it was
all he could do to keep it from ripping his throat open.
Coiling his legs, he kicked and knocked it back, gaining
the space he needed to heave himself at the table. His
fingers closed on the Spencer.

"Kill, Rufus! Kill!"

Chace fired as the dog leaped, fired as it crashed
down, fired as it started to get back up. The last shot sent
its brains out the other side of its head and it collapsed.
Chace took aim but there was no need. He kicked it. It
didn't move.

"So much for your hound."

Woman didn't respond.

Chace turned. He stepped over and poked her. The
knife wound had taken its toll; her lifeless eyes mocked
him. "That's all right," he told the body. "I won't get the
information I want but I can still put you to good use."

Chace bent and gripped her wrists.

11

Cassie was feeding the chickens. She scattered hand-fuls from the pail without paying much attention. She was thinking of Chace and how much she missed him. The chickens had strayed over near the woodshed, and a sound from inside brought her up short. It was someone singing. There was no door on the shed. She poked her head in. "Grandpa?"

Jed sat with his back to the pile of logs and was about to tilt a flask to his mouth. "Cassie girl. What is that you've got there?"

"Chicken feed."

"I'm not hungry, but thank you." Jed chortled and drank and lowered the flask to his lap.

"What are you doing in here?"

"Hiding from your ma."

Cassie sniffed and said, "Is that liquor I smell?"

"It's not chicken feed," Jed said, and chortled anew. "Which is why your ma will blister my ears, she finds out I'm sucking bug juice down."

"Where did you get it?" Cassie asked.

Jed raised a finger to his lips. "Shhh. Don't tell her but I have a couple of bottles in my saddlebags. I use them to fill this." He waggled the flask. "It's less con—" He stopped. "Less conspic—" He stopped again. "It's easier to hide."

"I never knew you were a drinker."

"Afraid so, girl. I used to partake on social occasions and that was all. But after my Mary died I took it up and now I can't seem to stop." Jed held out the flask. "Care for a swig?"

"I should say not. Ma would roast me alive."

"That's the trouble with Erna," Jed said sadly. "She never truly lets her petticoats down."

"Grandpa!"

"Well, she doesn't. I love her dearly, you understand. She's been a good wife to Buck and a good mother to you three kids, but she is so god-awful serious all the time."

"That's a fine thing to say with my pa and Uncle Granger and Uncle Fox missing and my brother off hunting them." Cassie started to back out. "I have half a mind to tell Ma on you."

"Wait!" Jed came to the opening. "Please don't. She might want me to leave and I promised your brother I'd look after you women while he's gone."

"You can look after us real good from in the wood-shed, can't you?" Cassie sarcastically asked. "You should be ashamed of yourself."

"I am, girl. I truly am." Jed held the flask out. "Are you sure you wouldn't care for a swig?"

Cassie scrunched up her nose. "I've never had the taste for it. Ma says hard spirits are the Devil's brew."

"She would. When she looks in the mirror she sees a halo over her head. The rest of us won't get ours until we see our Maker, if then."

"Oh, Grandpa."

"Here." Jed pressed the flask to her hand. "Just one sip. It won't harm you. I promise."

Cassie took the flask and looked at it uncertainly. She knew her father liked to imbibe on occasion. "I take a sip, you'll stop pestering me?"

"As God is my witness," Jed said solemnly.

"Just to make you happy, you understand." Cassie raised the flask and took a tiny swallow. It tasted terrible but she forced it down. Almost immediately a burning sensation spread from her throat to her tummy, her eyes began to water, and she had an impulse to blow her nose. Coughing and dabbing at her face with her sleeve, she said, "How can you drink this stuff?"

"It gets easier. Try another swallow."

"Not in this life." Cassie gave the flask back. "No wonder Ma says it's the Devil's work. Only the Devil would think a thing like this tastes good enough to drink."

"You'll change your mind," Jed predicted. "Wait and see."

Cassie noticed that the warmth in her belly was spreading and with it a surprisingly pleasant sensation. "I better get back in."

"You won't tell?"

"I can't promise," Cassie said. "Ma has a right to know about your shenanigans."

"Just don't let her smell your breath," Jed advised. "She does, she'll know you've been drinking, too."

"What are you talking about?" Cassie held her hand close to her mouth and breathed and sniffed. Sure enough, she could smell the whiskey. "So that's why you wanted me to take a sip. You tricked me, Grandpa."

Jed chuckled, and swallowed. "I'm sorry, girl, but I gave my word to your brother. You'll just have to put up with me until he gets back."

Cassie stalked off. She was mad at being duped. That he was a heavy drinker disturbed her. She wondered what other secrets he was hiding. She hung the pail on a hook in the barn and went into the cabin.

Scarlet was at the table eating soup.

"You're up and around," Cassie said in delight, her uncle momentarily forgotten. "How are you feeling?"

"Not as terrible as I have been. But I won't be my old self for a long while yet." Scarlet's face clouded. "I'd feel better if Pa was back. I'm worried something happened to him, and all on account of me."

"You?" Cassie said. "It was the Harkeys who, well, you know. They're to blame."

Erna came out of the bedroom carrying her knitting bundle. "Done with the chickens? You didn't happen to see your grandfather out there, did you?"

"No," Cassie fibbed.

"That man. I swear," Erna said. "He keeps disappearing. I'm beginning to think he doesn't like my company."

Cassie sat across from her sister. She tried not to stare at the bruises. They had faded some, but Scarlet still looked like a black-and-blue quilt. At least the swelling had gone down. "I wish I was a boy."

Scarlet spooned chicken soup into her mouth. She chewed and swallowed and asked, "What brought that on?"

"If I was a boy I could have gone with Chace. He only

didn't let me because I'm his sister." Cassie wasn't saying anything new; she had long regretted she was born female and not male. Men got to do more and have more fun. They hunted, they fished, they went to taverns and saloons. The women mostly stayed at home and did chores.

"You're just about a boy as it is," Scarlet said. "Oh, you wear a dress, but you don't act like a girl at all. You don't do up your hair and you don't care about your face. You'd rather be off with Chace in the woods."

"He's my twin."

"So? He's a boy. You're supposed to be a girl. Why you have to do everything he does is beyond me."

Cassie dug at the table with her fingernail. "I wouldn't expect you to understand. You're just you."

"What on earth does that mean?" Scarlet asked in mild exasperation. "I swear. Sometimes you act like you and him are one and the same."

"We are."

Erna was in her chair by the fireplace preparing to knit. She clacked her needles and remarked, "Folks say, Scarlet, that twins share a bond. That they're like two sides of the same coin."

"That doesn't excuse her acting like a boy," Scarlet said. "A girl is a girl. In a city they'd laugh her to scorn."

"I don't care what other people think," Cassie said. "I am me. I have to do as I want to do, not as others want me to."

"You talk plain silly sometimes."

"Now, now," Erna said.

"Maybe I can explain it so you'll understand," Cassie persisted. "I've given it a lot of thought and I have an idea how it works."

"How what works?"

"Being a twin." Cassie sat back. "I look so much like Chace that he could be me and I could be him if I didn't have girl parts and he didn't have the part that only boys have. But it's not just our bodies. We're alike inside, too. Our minds and our hearts are alike even though they are in two bodies. Entwined, you might call them."

"That's just not true," Scarlet said. "You don't act like him in everything. And your minds are nothing alike. You worry all the time and he doesn't ever fret about anything."

"He just holds more of it in than I do. Maybe one day he'll let it out and then you'll see."

Scarlet turned in her chair. "Ma, do you have any idea what she is talking about?"

"I think I do," Erna said thoughtfully. "Twins are special. Your father and I were so happy when—" She stopped and grew downcast. "God, I wish he was here now. I wish he never went to see Ezriah Harkey."

The door opened with a crash and all three of them jumped. Jed walked in and snorted in amusement. "Sorry, ladies. I reckon I don't know my own strength." He carefully closed it and came over to the table, moving as if he were on the pitching deck of a storm-tossed ship. Pulling out a chair, he sank down and placed his elbows on the table and his chin in his hands. "Miss me?"

"My God, no," Erna said.

"Excuse me?" Jed replied.

"You're drunk."

"I am not."

"Don't sit there and lie to my face. I know drunk when I see it and you have been hitting a bottle."

Jed straightened and squared his shoulders. "It was only half a bottle, I'll have you know, by way of a flask."

"You admit it?"

"I'm not ashamed of a nip now and then. They lighten my day, and Lord knows, some days need lightening."

Erna placed her knitting in her lap and frowned severely. "Jedediah Shannon, you ought to know better. I won't have this, not under my roof. You want to drink, you can just go home and guzzle."

"I can't leave even if I wanted to, which I don't." Jed reached across and patted Cassie's hand. "I have my granddaughters to think of."

"It's them I'm concerned about," Erna said. "I won't have them see you like this."

"Like what? You make it sound as if I am falling-down drunk. I'll have you know my head is clear as can be." Jed held up several fingers. "How many do you see?"

"Three."

"There. See?" Jed chuckled and put his chin back in his hands. "So, what's for supper?"

Cassie laughed. He was a hoot. Her mother, though, had that look she got when she was on the verge of throwing a fit.

"Jedediah, I'm not asking you. I'm telling you. I don't want you here in that condition. Go off somewhere until it wears off and then come back."

"Daughter-in-law, you're casting me out?"

"I am."

"Please, Ma," Cassie intervened. "Don't make him go. Can't we get some coffee into him?" She recollected her pa saying once that coffee helped after a man had too much to drink.

"I don't hold with liquor, girl," Erna said. "I don't hold with it at all. It is one of mankind's trials, a brain-child of the Tempter to lure us into wicked ways."

"Oh, brother," Jed said.

"It is," Erna said. "And don't you dare make light of heaven and hell. I don't hold with skeptics, neither."

"Jesus drank wine," Jed said.

"That he did. But nowhere in the Bible does it say he drank so much he couldn't walk straight or think straight. And he didn't do it behind his family's back."

"I was being considerate," Jed said. "I didn't do it in front of the girls for their sake."

"I thank you for that. But it doesn't change the fact you are slurring your words. Go out to the barn and sleep it off. Come morning you should be yourself. I'll fix you breakfast and we'll forget this ever happened, provided you promise never to do it again."

Cassie said, "Why not make him sleep in the chicken coop? Punish him good."

"That's enough out of you."

"It's *Grandpa*," Cassie said. "You can't just throw him out."

"I can and I did."

Jed pushed back his chair and stood, unsteadily. "That's all right, little one," he said to Cassie. "I respect your ma even if she doesn't respect me. I'll go curl up with the cows. They won't think ill of me for being human."

"Is that your excuse?" Erna asked.

"I don't need one," Jed said. He swayed to the door and put his hand on the latch. "I'm truly sorry, Erna. It's just that I miss my Mary so."

"I know," Erna said.

"There are days the hurt is more than I can bear."

"Get some sleep, Jedediah."

The door opened and closed, and Cassie said, "That was mean, Ma. I hope you're happy."

"No, child, I'm not. I'm worried sick about your father and I'm worried sick about your brother and now I'm worried sick about your grandfather, too. God help us, but I think the Tempter is out to strike the men of our family down."

"Chace won't let anything happen to him. He promised me."

"Let's hope he keeps that promise, then."

12

It was the afternoon of the third day.

Chace was on the roof, flat on his belly. He had been there since dawn. A whinny alerted him that someone was coming and he raised his head high enough to see over.

A heavyset man had drawn rein a ways out and was staring at the dead dog. Of a sudden the man yanked a shiny Henry from the saddle scabbard and smacked his pudgy legs against his sorrel. He came at a trot, staring at the cabin, and didn't see the woman lying in the grass until he was almost on top of her. Hauling on the reins, he gaped in horror and bleated, "God in heaven, no." He glanced all around, slid off his horse, and squatted next to the body. "Woman," he said. "Who could have done this to you?"

Chace rose onto his knees and shot the man where the right wrist rested on the right leg. As he expected, the slug cored the arm and the leg, both, and burst out the back, spraying the ground with blood and gore.

The man cried out and fell back, clutching himself.

The Henry fell in the grass. He was too hurt to think of grabbing for it and instead rolled back and forth in agony.

Chace moved to the edge of the roof. He trained the Spencer on the man's beet-red face. "When you're done caterwauling we have to talk."

The man stopped rolling but it took an effort. His face was a study in concentration. Blood flowed from between the fingers he'd clamped on his wrist. The leg wound was bleeding, too, a lot worse. "Who . . . ?" he rasped, his teeth clenched against the pain.

"The handle is Chace Shannon. I take it you're Ezriah Harkey?"

"It was you who killed my wife and my dog, wasn't it, you little bastard?"

"Don't be casting stones," Chace said. "Or have you so soon forgot my pa and my uncles?"

Ezriah tried to sit up but fell back and groaned. "Goddamn you." He uttered a string of swear words.

"Shuck the knife on your hip," Chace instructed.

Ezriah Harkey glared.

"Do it or I'll shoot your other wrist." Chace raised the Spencer. "Your other leg, too."

Reluctantly, Ezriah complied, tossing the knife well out of his reach. "Happy now?"

"Not by a long shot." Chace coiled and dropped. He landed lightly, the Spencer centered on the patriarch. As he unfurled, he said, "You and me have a lot to talk about, so we might as well get to it."

"Talk, hell. I'm bleeding to death. You need to fix me up before I'll say a damn word."

"I should have thought you'd have gotten the point

by now," Chace said. He rammed the Spencer's stock against the man's forehead.

Ezriah fell back and howled like a kicked hound. His curses blistered the air. When he subsided he lay panting and glaring. "If it's the last thing I ever do, I'll see you dead."

"You don't catch on quick to things at all." Chace picked up the Henry and leaned it against the cabin. "I'll give you a minute to collect your wits."

"You damned kid," Ezriah growled. "You think this is some game but it's not."

Unruffled, Chace responded, "Where's the game in your kinfolk raping my sister? Where's the game in you and your wife killing my pa and Uncle Granger and Uncle Fox? Where's the game in me killing your missus? Where's the game in the other Harkeys I'm fixing to kill?"

"You have killing on the brain, boy," Ezriah said. "You were lucky with me and probably lucky with Woman, but you won't stand a prayer against the whole Harkey clan."

"How will they know it was me? You won't be around to tell them."

"Do it and get it over with, then," Ezriah said defiantly. "I'm not afraid to die."

"Because you expect it will be quick. But it won't. Not unless you tell me what I need to find out."

"I won't tell you a thing."

"The names of those as raped Scarlet. Their names, and where I can find them."

"Not on your life," Ezriah said. "Not now, not ever."

"You are a puzzlement," Chace said. "Or do you naturally bluster a lot? Try to get this through your head: You don't have a say in anything anymore. You gave up that say when you took my pa from me. You hadn't done that, I might have let you live."

"Listen to you. Talking like some big he-bear when you ain't nothing but a cub."

Chace reached behind him and drew the Arkansas toothpick. He let the sun play over the blade. "I reckon there's only one way." Lunging, he slashed the tip across the old man's left eye.

Roaring and swearing, Ezriah thrashed back and forth, one hand over the socket. "What have you done, damn you?" he howled. "What in God's name have you done?"

Chace wiped the toothpick on the grass and slid it into his sheath. He leaned against the wall and gazed at a pair of buzzards circling high over the dead dog and the dead woman. Raising the Spencer, he sighted on the biggest, then grinned and lowered the rifle. He watched a black ant crawl out of the cabin with a piece of bread in its pinchers. He turned and looked inside at the stove and then at Ezriah Harkey, who was still tossing about and had smeared red over much of his face and clothes. "Are you about done?"

Presently Ezriah stopped thrashing and lay still save for the twitching of his skin and jaw muscles. When he spoke his voice sounded far away. "What kind of monster are you, boy?"

"Says the man who killed my pa."

"I did that to protect my clan."

"If that's your excuse it's good enough for me. You're the head of the Harkeys. I do you in, I'm doing my own clan a favor."

Ezriah focused his remaining eye on Chace. "This doesn't affect you at all, does it?"

Chace was watching the ant. It had come to a hole and was about to go down. Another ant came out, they touched antennae, and the second ant started toward the cabin.

"Didn't you hear me, boy?"

"Are you ready to tell me who jumped my sister in Harkey Hollow?"

"Go to hell."

Chace took the Henry and the Spencer and went inside. He placed the Henry on the table. He poured the water from the pitchers into a pot and set the pot on the stove and kindled a flame. When he came back out, Ezriah Harkey was shakily crawling toward the discarded knife. Chace walked around him and picked it up and threw it so far it would take a month of Sundays to get to.

"I hate you," Ezriah said.

"You'll hate me a lot more before too long," Chace predicted. He hunkered, the Spencer across his legs. "Who's next in line to lead the Harkeys if something happens to you?"

"Ask my wife, you son of a bitch. Oh. That's right. You can't since you killed her." ———

Chace shrugged. "It's your last day of breathing. Whether you do it with dignity is up to you."

"What the hell do you know about *dignity*?" Ezriah raged. "You're wet behind the ears yet."

"I know I don't want to die like you're going to die."

Ezriah had nothing to say to that.

Chace scratched his chin and asked, "What was it like in the old days? Before the truce was agreed to?"

"Why ask me?"

"Because you were there. Because my grandpa won't talk about it unless I beg, and that gets tiresome."

Ezriah settled back. Great weariness marked his face and his posture. "I reckon I might as well. I have nothing to lose, as short as my stay in this world is." He put a hand over his ravaged eye and groaned. "It wasn't nice like it has been while you were growing up. It was ugly. Harkeys killing Shannons and Shannons killing Harkeys. It got so I couldn't turn around without hearing that someone or other had died. I got sick of it. So sick, I was happy to agree to a truce." He stopped and groaned louder. "Talking takes a lot out of me."

"We're not going anywhere."

"You're a caution, boy. But as for the truce, I'd been feuding all my life, so it was hard at first not to shoot a Shannon on sight. Then I realized that if I couldn't control my urges, how could I expect other Harkeys to?"

"With me it's not an urge so much as a means to an end," Chace said. "The end is to spare the Shannons more grief, and the only way I can see is to wipe you Harkeys off the face of the earth."

"You alone?" Ezriah said, and uttered a mocking squeal. "That's a tall order for someone barely old enough to shave." He grimaced and lowered his hands. "I hope you rot in hell for this." The eyeball was slit crosswise and a pale fluid was leaking out. When he blinked the whole eye trembled.

"All you had to do was answer." Chace paused. "I'll be fair and warn you: You're going to have more choices to make pretty soon."

Ezriah closed both eyes and rested his cheek on the ground. He said something.

"I didn't quite catch that."

"Do you have a shred of mercy in your soul?"

"Not a lick," Chace said.

"Buck told me he was Jed's boy. That makes you Jed's grandson. He's a kind man, your grandfather. He always puts others before himself. That's why he wanted the truce, to spare his clan." Ezriah looked up. "How come you're not more like him?"

"I'm not like anyone," Chace answered. "I'm me." He saw more ants file out of the hole and march toward the cabin "I take that back. My sister might be, although I hope not, for her sake. It would be a shame for her to end up with the law after her like they will be after me."

"For killing us Harkeys."

"A whole bunch of you," Chace said.

Ezriah swallowed and raised his good arm to his forehead. "What have I set loose on us?"

"I'm just a person, like everybody."

"Not from where I lie."

Chace grinned. "I like your sense of humor. It's as grim as my own."

"You're too young to be grim," Ezriah said.

"It's not the age. It's what we do and how we think. And I'm a thinker. I may not look it or show it, but I think about everything. I spent days thinking about how I was going to do you in."

"You aren't right in the head."

"I've wondered. But I see it the opposite. I see people who pretend the world is wonderful and warm. Take my ma, for instance. I love her dearly but she wears blinders. Her daughter, raped, and she thinks the good Lord is watching over us and wants me to give thanks at the supper table." Chace pointed. "People are like these ants. They dig holes for themselves and think the hole is the whole of creation."

"You're confusing the hell out of me."

"I doubt that. You're a crafty devil. You must have known about your kin and my sis but you didn't come to my grandpa and ask his pardon. No, you stayed put, knowing full well someone would come, and when my pa and his brothers showed up, you killed them so they wouldn't go after those who are to blame."

Grunting and wincing, Ezriah said, "Has anyone ever told you that you are old for your years?"

"How many Shannons have you turned into maggot bait, not counting my pa and my uncles?"

"Two others," Ezriah answered without hesitation, "back during the feuding days."

"How did you feel after?"

"Twinges of guilt. It had to be done but I can still see their faces. Sometimes I wake up at night in a cold sweat over it."

"I hear that's how most folks are," Chace said. "Not me. I pushed a drunk out of a hayloft a few years back and never felt a thing. That's when I had a decision to make."

"I feel so weak," Ezriah said. He closed the cut eye and rubbed his cheek. "What decision?"

"Whether to put on blinders like everyone else or go through life without them."

"No need to ask what you decided."

Chace stood and looked inside. "Don't go anywhere. I'll be right back."

"I wish I were dead," Ezriah said.

Chace went to the stove. The water was bubbling. He

took a towel and gripped the handle and carried the steaming water outside. He stood over Ezriah and tilted the pot but not quite enough that the water would spill out. "You know what I want."

"I would if I could."

"The names of them who raped Scarlet, and where they can be found. The name of whoever will be head of your clan with you gone. Tell me and I give you my word: one shot to the brain. No pain. No suffering. Don't tell me and this water is only the start. I've got my knife and I saw an ax and if I have to I'll even use the ants."

Ezriah Harkey trembled. "I can't. I'm sorry."

"It's not that you can't. It's that you won't," Chace corrected him. "Last chance. Now, or an hour from now, it's all the same to me."

His good eye misting over, Ezriah said, "God in heaven, help me. Don't let him do this."

"You and my ma," Chace said, and upended the pot.

13

The water hole was a favorite haunt of the Harkey boys on hot summer days.

Only the boys went there. Girls weren't allowed. The boys liked to swim with little or nothing on, and girls weren't to see boys naked.

Rabon and Woot showed up about one in the afternoon. By then nearly a dozen other Harkeys were already there, swimming and diving from a high bank, and joking and laughing. Half were bare-assed. The rest wore pants.

Rabon was the biggest. He swaggered a lot and pushed the smaller boys around. Once Rabon held another boy under the water so long that when Rabon finally let the boy up for air, the boy barely made it to land and lay sucking in air and wretching for minutes. Rabon laughed heartily.

From a thicket near the pool, Chace saw and heard everything. Several times he raised the Spencer and centered the sights on Rabon's hairy chest and lightly touched the trigger, but didn't squeeze, and whispered to himself, "Bang, you're dead."

Two other of the boys fit descriptions Ezriah had given Chace of those who were at Harkey Hollow the day Scarlet was raped. One, nicknamed Scooter, was a close cousin to Rabon and Woot. The other was Jimbo, the boy who had tried to stop them and been knocked down.

The swimmers stayed most of the afternoon. When they tired of the water, they lazed on a large flat rock, soaking up the sun. They talked about girls and their folks and girls and hunting and girls and fishing.

Chace heard every word. His interest perked along about four when one of the boys mentioned that he'd heard a girl by the name of Mabel would do it with anything in pants. "I aim to have her myself," the boy bragged. "I hear she is as fine as can be."

"You want fine," Scooter said, and snickered, "you should have had that Shannon girl. Lordy, she had a nice body. Didn't she, Rabon?"

Rabon was on his stomach with his arms crossed and his cheek on his arms.

He grunted.

Woot laughed and said, "She was a panther, that gal. Fought us tooth and nail. I still got the marks." He raised an arm to show thin scars.

"I wish I'd been there," said the boy who had brought up Mabel.

"It was wrong," Jimbo said.

Rabon raised his head. "Don't you start. I got into trouble over you. My pa didn't like that I hit a girl."

"Your pa has sense."

Rabon pushed onto his elbows and his dark eyes glittered. "I can do it again. I can hit you until you beg me to stop and I'll keep on hitting you anyway. That what you want?"

"No good will come of that day," Jimbo remarked. "My pa is worried it will set off the feud."

"Worrywarts, the both of you," Rabon said. "Has anything happened? Have the Shannons been crying for Harkey blood? No and no. I bet that girl didn't even tell anyone."

"You beat her so bad, it was plain."

"That she was beat, yes, but not the other," Rabon countered. "She'll keep her mouth shut about that."

"Out of shame?" Woot said.

"That, and secretly I bet she liked it," Rabon said with a smirk.

"She was crying," Jimbo said.

"So? She could like it and cry, too. You don't know much about females, do you?"

"I know they don't like to be raped."

"Shut the hell up," Rabon snapped. "Better yet, get the hell gone before I come over there and pound your face in. I mean *now*."

The other boys looked at Jimbo. He silently rose and moved to the end of the flat rock and looked back. "There are days," he said to all of them, "when I'm ashamed to be a Harkey." Off he walked, his head held high.

"God, I hate him," Rabon said. "If he wasn't kin I'd beat him to death."

"I'd help," Woot said.

Scooter spat and commented, "His family always has been different. It's his ma, always on her high horse about being nice to everyone."

"Nice, hell," Rabon said. "You don't be nice to your enemies, and that girl was a Shannon."

"I hope we spot her in Wareagle someday," Woot said. "We could jump her and do it again."

"Not in Wareagle we can't," Scooter said. "Old Ezriah would have us caned, or worse."

"I ain't afeared of him," Rabon said. "I ain't afeared of anyone."

"Never said you were," Scooter said.

No more was said about Scarlet. The boys talked about a horse race they had seen and a big corn snake one of them had killed and how they were looking forward to the fair in the fall. Singly and in pairs they drifted away to home until only Rabon and his brother and Scooter were left. They were reluctant to leave.

The sun was above the trees to the west when Woot sighed and said, "I reckon we better be on our way. Pa will be mad, we get home after dark."

"I just don't want to have to listen to Ma nag us," Rabon groused. "That's all she ever does."

"Females are good at that," Scooter said. "My ma is always on me about picking up after myself and not using all the leaves in the outhouse."

"Your ma can't hold a candle to ours when it comes to nagging," Woot said.

"Every word out of her mouth is nag."

Rabon swore. "What Pa saw in her I'll never know." He jabbed a thick finger at his brother and his cousin. "You ever tell anyone I said that and I'll stomp you."

"Hell," Woot said. "I feel the same as you."

"I'll never tell," Scooter said.

Chace followed them on foot. He made no more noise than a cougar. The three took a path that wound through the heavy woods. They walked in single file, Rabon, then Woot, and then Scooter. Chace came up behind them. They didn't once look back. Rabon and Woot went around a bend. Before Scooter could reach it, Chace was on him. He brought the Spencer's stock down hard on the back of the boy's head and Scooter folded like a broken cornstalk and never uttered a peep. Stepping over him, Chace cat-footed to the bend and made sure the brothers were still moving along before he trailed after. They were talking about how hungry they were and Woot was saying as how they were to have possum for supper and he loved possum meat. Woot was bigger than Scooter, so Chace clubbed him twice and Woot collapsed.

Rabon heard, and turned. "What the hell?"

Chace didn't point the Spencer. He didn't demand Rabon hold up his arms or warn him to be quiet. He sprang, holding the rifle by the barrel, and swung before Rabon could collect his wits. His first blow caught Rabon on the jaw and made him stagger. His second blow split Rabon's ear, and Rabon's knees started to buckle. His third blow brought Rabon down, unconscious.

Chace hit Rabon again to be sure he stayed out, careful not to swing so hard he killed him. He clubbed Woot and Scooter, too, as he went past them and back along the trail to the water hole and beyond into the thicket to where he had tied Enoch. He rode to where the three boys lay, cut strips from their clothes, and bound them, wrists and ankles. One by one he threw each over Enoch and took him to the watering hole and dumped him and went back for the next. Then he hunkered and waited.

The sun was setting. Shadows crawled from under the trees, and grew. The songbirds stopped warbling and the butterflies sought cover. In the distance a dog howled.

Rabon came around first. He made a sound like a pig rooting in the dirt and his head jerked up and he looked around in mild confusion. "Where? What?" he said, and saw Chace. "You! You hit me."

"How do you do?" Chace said.

Rabon went to rise and realized he couldn't move his arms or legs. He glanced over his shoulder at his wrists, and swore. His muscles bulged until he was red in the face and he hissed like a mad cat.

"I tied you real good."

"Who the hell are you?" Rabon snarled. "What's this about?"

"Think about it," Chace said.

"Think about what? I want to know who you are and I want to know *now*." Again Rabon tried to get up and made it as far as his knees. "Answer me, you son of a bitch." He saw the other two. "My brother and my cousin. What are you fixing to do to us?"

"Figured it out yet?"

Rabon uttered a fiery string of oaths. He was so mad, his body shook and spittle dribbled down his chin.

Chace rose and stepped to the pool. Dipping a hand in, he wet his lips and his neck and his brow. He came back and squatted in the same spot just as Scooter groaned and rolled over.

"Rabon? What's happening?"

"Sit up and see for yourself."

Struggling, Scooter did. He sucked in a breath when he set eyes on Chace. "A Shannon, by God. Here, of all places."

"What?" Rabon said.

"His hair and his eyes. He's a Shannon. Let me guess. Her brother or a close cousin or a boyfriend."

"Brother," Chace said.

"Whose brother?" Rabon demanded, and blinked.

"Wait. That bitch from the Hollow? Is that what this is about?"

"The light dawns."

Hate contorted Rabon's brute face. "Here to get even—is that it? Stupid bastard. Hurt us and you'll never make it out of Harkey country alive."

"The important thing is that this is the last day of your life," Chace said quietly. "And the next time a Harkey boy comes on a Shannon girl, he'll think twice about doing something to her."

"If my hands weren't tied . . ." Rabon said.

Scooter was studying Chace. "What I want to know is how you found us here."

"Ezriah told me."

Rabon snorted in amusement. "My grandpa? What do you take us for? He'd never do a thing like that."

"He would if the skin on his face was blistered from scalding hot water and the fingers on his left hand had been chopped off one by one and he was about to have his pecker cut off, too."

"God," Scooter said.

Confusion replaced Rabon's amusement. "What are you saying? That you did that to my grandpa?"

"That and more," Chace said, "before I put him out of his misery. Him, his wife, their dog."

"You're lying," Rabon said stubbornly. "You're making it up. Hell, you're younger than me, from the looks of it. You couldn't ever get the better of my grandpa. He's tough, that old goat. Tough and smart."

"Not smart enough," Chace said.

"It won't work. You can't scare us with lies."

"All she wanted was blackberries. You could have scared her a little, had fun, and let her go. But no. You took her. You hurt her. You did the worst thing a man can do to a woman and then you thought—what, you would get away with it?" Chace moved to where Woot lay.

"What are you doing?" Rabon asked. "Get away from my brother! You hear me?"

Chace set down the Spencer, slid his hands under Woot's arms, and dragged him to the pool. He sat on Woot's chest and put his foot against Woot's cheek and pushed Woot's face in the water. For several seconds nothing happened. Suddenly Woot exploded into movement, heaving up and coughing and sputtering. Chace let him raise his head out.

"What? Who?"

"Leave him be!" Rabon raged.

Woot looked scared. He spat out water and sneezed and asked, "What are you doing to me? What's this all about?"

"Remember the girl from the Hollow?" Chace said. "This is for her." He jammed his foot against Woot's chin. Woot tried to jerk his head away but Chace thrust out and down, submerging Woot's face. Woot sought to lever upward and Chace locked his leg and pressed harder. He kept on pressing as the body under him heaved and twisted. The water roiled and churned. A swarm of bubbles rose to the surface. Rabon swore nonstop. Scooter begged Chace to stop. Then it was over. The bubbles stopped rising. The water stilled. The body went limp.

Rabon was almost beside himself. "I'll kill you!" he shrilled. "You hear me, boy? I will by God kill you!"

Chace rose and roved about, searching. He found a rock about the size of a walnut and moved to Scooter, who was as pale as a bedsheet.

"What are you fixing to do? Beat me to death?"

"No," Chace said, and pushed him onto his side. Scooter cursed and attempted to swing his legs, but Chace slammed him onto his back and dropped, knees first, onto Scooter's stomach. Scooter cried out, his mouth gaping wide.

In that instant Chace rammed the rock into Scoother's mouth, shoving it down as far as he could and yanking his fingers out before he was bit. He clamped one hand over Scooter's mouth and with the fingers of his other hand pinched Scooter's nose shut. Scooter's eyes were white saucers. He coughed and choked and bucked and made sounds no human ear should hear. Tears streamed down his face. He arched his back and stiffened, and died.

Chace slowly rose. He slowly turned and slowly stepped to Rabon, who was slick with the sweat of raw fear and quaking from head to toe. "Your turn."

14

The cabin was small. In the clearing in which it stood were a dozen stumps from the trees chopped down to build it. No one had bothered to clear the stumps. Just as no one had bothered to fence in the chicken coop or put a roof on the outhouse. Pigs nosed in the dirt. A cat with three legs hobbled about meowing.

Chace leaned against a maple. He was cradling the Henry that had belonged to his uncle Fox; the Spencer was tied on Enoch. Chace ran his hand over the shiny brass receiver.

The latch moved and the front door opened and out came a girl barely ten years old. Her dress needed washing and her feet and arms were filthy. She was toting a wooden bucket. Humming to herself, she headed for the creek that flowed past the maple.

Chace eased back from sight. He heard her footfalls and a splash and peeked out. The girl had dipped the bucket in the creek. Holding the Henry in one hand behind the tree, Chace stood so she could see him, smiled his warmest smile, and said, "It sure is a hot one, ain't it?"

The girl gave a start and nearly dropped the bucket.

Scrambling to her feet, she blurted, "Who are you? What are you doing here?"

"I'm a friend of your brother's," Chace said. "Is Chub home by any chance?"

"He's inside eating," the girl said. "Practically all he ever does is eat."

"Would you send him out?"

"I'll do better." She turned and cupped a hand to her mouth and bellowed loud enough to be heard in Texas, "Chub! There's a boy to see you! A friend of yours." She stopped. "I didn't catch your name."

The latched rasped and the door opened and out stepped a boy of fifteen with a roll of flab for a belly. He was eating a roast chicken leg. "What was that, Myrtle?" he hollered with his mouth full.

Chace whipped the Henry to his shoulder. He aimed at the center of Chub's forehead, thumbed back the hammer, and fired. He did it so swiftly, Chub had no chance to react. The slug smashed into Chub's face and sent him stumbling against the jamb.

Myrtle threw back her head and screamed.

"Have a nice day," Chace said to her. Smiling sweetly, he melted into the greenery.

Lincoln Harkey lived on a piney ridge with his ma and two brothers. Their cabin was well made. They had grass and a flower garden and not one but two dogs lazing under the overhang with their tongues lolling. Several mules were in a corral made of saplings and half a dozen geese were honking at a squirrel that had sought sanctuary in a tree.

Flat on his belly next to a briar patch, Chace held the Henry to his shoulder. He already had the hammer thumbed back. He stared at the cabin and only the cabin. Even when a hornet alighted on his arm, he kept watching the cabin. The hornet flew off. Muffled voices told him someone was home.

The door opened. The boy who came out was tall and lanky and had the Harkey shock of hair. Behind came two others, all enough alike that it was obvious they were brothers, and close in age. They were toting squirrel guns, older single-shot rifles.

Only one of the three had been at Harkey Hollow that day, according to Ezriah. Lincoln, the oldest, had helped hold Scarlet down and taken his turn after Rabon and Woot. "But which one is him?" Chace said to himself. He couldn't tell.

The trio went to the corral and brought out three mules. They were going somewhere. They were bantering, relaxed. Dispensing with saddles, they climbed on and rode off bareback.

Chace hurried to Enoch, swung up, and used his heels. Chace stayed a good way back but not so far he'd lose them. They headed to the southeast. The only thing Chace could think of in that direction was Wareagle.

Once he was convinced that they were indeed making for town, Chace swung wide and rode at a gallop. After half a mile he reined to a point in front of them and dismounted. "Stay put," he said to Enoch. He let the reins fall and slipped behind a spruce.

It wasn't long before the undergrowth crackled and they were there. The one in the lead hauled on his reins and regarded Enoch with a mix of curiosity and puzzlement. He said something to his brothers, who came up on the other side. Together they climbed down and together they advanced to Enoch.

"Sure is a fine mule," said one.

"Where's whoever owns it?" wondered the second.

The third reached for the reins, but Enoch pulled away. "I think I'll claim it for my own."

Chace moved from behind the spruce with the Henry leveled. "Think again."

The trio turned, and froze. The barrels of their rifles were pointed at the ground.

"No need for that," said the brother who had tried to grab the reins.

"Which one of you is Lincoln?"

"Why do you want to know?" the same brother asked.

"I have something for him."

The second brother glanced at the other two. "Don't say a word. Look at him close. He's a Shannon, by God."

"In Harkey country?" marveled the rein grabber.

Chace sidled to the right so he had clear shots at all three. "I'm only after Lincoln. The other two can go on home or jump in a lake for all I care."

"We'll never say which one he is," said the third. "So unless you aim to shoot all three of us, you'd best light a shuck."

"Drop your rifles," Chace commanded.

"No," said the first one.

The second shook his head. "You're in a pickle, Shannon. You can't shoot all three of us before one of us brings you down."

"Not all three you can't," agreed the third.

The first one said, "You're the one who should drop *his* rifle."

"Damn stupid Harkeys." Chace shot the first one

in the head and the second in the head, but the third bounded for the brush and made it under cover as Chace was taking a bead. Darting behind the spruce, Chace jacked the lever to feed another cartridge into the chamber.

From out of the growth came a pounding sound, as if the surviving brother was so mad, he was striking the ground.

"Are you Lincoln?" Chace called to him.

The pounding stopped. "Whether I am or I ain't, you're dead. You've done killed my brothers."

"All they had to do was say," Chace said.

"Kin never betrays kin. You must not have a brother of your own or you would know better."

Chace swiveled toward where the voice was coming from. "I have a sister and Lincoln raped her."

"I'd do it again and make you watch if she was here." And Lincoln Harkey laughed.

Staying low, Chace ran from the spruce to a cluster of tall grass. As he threw himself down, a rifle boomed and pain seared his right arm. The brother whooped, but the slug had only torn Chace's sleeve and barely creased his skin. He stayed down and groaned as if in torment.

Lincoln did more laughing. "You came all this way, Shannon, and for what? To die alone."

Chace didn't answer. He snaked a few yards to the right. The woods had gone quiet. A fly winged past, its buzzing unnaturally loud. A beetle crawled along. He stayed motionless save for his eyes and a slow turning of his head. It was a full ten minutes before a shape that was not part of the landscape caught his eye. The shape was prone and crabbing toward where he had fallen.

Lincoln was good; he moved slowly and he made no

sound. His only mistake was he assumed Chace had been hit hard.

Chace inched the rifle to his shoulder and took aim. He didn't shoot until he saw the head clearly and then he put a slug into one of the dark eyes, into the pupil, and the body flopped once and was still. Rising, Chace confirmed the kill. He went to Enoch and climbed on. "Only one left."

There were poor Harkeys and there were well-to-do Harkeys. One of the well-to-dos was Thaddeus Harkey, whose farm covered hundreds of acres.

Instead of a cabin, the family lived in an honest-to-goodness house with three floors and a slate roof. Thaddeus even had four hands who worked for him. His family consisted of his wife, three daughters, and a boy named Festus.

There was no cover near the house save for a few trees. Chace surveyed the situation from a quarter of a mile away and said, "I guess we do this the hard way." He clucked to Enoch.

None of the hands working the fields paid much attention. A girl of ten or so was on a swing under a maple. Another girl, slightly older, was playing with a puppy. A woman was hanging laundry on a line. She stopped hanging and dried her hands on her apron and came over, smiling.

"Hello, stranger."

Chace smiled, too, his best and warmest smile, the smile that Cassie said lit him like the sun. "Hello, ma'am. Would your boy Festus be to home?"

"I'm afraid not," the woman said. "Him and his pa

went to Wareagle yesterday and won't be back for a week."

"You don't say."

"What do you want to see him about?"

Chace held out the Henry. "This. I was told he might be interested in buying it."

"A rifle?" The woman nodded. "I can see why. Festus loves to hunt and loves his guns and that one is a beauty."

"Yes, it is," Chace agreed. "It's a shame I have to part with it."

"Who told you he might buy it?"

"A man in town." Chace sighed. "Appears I've come all this way for nothing. I could have stayed there and waited for your son to come to me."

"Would you like some tea or lemonade or maybe a johnnycake before you head back?"

"Thank you, ma'am, but it's a long ride and I'd like to find Festus sooner rather than later." Chace tipped his head and reined around. He stuck to the dirt road. That night he camped beside it and made a small fire. He cleaned the Henry and the Spencer, and when he was done, he set them side by side. "I am rich with rifles," he said, and laughed.

Later Chace lay on his back with his head propped in his hands and gazed at the stars. Right before he fell asleep, he said softly, "My sweet twin."

The next dawn found him under way. It was half a day's hard ride to Wareagle. He passed a fair number of travelers but they paid him no mind.

Finally he arrived, dusty and weary, at the end of Wareagel's main street.

The only place that had rooms to let was the tavern. Chace tied Enoch at the hitch rail and strode in with the Henry at his side. To the right of the front door a woman was behind a high counter scribbling in a ledger. To the left was an archway into the dining room.

"You look a little young for liquor, young man," the woman said. "Or is it a room you're after?"

"I'm looking for a friend of mine," Chace added to his lies. "Name's Festus Harkey. He'd be staying with his pa, Thaddeus."

"They are here, in fact," she confirmed, and nodded at the archway. "Went in about ten minutes ago."

"I'm obliged."

The tavern served food as well as liquor. People came just to eat and there were couples and single townsfolk. Only one table had a man and a boy, over in a corner. Both were dressed fine, by Wareagle's standards, in Sunday-go-to-meeting clothes, and were hungrily attacking thick slabs of beef with their forks and knives.

Chace stopped a few feet from them so he had room to use the Henry.

"Festus Harkey," he said.

Father and son looked up. The father was middling height with sloped shoulders, the son Chace's age, or thereabouts, his hair slicked down and his face scrubbed clean.

"Something we can do for you?" Thaddeus asked.

"I'm here for your boy."

"Do I know you?" Festus said.

"You know my sister. You and Rabon and Woot and others raped her in Harkey Hollow a while back. All of them are dead except for you and now your turn has come."

Father and son turned to stone with their knives and forks in their hands.

Then Thaddeus shifted uneasily and said, "You can't be serious. My son would never rape anyone."

"Ezriah said different," Chace said.

"My uncle told you this?" Thaddeus turned to his son. "Festus? Tell me he's mistaken. Tell me you didn't."

Festus set down his knife and fork. He kept his right hand on the table and started to inch his left hand under it.

"Festus? You answer me," Thaddeus said.

The boy heaved out of his chair and brought his hand up, holding a pocket pistol. He was fast but he didn't have it pointed when Chace fired from the hip and put a slug into Festus's gut. Punched back by the impact, Festus doubled over and Chace shot him in the face.

Thaddeus sat paralyzed with disbelief.

Chace started to back away and stopped when a gun hammer clicked behind him. He glanced over his shoulder.

From one of the other tables a man had risen. He was holding a revolver and he was wearing a badge.

15

Cassie paced back and forth near the chicken coop, her arms across her chest, her head bowed. She had been pacing for a good ten minutes. Every now and then she would stop pacing and stomp a foot. She had just stomped when someone coughed.

"You mad at the chickens for not laying eggs?"

Jed had come from the barn. Bits of straw clung to his buckskins and stubble speckled his chin. He wasn't swaying, but his eyes were bloodshot and unfocused.

"You're drunk still," Cassie said.

"Only partly," Jed admitted. "I handle my shine fine. Your ma had no call to throw me out like she did."

"All this time you kept it hid from me."

"What a man does when he is alone is his business," Jed said. "So what if I drink a little if it doesn't hurt anyone?"

"I have a hurt of my own," Cassie told him. "Chace."

Jed came closer. "You've had word? Is he all right? Or did the Harkeys get their hands on him?"

"It's a feeling I have," Cassie said.

"A feeling?"

"Yes. A feeling he is in trouble. Or is going to be."

"He's in Harkey country," Jed said. "You only now realize that he's in danger? God, girl. Why do you think I was so dead set against it?"

"It's more than that," Cassie said angrily. "I can feel what he's feeling. Usually he doesn't let his emotions out so I don't feel much but it just came over me that he needs me and needs me bad."

"A feeling," Jed said again, his skepticism thick enough to cut with a butter knife. "Will you listen to yourself? He's miles from here. It's only in your head."

"You're saying I'm imagining it?" Cassie knew her sister scoffed at the notion and her mother had doubts she never voiced. "I figured you would believe me if anyone would. I guess I figured wrong." She went on pacing.

"I'd like to," Jed said, "but I've seen too much foolishness in my day. People believe what they want even when it's not true."

"Oh, Grandpa," Cassie said.

"Don't take that tone, girl. You, your brother, I love you both dearly. I'd do anything for you. You know that. But don't expect me to believe you can feel your brother from far off."

"Go back into the barn and suck on your flask. I'd rather be alone."

"That's harsh," Jed said.

"I don't care. You come out here and call me a liar, what do you expect?"

Cassie turned her back on him and went around the chicken coop. She walked to the orchard and stood under an apple tree. Bees buzzed around a few early fallen apples and a pair of wrens flitted in the branches.

She stomped her foot again and said out loud, "I have to find out."

Cassie couldn't take the not knowing. She circled to the coral, careful to keep out of sight of the cabin windows. She brought out her mule, Bessie, and slipped on a bridle but didn't bother with a saddle. She had been riding bareback since she could remember. She walked Bessie until she was sure her mother wouldn't hear, then mounted and galloped off. She wasn't sure which direction so she just rode north a short distance and stopped. Closing her eyes, she concentrated on Chace. She pictured him in her mind. The special feeling came over her, stronger than ever. She let it wash through her whole being. It was like sinking into a tub of wonderfully warm water, only it was on the inside of her, not on her skin. She felt a pull, like an invisible rope, a sense that she should head east.

That was the direction she reined. She had gone half a mile when she realized where she was being pulled.

Toward Wareagle.

"No sudden moves—you hear?" said the man wearing the badge. He was slight of frame but muscular and wore store-bought clothes, including a vest. He had spurs on his boots and a belt with a big buckle. His revolver was a new Colt. His face was dark from a lot of riding in the sun and he appeared to be upwards of thirty.

"Who might you be?" Chace asked. "You're not Sheriff Wyler. I've seen him. He's a dumpling and a half."

The man grinned. "Wyler does like to eat, sure enough. I'm one of his deputies. Nick Fulsome. I'm placing you under arrest."

"It was self-defense. He drew on me."

"I saw the whole thing," Deputy Fulsome said. "I want you to set down your rifle and hold your hands out from your sides and stand real still."

The tavern was as quiet as a tomb. Everyone had stopped eating and talking and was staring.

"Sure, Deputy." Chace set the Henry on the floor and extended his arms. "I'm as peaceable as a kitten."

"You weren't a minute ago. What was that about, anyhow?" Deputy Fulsome asked. He was wary but not overly so, doing something he had done a hundred times. "I didn't catch what you and him were talking about."

"I can't say."

"You'll have to, in court. If you don't they'll throw you behind bars."

A strangled cry caused Chace to turn his head.

Thaddeus Harkey was clutching Festus and choking down grief. "No," he wailed. "No, no, no, no." He came out of his chair and put a hand on the hilt of a knife on his left hip. "You killed him. Made up a story and killed my boy."

"It wasn't made up," Chace said.

Thaddeus jerked the knife out. "My boy would never do what you claimed. Not a thing like that, he wouldn't. I raised him good, raised him proper." He took a step.

"Hold it right here," Deputy Fulsome said loudly. "And let go of that pigsticker."

"He shot my son," Thaddeus said. "I have the right."

"Not to kill him, you don't," the lawman said. "You can testify against him in a court of law, and if the judge and jury see fit, you can watch him swing from a gallows. But you can't do it yourself."

Thaddeus Harkey's face was contorted in fury and sorrow. He was a boiling pot fit to overflow with emotion.

With a loud cry he flung himself at Chace and raised the knife to stab. The boom of the deputy's Colt was loud in the room. Blood spurted from Harkey's wrist and his arm was whipped back and the knife went skittering.

"I warned you," Deputy Fulsome said.

Thaddeus bent, his wrist to his belly, tears filling his eyes. "I had the *right*," he said. "No law can take that from me."

"Calm down."

Thaddeus didn't seem to feel his wound or notice the red drops falling on his boots and the floor. "You shouldn't ought to have butted in. This is between us Harkeys and the Shannons."

"I won't tell you again." Deputy Fulsome sidled to put himself between the two of them. "Sit back down and I'll send for the sawbones."

Chace stayed still, his arms out, smiling. "Better listen to the tin star," he said to the enraged father. "You don't want to end up behind bars over a worthless no-account like your son."

Deputy Fulsome glanced at him. "Hush, you."

Thaddeus's lips curled back from his teeth like a rabid wolf's and he raised his good arm, his fingers hooked like claws. With a piercing cry he threw himself at Chace. Deputy Fulsome tried to push him back but Thaddeus grabbed both of the deputy's wrists and they grappled.

Instantly, Chace scooped up the Henry. He slammed the stock against Fulsome's temple and as the law dog started to crumple he rammed the muzzle into Thaddeus Harkey's gut. Both men went to their knees. Deputy Fulsome gamely attempted to raise the Colt and Chace hit him a second time. Thaddeus groped for Chace, hissing like a water moccasin. A sidestep, and Chace smashed him across the jaw.

No one else moved. No one spoke.

Chace pointed the Henry at Thaddeus. He touched his finger to the trigger but he didn't squeeze. Frowning, he backed to the archway and past the shocked woman at the front counter. "Anyone comes out this door, I'll shoot." Whirling, he rushed out and bounded to the hitch rail.

People had heard the shot. A number stared at the tavern and several men were coming toward it.

Chace swung up. He reined sharply and trotted to the east end of the main street and on to the first bend in the road. Once out of sight, he changed direction, plunging north into the forest and circling until he was west of Wareagle. He slowed to spare Enoch. Staying shy of the road, he took his time. "No one is after us," he said to the mule. "I reckon we got plumb away. I only hope no one recognized me."

The bright splash of sun, the warbling of birds, the green of the woodland, were a tonic. Chace smiled as he rode. "I did it," he said. "Accounted for all of them, and the patriarch besides. Pa would be proud of me."

Enoch flicked his long ears.

The day waxed. Chace had a mile to go when there was an intimation of trouble: the thud of hooves. Horses were coming fast. Chace veered to the crest of a low hill, rose in the stirrups, and shielded his eyes with his hand. He counted seven, riding hard. The lead rider wore a vest and on it something sparkled.

"That deputy has a hard head," Chace said, and used the reins and his heels. He headed northwest, away from home, galloping where the ground permitted and moving as fast he could where the forest was thick. The minutes and the miles fell behind him. He gained enough that he didn't hear the sounds of pursuit but not enough to feel safe.

The afternoon crawled into evening. Chace climbed to the high lines and drew rein atop a broad ridge. He scoured the darkening gray land below and spotted the string of pursuers well back but persistent.

"That deputy is taking this personal."

Enoch was tired and so was Chace but he pushed on until midnight. A large willow offered a haven from the wind. He stripped Enoch and lay on his back with the Henry on one side and the Spencer on the other. To the north a female fox gave voice to a cry that would bring every male fox within earshot. Closer, wings fluttered and a mouse squeaked. Gradually his eyelids grew heavy. He fell asleep to the music of the night and slept soundly until the crack of dawn.

Up at first light, Chace ate a few pieces of jerky. He left the Henry and the Spencer on the ground and threw on the saddle blanket and saddle. He was bending to pick up the Spencer when the undergrowth crackled and they were on him, bursting out on horseback. They didn't shout for him to throw up his hands. They didn't yell to surrender. They opened fire.

Chace spun and shot from the hip. A rider tumbled. Whirling, Chace vaulted onto Enoch. A swarm of leaden wasps sought him as the mule broke into motion. Chace's ear stung. His upper arm flared with pain. A slug dug a furrow in Enoch's neck. Then they were in the trees and the shots were missing, but it was close.

"After him, boys!" Deputy Fulsome hollered.

Chace glanced back at the Henry, lying where he had left it. Then he rode as he had never ridden. The mule had always been fleet and surefooted; now both were put to the test. The posse came on swiftly, determined to overtake him.

Chace lost track of time and where he was. The position of the sun showed he was heading southwest. Not the direction he wanted but it would have to do.

When next he looked over his shoulder, all save two had fallen behind. One was Deputy Nick Fulsome. The other was a townsman, by his clothes, but a damn good rider.

Chace reined to avoid a tree. So far Enoch was holding his own. Mules generally didn't tire as easily as horses so if he could stay ahead long enough the horses would play out.

Out of nowhere a steep slope unfolded below him. Chace started down much too fast. Enoch stumbled, recovered his balance. A tree loomed and Chace reined to avoid colliding with it. They were halfway down when a horse whinnied shrilly.

The townsman had misjudged. His bay went down, squealing as it pitched into a roll. Rider and horse crashed against a boulder and even that far away Chace heard the sharp *crack* of bone. The townsman's bowler bore the brunt and the man flopped head over feet and slid to a rest, the bowler a ruin and his head pulped to mush.

Deputy Fulsome didn't stop.

Chace reached the bottom and a flat stretch. He goaded Enoch and the mule didn't disappoint. But when the lawman came to the flat, his buttermilk proved to be

four-hooved lightning. Fulsome was soon in pistol range
and whipped up his Colt. He was smiling, confident he
was about to bring Chace down.

Snapping the Spencer to his shoulder, Chace twisted
in the saddle and banged off shot after shot. It was impossible to hold the rifle steady and nearly impossible to
aim; he did the best he could. At the last blast Deputy
Fulsome flung out an arm and toppled over the back of
the buttermilk. When next Chace looked back, the lawman was sitting on the ground, a hand to his shoulder.

"I know who you are, boy!" he shouted. "I'll be coming for you!"

Chace galloped on. Half a mile farther he brought
Enoch to a stop and sat listening and scanning his back
trail.

There was no one after them.

"We did it," Chace said. "Or, rather, you did." He patted Enoch and let out a long breath. "It was a close one."
He began to reload. He took the tubular magazine from
the stock and plucked a cartridge from his cartridge belt.
His brow puckered, and he said, "Do you reckon he was
telling the truth about knowing who I am?"

Enoch blew and nipped at the grass.

Chace replaced the seven cartridges. He jacked the
lever to feed one into the chamber and cradled the rifle
in the crook of his elbow. "If he does it changes things."

Enoch tossed his head.

"Yes, it does," Chace said. "It means I can't ever go
home again."

16

Cassie rode for all she and Bessie were worth. The feeling in her that she must get to Wareagle had become so strong it was scary. She had never felt like this. She kept saying to herself, "Oh, Chace, Chace, Chace." As she neared the town, she saw the street was filled with people. It made her think of a nest of riled hornets. Other Shannons were there, and a lot of Harkeys, mingling with the townspeople. As she slowed she heard a lot of loud talk. Many of the people appeared to be angry or upset. She stopped at the first hitch rail she came to, slid down, and tied Bessie off.

Staying close to the buildings, Cassie caught snatches of conversation.

The more she heard, the more troubled she became.

"...the gall, the rank gall. To ride in and shoot that boy dead. In broad daylight, no less. It's unthinkable..."

"...walked up and shot him. Right in the face, I hear. Then knocked out the deputy and ..."

"...father is over to the doc's. They say he'll be all right, but you've got to feel sorry for ..."

"...the boy thinking? Why in hell did he do it? This

will start the feud up again, and after years of living peaceable ..."

"... Sheriff Wyler is on his way. Word is the judge will issue a warrant for the boy's arrest ..."

Cassie's fear climbed. She spotted a cousin about her age under the overhang in front of the general store and hurried over. Struggling to stay calm, she took her cousin by the arm. "Matilda. What's all the fuss about? I just got to town."

Her cousin had been listening to two men argue. She jumped when Cassie touched her, and blurted, "You! Here?" She pulled Cassie around the corner. "How could he? My pa says there will be a lot of killing now."

"What are you talking about?"

"You don't know? Your brother shot Festus Harkey. Marched into the tavern and shot him dead, then lit out. A posse is after him."

Cassie's legs grew weak. She leaned against the wall and bowed her head. "Oh God."

"Why would Chace do such a thing?"

Without thinking, Cassie answered, "The Harkeys raped my sister."

Matilda gasped.

Cassie closed her eyes and groaned. This was terrible. Her twin, on the run from the law. She needed to be with him, to help him. She opened her eyes and looked up to ask her cousin which way Chace had gone—only Matilda wasn't there.

Cassie went to the corner. Matilda was over with her folks and some others, talking excitedly. One of them saw her and pointed and they all turned and Matilda's pa came over. His name was Orville and he was a big man and had always been nice to her.

"Is it true what my girl says? The Harkeys raped Scarlet?"

Cassie nodded.

"Why weren't we told? What was Buck thinking, keeping it secret? Where is he? I want to talk to him."

"He's gone," Cassie said. "Him and his brothers went to see Ezriah Harkey and never came back."

Orville's expression became grim. "Son of a bitch." He caught himself, and said, "Sorry, girl. Excuse me. The rest of our clan needs to know." He turned but stopped. "Tell your ma some of us will be out to your place. Tell her she's not in this alone." He patted Cassie's shoulder and hurried away to a knot of Shannons in front of the saloon.

Cassie had a sense she had done something awfully wrong. She didn't care. Her only worry right now was Chace. He came before anything else. She tried to think what she should do, how to find him. In a daze she wandered back down the street toward Bessie. Without looking she bumped into someone and said, "I'm sorry."

"You should be, girl, sneaking off that way."

Cassie looked up and pure joy flooded through her. "Grandpa!" she exclaimed, throwing her arms around him.

"I saw you riding away and came as fast as I could but couldn't catch you. What are you up to? Your ma will be mad as a wet hen."

Cassie hugged him close and said into his chest, "It's terrible. Chace is wanted by the law."

"Come with me." Jed took her by the hand and went into the store.

It was deserted except for Tom McKeevy, the owner, who was at the front window gazing out and running his hands over his white apron. He nodded at Jed. "This is bad. This is very bad."

"I just got here," Jed told him. "Can you give me the particulars?"

"The deputy was in to buy ammunition right before the posse rode out," McKeevy related. "He told me everything." McKeevy gave a short account of the shooting. "There were half a dozen witnesses. Your grandson goes on trial, he'll spend the rest of his days behind bars if they don't hang him."

"Which way did he head when he left?"

"I don't know. Deputy Fulsome will find him, wherever it was. Fulsome is a bloodhound when he's on a scent, and a good tracker."

"Thank you," Jed said, and led Cassie back out. "Festus Harkey. He must have been one of them as hurt your sister. Now I'm wondering how many others Chace got to before he tracked down Festus."

"What do we do, Grandpa? How can we help him?"

From out in the street came a furious bellow from a large slab of a Harkey, who had his hands on his hips and was glowering at a Shannon.

"That's a damned lie! You take that back. A Harkey would never do a thing like that."

The Shannon raised his own voice. "Scarlet Shannon was raped, I tell you. And it was you damn Harkeys who did it."

Jed turned on Cassie. "What have you done?"

New fear coursed through Cassie. She saw the large Harkey push the Shannon.

"Who have you told?" Jed gripped her by the arms. "Answer me! This is serious."

"Matilda," Cassie said. "I told Matilda."

Jed glanced along the street. More confrontations were taking place.

"You stay right here. You hear me? You're not to move. I've got to nip this in the bud before all hell breaks loose." He ran off.

Cassie sagged against the window. Her whole world was turning upside down. She yearned to be with Chace. She was a Shannon but he was her twin and he meant more to her than anyone.

More angry voices pierced the air. A fistfight broke out between a pair of Harkeys and a pair of Shannons. Two women started slapping each other and pulling at their hair.

"Oh God," Cassie said. No one from either clan was to ever cause trouble in town. The rule had been drummed into her from when she was six, and she'd taken it for granted everyone would always abide by it.

A townsman was trying to stop the fight. "Here now!" he shouted. "We'll have none of that in Wareagle."

Weapons were brandished. A Harkey pointed a rifle at a Shannon. A Shannon drew a revolver and trained it on a Harkey.

Cassie wrung her hands. This was her fault. She shouldn't have told her cousin. She prayed to God everyone would calm down and go home in peace. No sooner did she stop praying than down the street a Shannon clubbed a Harkey to the ground. "Chace, where are you?" she said softly.

A shot boomed, and bedlam erupted. Shannons attacked Harkeys and Harkeys attacked Shannons. Some used fists; some used knives. The crack of pistols, the loud blast of rifles, the curses, and the screams and the cries of panicked townspeople and terror-stricken children filled the street.

Cassie headed for Bessie. She had to get out of there, had to find her brother. She saw a Harkey go down, his throat slit. A Shannon fell, the top of his head blown off. It was as if all the hatred the two clans had pent up for the better part of two decades was being unleashed. Violence had spread the length and breadth of the street. A few people were trying to restore calm but it was hopeless.

Cassie looked for her grandfather but didn't see him. She avoided a pair of furiously battling men, skirted two women who were rolling in the dirt. Somewhere a baby was bawling. A small girl ran past, screeching, "My pa's been hurt! My pa's been hurt!"

Bessie didn't need goading. As soon as Cassie swung on, the mule was away from the rail and broke into a trot. Cassie thought she heard her name called and looked over her shoulder. Wareagle was a welter of confusion and bloodshed.

Townsmen were breaking the combatants apart but there were not enough of them to stop everyone.

Then Cassie was in the clear and had the road to herself. She couldn't stop thinking about Chace. With a posse after him he must be on the run. "I'll find you," she vowed aloud. She rounded a bend and four men were ahead, blocking the road. With relief she saw they had straw hair and blue eyes and drew rein, saying, "Out of my way. I'm in a hurry."

"Ain't you Buck's girl?" one asked.

"What's your rush, little one?" another wanted to know.

Cassie's head was in such a whirl she couldn't remember their names. She didn't see them but once or twice a year and then only in town. "The feud," she said.

"What about it?" asked the third man.

"Harkeys are killing Shannons in the street," Cassie said, and pointed back toward Wareagle. "I got out of there before they killed me."

All four looked at one another and then at her, disbelief writ on their faces. "As pranks go, that's poor," said the first man.

"It's no prank." Cassie wanted them out of her way. "You don't understand." In a rush of words she told them everything: Scarlet being raped, her pa gone missing, her brother shooting a Harkey, and the chaos.

"God Almighty," one exclaimed. "I think she's telling the truth."

"We have to go see," said the first one. "Our kin might need us."

Cassie stayed where she was as they raced by. One yelled for her to follow but she did the opposite; she continued west. Half a mile on was a meadow abundant with wildflowers. She had gone there often to catch butterflies when she was little. She reined off the road and across the meadow to a belt of trees. Dismounting, she sank to her knees. "Oh, Chace," she said, and her eyes moistened. A tear trickled down her right cheek. More flowed, until she couldn't stop. She covered her face with her hands, crying as much over Chace as over her pa and her uncles and Scarlet and what she had caused in Wareagle. She cried until she had no tears left and all the vitality had drained out of her.

Cassie curled on her side and sorted her thoughts. The important thing was still Chace. But how to find him with him on the run? She concentrated on him and on nothing else. Slowly a familiar feeling came over her. She should continue west. Something told her that if she did, eventually she would find him.

Cassie climbed back on Bessie. She never questioned her feelings, not where her brother was concerned. She emerged from the trees and was across the meadow and almost to the road when another rider galloped up. "Grandpa!"

"You shouldn't have run off," Jed said sternly.

"I couldn't stay. I'm sorry. I have to find Chace."

"Your brother can wait. I want you home with your ma. You're to stay there until you hear from me."

"No," Cassie said.

"Don't sass me. I'm not in the mood." Jed brought his mule alongside Bessie. "People died back there because of you. You should have kept your mouth shut about Scarlet."

"Don't lecture me. The only one I told was Matilda. She told her pa and it got out of hand." Cassie paused. "Shouldn't you be in back in town with them and the rest of our kinfolk? You're the head of our clan, after all."

"Don't *you* be lecturing me," Jed said gruffly. "I did what I could. Then I saw you light a shuck and I came after you."

"I'm just one Shannon," Cassie said.

"You're also my favorite granddaughter." Jed gestured. "Do as I say and head home. With you safe I can go back and sort things out. Tell your ma I'll likely stay in town overnight."

"If that's what you want," Cassie said. She dutifully lifted her reins and rode off without looking back. At the fork that would take her south to the cabin she continued west instead.

Cassie would find Chace and they would work out what to do. Since they had been knee-high to bedbugs, they had always solved their problems together. Two minds as one; two hearts as one. That was how it would be for as long as either drew breath. She didn't expect her grandfather to understand. Nor her ma or her sister or anyone else, for that matter. Only another twin would. Only another twin *could*.

Cassie liked that she and Chace were so close. It was comforting to have someone who thought the same and felt the same. She was never alone, even when they were separated, like now, because he was always with her, always a part of her just like her arms and legs. The particulars of how was a mystery; it just *was*.

The sun was low on the horizon when Cassie gave thought to stopping for the night. Only then did she realize that she didn't have any food or blankets or a weapon to defend herself with. There was Bessie and her and the dress she was wearing and that was it.

Cassie didn't care. She would trust in the Lord to watch over her. Her ma was always saying as how God looked after those who looked up to Him. It made her think of the big difference between Chace and her; he didn't believe as she did, not wholeheartedly. She'd asked him once why not and he replied that he'd had doubts ever since Uncle Granger's baby girl died of the croup. As Chace had put it, "What kind of a God kills babies?"

Cassie didn't know why things were the way they were. All she was sure of was that she would find Chace or die trying.

17

It was hard being a patriarch, Jedediah Shannon thought to himself. It was hard being responsible for so many lives. He'd never asked to be head of the clan. It had fallen to him when his father was shot by a Harkey.

The damned Harkeys.

Jed often mused on how different his life would have been if not for the feud. He never did like to kill and hated that so many others lost their lives over something so stupid as hate. That was how he once described the feud to his pa: *stupid*. Especially given as how no one could recollect what started it in the first place. But there the two clans had been, grown men and not so fully grown men, going around shooting at one another and lying in ambush and murdering one another with guns and toothpicks and bowie knives.

Jed was proud of ending the bloodshed. That day he ran into Ezriah Harkey at the general store was a sign from above. Ezriah had been just as sick of the killing as he was. So they came to an agreement and shook hands, and just like that, the feud was over. Until now. Until Scarlet had to go and do something dumb and Buck had to prove something to himself by refusing help and then Chace had to go and shoot that Harkey in the tavern. Now here they were, the feud broken out again, and Jed miserable. Twenty years of peace forgotten as if it never was. The best and grandest thing he had ever done, shot to pieces.

Jed shuddered to think how many more had their wicks snuffed out in the Wareagle fight. When he'd lit out there had been five on the ground and several more wounded. He should have stayed. As head of the clan he was obligated to tend to his kin. Instead he had gone after Cassie. He had no choice. He truly did adore her more than any of his grandkids. He adored her even more than he had adored his own sons, and that was saying a lot.

Jed hung his head in despair. His sons. Buck and Granger and Fox should have been back days ago. He'd held out hope but there was no denying the truth; he wouldn't ever set eyes on them again. They were dead. That was another reason he'd gone after Cassie; he didn't want to lose her, too. Losing three sons was trial enough.

Jed drew rein. He opened a saddlebag and found his silver flask. Taking a swig, he smacked his lips. His thinking juice, he liked to call it. He savored another swallow. By rights he should be fanning the breeze to Wareagle, but there he sat, drinking and pondering. *What's the matter with me?* he asked himself. The answer was as plain as his nose. Maybe it was his years. Maybe it was losing his beloved wife, Mary. Maybe it was losing his boys. But God help him, he didn't want to be patriarch anymore. "Hell," he summed up his sentiments.

It was dark when Jed reached the cabin. He wearily

dismounted and went in without knocking. Erna was in her rocking chair, knitting. Scarlet was at the table playing cards. "Where are Chace and Cassie?" he asked.

Their confusion spiked a dread certainty. Jed turned to go but stopped. He placed his forehead against the jamb, and sighed. "If it ain't chickens, it's feathers."

Erna set her needles and yarn down and stood. "What is going on, Jedediah? Where are my children?"

Jed bid her sit at the table. He related all he knew, leaving out only the grislier details of the clash in Wareagle and saying nothing of his great fear for Chace and Cassie beyond. "I think Chace is on the run and Cassie went to find him."

Erna listened stoically. "First my husband and now my two youngest," she said with great sadness. "Is there no end?"

"At dawn I'll set out after the twins."

"I'll go with you."

"Is that wise?" Jed asked diplomatically. "What if they show up here? And how about Scarlet?"

"I can take care of myself," Scarlet said.

"You're still not yourself," Jed noted. "And with the Harkeys on the rampage, you shouldn't be alone."

"They wouldn't dare come this far into Shannon country," Erna said.

"Your husband and your son went as far into theirs," Jed argued. "Nothing is as it was. They could strike anytime, anywhere."

"I'm not comfortable with sitting here twiddling my thumbs," Erna persisted. "I'm their mother."

"You have every right to come if you really want," Jed said. "But I can ride faster and I know these mountains better than just about anyone." He had her there.

"I'll think about it while I fix supper," Erna said. "We held off eating in case some of you showed."

Jed had little appetite but he let her feed him potato soup and boiled chicken and green beans. He dearly desired to wash it down with whiskey but he kept the flask in his pocket.

Scarlet didn't say one word the whole meal. Afterward, as Jed sat puffing on his pipe and Erna was washing the dishes, Scarlet folded her hands on the table and said, "This is all my fault."

"Not hardly," Jed said.

"I was the one went to Harkey Hollow. I brought this down on our heads." Scarlet's eyes mirrored inner pain.

"How were you to predict?" Jed said. "You were careless, yes, but the truce was in effect longer than you've lived. You can't be blamed for not taking it as serious as you should."

Erna said over her shoulder, "If it's true my Buck is gone, then I'm glad the truce is broken. I aim to avenge him and kill me a few Harkeys. An eye for an eye, just like in the Bible."

"That's no way to talk," Jed said. "Not with you a mother and a woman and all."

"Why, Jedediah Shannon," Erna said. "Are you suggesting a female can't stand up for her clan the same as the males?"

"Don't put words in my mouth."

"Then what? I'm supposed to forgive and forget? After what they did to my Scarlet? After they've probably gone and killed my Buck?" Erna's voice broke.

Jed's mouth was so dry he couldn't wet his lips. He put his hand to his pocket and drew it away.

"I agree with Grandpa," Scarlet said. "Not because

you're female but because if I lose you and the law catches Chace, it'll be me and Cassie all by ourselves."

"Listen to her," Jed said to Erna. He got up and walked to the water pitcher and filled a glass. He gulped half down. It didn't help. His mouth was still dry and his arm and leg muscles were twitching. "Not now," he said under his breath.

"What was that?" Erna asked.

"I've got to put my mule in the corral." Jed hurried out and took hold of the reins. He wasn't quite to the barn when the shakes hit. Unable to stay on his feet, he dropped to his knees and pressed his arms to his gut. It was the worst attack of many. He shuddered and shook and gritted his teeth, the sweat pouring from his pores. The last time had been at his place before he set out to see Buck.

The attack passed. Jed pushed erect and shuffled to the gate. He was so weak he had to try twice to open it. Stripping the saddle was a chore and a half.

His Sharps over his shoulder, he retraced his steps. As he came around the cabin a gun muzzle was shoved against his ribs.

"So much as twitch and you're dead."

Jed froze. There were two of them, both with black hair and bushy brows and Winchesters. "What do you want?"

"As if you don't know," said the Harkey who had jabbed him.

"If I did I wouldn't have asked."

"We want the boy called Chace," said the other. "He's to blame for today and we know he lives here." He took the Sharps. "Inside, old man. Go slow or we'll blow holes in you."

Jed felt no fear, only anger. Not anger at them but at himself for being taken unawares. "Chace ain't here," he said.

"As if we'd take your word for it," the Harkey holding the rifle said. He jabbed Jed hard. "Get going."

His anger climbing, Jed stepped to the door and gripped the latch. He contemplated resisting but now wasn't the time. He went in, saying, "Stay calm, ladies. We have visitors."

Erna and Scarlet were at the table. When they saw the Harkeys, they stood in alarm and Erna said, "What's the meaning of this?"

The Harkey who had taken the Sharps moved past Jed to the bedrooms. He peered into each and turned and shook his head. "No one else here, Joe Earl."

"Damn," Joe Earl said. "I want that son of a bitch so bad, Arlan, I can taste it."

Erna bristled. "Watch your mouth. I won't have that kind of talk in my house."

"You must be the bastard's ma," Joe Earl said. He nodded at Scarlet. "You must be his sis." He poked Jed with the rifle. "Grandpa, right? Got a name to go with that gray hair?"

Jed told him.

The one called Arlan came to the table. "Jedediah Shannon?" he repeated, his eyebrows meeting over his nose. "Wait. Ain't you the head of all the Shannons?"

"That he is," Erna said before Jed could answer. "And if you know what's good for you, you'll get out of here and leave us be."

"Shut up, bitch," Joe Earl snapped. "Your son shot one of us today and three more Harkeys were killed in the fight, after."

"That's right," Arlan chimed in. "We also got word right before we left Wareagle that other Harkeys have been killed off in the hills, and we think maybe your son had a hand in them, too."

"So we'll just wait for him to come home and do to him as he's been doing to us Harkeys," Joe Earl informed them.

"The law is after him," Jed said. "He's likely halfway to anywhere by now."

"We'll wait anyway."

Arlan was staring at Scarlet. "You sure are pretty, gal. But what in tarnation happened to you? You're all black-and-blue. Did your folks beat you for misbehaving?"

Erna was livid, her fists clenched at her sides. "She was raped by you rotten Harkeys, is why! That's what started this, not my boy shooting one of you vermin."

"I'd be careful with the insults," Joe Earl warned.

Erna took a step toward him. "You bust in my house. You hold a gun to my father-in-law. You threaten women."

"Erna," Jed cautioned.

Erna took another step. "You're scum," she growled at Joe Earl. "Just like all you Harkeys. Us Shannons should have wiped you off the face of the earth when we had the chance. I'm glad my son killed some of you." She grinned fiercely. "Do you hear me?"

"I hear you fine," Joe Earl said, and shot her.

Jed had been inching his hand to his right hip. He was surprised at how careless they were, not taking his knife. As the Winchester blasted he drew his bowie and spun, thrusting up and in and sinking the big blade to the hilt in Joe Earl's belly. Joe Earl bleated and his eyes widened and he tried to draw a pistol but he was dead on his feet.

Yanking the bowie out, Jed spun toward Arlan, who was leveling his rifle.

Scarlet leaped between them. She grabbed the barrel and went to push it aside just as it went off. The slug ripped through her chest and she staggered back and looked down at herself in disbelief. "Grandpa?" she said, and her knees gave out.

Arlan appeared as stunned as Jed. Belatedly, he brought the Winchester up, but Jed was already in motion. He came around the table, and kicked. Arlan was knocked back. Jed was on him in a long bound and grabbed the barrel as Scarlet had done, only Jed shifted sideways so if the rifle went off he wouldn't be hit. He slashed at Arlan's neck but Arlan grabbed his wrist. Locked together, they grappled, each seeking the upper hand. Jed let go of the Winchester and punched Arlan in the throat. Arlan grunted and made strangled sounds but held on to Jed's wrist. Jed grabbed the barrel again and they moved back and forth and around and around in a grotesque mimicry of a dance. Jed broke the stalemate by kicking Arlan in the knee. Arlan swore and sagged. Jed tore his wrist free and slashed twice, cutting so deep he nearly severed the head from the body. A fine red spray ruptured from the near stump of a neck.

Jed moved to Scarlet. She was on her side, still breathing, tears in her eyes, her cheeks wet. He cradled her on his legs.

"Grandpa?"

"I'm here, girl." Jed gently squeezed her arm. A spreading stain on the front of her dress and her pallor were harbingers of the worst.

"I'm cold, Grandpa," Scarlet said. She looked up at him and gasped and went limp.

Jed went to Erna. She was facedown. He carefully rolled her over and her eyes opened.

"How bad is it?"

Jed looked at the wound. She had been shot down low and there were only a few drops of blood on her dress. "I can't tell."

Erna swallowed and said weakly, "It feels like my insides are tore up. Is Scarlet all right?"

"She's fine," Jed lied.

"Take care of her. The twins, too. Find them and bring them back and see to it they turn out decent."

"I will," Jed said. Grief filled him, grief and something worse, but he held them back. Not yet, he thought.

"I'll be with Bucklyn soon," Erna said, and smiled. "Any message I can give him for you?"

"I love you both," Jed said.

"Take care of yourself, Jedediah. Take care of my babies, too." Erna reached up but her hand never reached him. She arched her back and gazed up at the ceiling and said, "There's a light." Then she deflated like a punctured water skin.

Jed felt dizzy. He stood and leaned against the table and took his flask from his pocket. He opened it and upended it and sucked the whiskey as if it were the elixir of life.

When he lowered it, the tears started.

18

The tavern was in the middle of the wilds. The last town was thirty miles back. The next, according to a sign on the front of the tavern, was twice as far. The sign, bathed by light from the front window, read *Barnaby's. Last food and drink for sixty miles. Served six a.m. until midnight. Lodging available upon request. Horses and mules put up, extra. Lucius Barnaby, Prop.*

Chace wrestled with the sign, saying the words out loud. Those he didn't know, he guessed. Climbing down, he tied Enoch and climbed the steps. He idly swatted dust from his clothes and opened the door. He held the Spencer in his left hand.

A spacious room glowed yellow with the light from several lamps. Tables were to one side, to the other a bar. A balding man with no chin and thick arms was wiping a glass with a cloth. He smiled and beckoned.

"Come in, boy, come in."

Chace went over. He stood so he could see the door and set the Spencer on the top of the bar.

"I was just about to close," the man said. "I'm Lucius Barnaby, in case you haven't guessed."

Chace didn't say who he was.

Barnaby shrugged and went on smiling. "You look a little young for liquor but I don't judge. I never judge. That's in the Bible, you know. 'Judge not, lest ye be judged.' Do you judge, boy?"

"Yes," Chace said.

Barnaby's right eyebrow crooked upward. He set down the glass and draped the cloth over his shoulder. "What will it be, then?"

"Food. I'm not particular. It doesn't have to be hot. Cold meat. Cold stew. A handful of carrots if that's all you've got."

"Famished, are you? Well, I reckon I can do better than carrots." Barnaby gestured at the tables. "Why don't you take a seat? Usually I don't do food so close to closing, but for a handsome boy like you I'll make an exception." He winked and patted Chace's hand. "Give me ten minutes or so."

"I'm obliged." Chace chose a table in the corner. He placed the Spencer on it, turned a chair around, and straddled it so he was facing the front door. He ran a hand through his hair and across his chin, and yawned.

From in back came singing and whistling. A pan banged. There was loud clattering.

Chace reached behind him and drew the Arkansas toothpick. He flicked at spots of dry blood with a finger-nail, then tested the edge by lightly running it along his little finger. A thin red line welled. He wiped the blade on his pants and slid it back into the sheath.

When Barnaby reappeared he was carrying a large tray. He hummed as he brought it over and set it on the table. "I went to extra effort on your account, boy. I want you to appreciate that." He set out a plate and silverware and several dishes steaming with food. "It's not fancy but it's filling."

"How much?" Chace asked.

Barnaby did more winking. "For you, handsome boy, not a penny. It's on the house." He moved toward the front. "I better lock up. Don't worry. I'll let you out when you're ready to leave."

In addition to a pot of coffee, the meal consisted of half a macaroni pie with shallots, a side of turnips, and a thick piece of peppermint cake. Chace ate heartily, washing every other mouthful down with coffee.

The proprietor was looking out the window. He gazed up the road and then down the road, and nodded to himself. Then he came over, wiping his hands on his apron. "That mule of yours is tuckered out. Been doing a lot of hard riding, I take it."

Chace spooned macaroni into his mouth.

Barnaby held his right hand palm out. "It's none of my business, I know. But if I was to guess, I'd say you're on the run."

"You're right," Chace said between chews. "It's none of your business."

"Of course, of course." Barnaby pulled out the chair across the table and sat. "Maybe I can be of help, though."

"Why?"

"Why help you when I don't even know you? That's just how I am. I was young once. I remember how it was. If you're in trouble you can confide in me. I won't tell a soul. Honest."

Chace speared a turnip with his fork. "I've killed pretty near a dozen people and the law is after me."

Barnaby chuckled. "That's a good one. A boy your

age . . ." He caught himself. "Hold on. You're not funning me?"

"It might be more. I shot a posse man and he went down but I can't say as he's dead." Chace chewed the turnip. "You're a good cook."

"Good God."

"You make this pie yourself?" Chace asked.

Barnaby nodded and licked his lips. Sweat broke out on his balding pate. "Can I ask who?"

"No."

"Can I ask why?"

"The why doesn't count. All that matters to the law is the doing."

"True," Barnaby said.

Chace refilled his cup with coffee. "I shot a deputy, too, but he's still breathing. It's him who will dog me. I doubt he took kindly to lead in his wing."

"I imagine not." Barnaby gazed at the window and drummed his fingers on the table. Sweat now glistened on his face and neck. "When I said trouble I had no idea."

"Now you do." Chace smiled and spooned more macaroni. "My ma hardly ever made macaroni pie and hers wasn't as good as yours. You should be a cook."

"If I cooked I'd have to work in a restaurant or a hotel and be around people and I'm not much of a mingler. To be honest, I don't like people that much."

Chace put his hand on the Spencer. "You like handsome boys."

A bead of sweat ran down Barnaby's nose and dripped off the end onto the table. "That wasn't what you think."

"We should always say what we mean and make it

plain," Chace said. "People take things wrong, they might shoot you."

Barnaby glanced at the Spencer and took the cloth from his shoulder and mopped his face. "I'm too nice for my own good." He started to get up.

"No," Chace said.

Barnaby sat.

Chace finished the pie and the turnips and began on the peppermint cake. The cake was dry and broke apart when he forked it. He put the fork on the plate and pushed the plate away. "So if you were me, what would you do?"

"Make myself scarce in these parts, but that goes without saying." Barnaby rubbed the chin he didn't have. "Your best bet is a city. Be another face in the crowd. Texas is as good as anywhere and it's not that far. Dallas. Houston. San Antonio. Or maybe Galveston. I hear it's booming and there are lots of jobs to be had."

"Galveston," Chace said.

Barnaby nodded. "It's on an island. Has gaslights and an opera house and everything. You could lose yourself, easy. No Arkansas lawman would think to look for you there."

Chace downed the last of the coffee. "How do you know so much about it?"

"Folks stop here regular," Barnaby said. "I hear a lot of things. Were it me hiding out, that's where I'd go."

Pushing his chair back, Chace set the Spencer in his lap. "Here's my problem. Do I trust you, mister?"

"I said you could."

"Saying doesn't make it so." Chace stood, and Barnaby paled and spread his hands on the table.

"Listen to me, boy. I have no love for the law. I was in

trouble a few times when I was your age so I know how life goes."

"How many folks did you send to their reward?"

"Well, none. But not because I didn't want to." Barnaby's face dripped sweat. "I don't have your grit, I guess. I can't just go and shoot someone. I'm too afraid of being put in prison."

Chace came around the table but stayed out of reach. "Let's say I believe you. Let's say I go my way and a month from now a lawman is on my trail and I find out it's thanks to you."

"Yes?" Barnaby said when Chace didn't go on.

"It would rile me."

"I have no hankering to die."

"I hope so, for both our sakes." Chace walked sideways to the door and out into the cool of the night. He unwrapped the reins and climbed on Enoch and rode on down the road.

"I have just made a mistake," he said.

It was an hour or so past midnight by Cassie's reckoning when she spied the tavern. It sat by itself, a lonely haven for wayfarers. A single glow showed in a window at the back. She was tired and hungry and had nearly ridden Bessie into the ground. She had to stop even though she didn't want to.

Cassie went to the door and raised her fist to knock, and hesitated. It was late and the people inside might be asleep and it would be rude of her to wake them. But unless she got some rest and nourishment, she would be useless. She knocked loudly. No one came so she knocked louder. She thought she heard sounds and the front window flared with light. There was a sign but she didn't bother reading it.

"Who's there?" a man's voice asked. He sounded half afraid.

"Me," Cassie said.

"A girl?"

A bolt rasped and the door opened a crack and an eyeball peered out at her. The man the eye belonged to said, "I am dreaming."

"What?" Cassie said. "No, you're not. I'm real and I'd like something to eat and a bed to sleep in. This is a tavern, ain't it?"

The door opened wider. "You look just like—" The man stopped. He had a shiny head and was wearing a nightshirt and holding a small lamp. "I'm Barnaby," he said.

Cassie told him who she was. "Can I come in or not? I know it's late and I'm sorry."

The man raised the lamp higher and poked his head out and gazed the length of the road. "You alone?"

"Yes, sir." Cassie didn't see what that had to do with anything. A traveler was a traveler.

Barnaby stepped back and held the door wide. "Come on in. If I seem surprised it's because I've never had a girl your age show up at my door this late and all alone. But you are more than welcome."

Cassie entered. The room smelled of food and tobacco. "Is your wife to bed?"

Barnaby was studying her as if she was a mystery he wanted to solve. "My wife? Oh yes. She's sleeping. I was just about to turn in myself when you knocked." He closed the door and threw the bolt.

"Why'd you do that?"

"Common sense. I don't care to be robbed or have my throat slit while I sleep."

"Is there any chance I can get a bite to eat?" Cassie's mention of food caused her stomach to rumble. "You can hear how hungry I am."

"That I can." Barnaby grinned in amusement. "I have some cold turnips and leftover peppermint cake. In the morning I can fix you a proper breakfast."

"Doesn't your wife cook?"

"By me I meant her." Barnaby set the lamp on a table. "Why don't you take a seat? I won't be long."

Cassie gripped the edges of the chair and bowed her head. She hated the delay. She wearily closed her eyes and a feeling came over her, the warmth she always felt when Chace was near. She glanced about her at the empty room and shook her head at how ridiculous she was being. Wishful thinking was all it was.

She yawned and fidgeted and hoped the man would hurry.

The plate he brought also had a slice of bread smeared with butter and several crackers. He had also thought to bring a glass of milk.

"It's not much," he apologized.

"It will do." Cassie ate like a famished wolf. The turnips weren't cold as he had said but slightly warm as if they had recently been cooked. She'd never been all that fond of turnips but her belly wasn't as choosy. The man sat at the next table, watching. He didn't say a word. She didn't like being stared at but it was his tavern. When she was done she pushed the plate and empty glass away. "I'm awful grateful."

"Are you riding on?"

Cassie wanted to. Her compulsion to catch up to Chace was like a rope around her heart, pulling her. "Not until daylight. I can use some sleep. But there's something you should know. I don't have any money to pay you."

Barnaby said a strange thing. "Gall must run in your family."

"I'm good for it, though," Cassie made her case. "You tell me how much it is and I'll see it gets to you if it takes me a month of Sundays. I'm honest, mister. Truly I am."

"I believe you. So I'll tell you what I'll do. In the morning you can wash the dishes I didn't get to today and we'll call it even. How would that be?"

Another delay Cassie would rather not have. Still, she wouldn't owe him anything, and he was being kind. "We have a deal."

Barnaby smiled and picked up the lamp. He led her down a narrow hall, past several doors. One was open and Cassie saw a bed and a dresser and a rug on the floor. He came to the last door and opened it and stepped aside.

"After you."

Cassie stepped past him and took two steps in and stopped. It wasn't a room, it was a big closet with shelves lined with canned goods and spare blankets and whatnot. She started to turn and the door slammed shut behind her, plunging her in darkness. "What are you doing?" She groped for the latch but there was none. The door only opened from the outside. Fear gripped her and she called out, "Mister? What are you up to?"

"What do you think, girl?" Barnaby replied, and laughed.

19

Deputy Nick Fulsome was lying in bed in a spare room on the second floor of Doc Witherspoon's when Sheriff Aldo Wyler waddled in. Wyler wore a tailored suit and polished leather boots and a hat that never had a speck of dust. Wyler walked to a chair and contemplated sitting in it and stepped to the bed instead. "Well," he said.

"Well yourself," Nick sulkily responded.

"You went and got yourself shot."

"No wonder you're the sheriff. You don't miss a thing."

Wyler frowned, a feat in itself as his face was a great moon of fat. "You're the only one in the world I will take that from. Do you want to know why?"

"I'm the only deputy you have who is worth a damn."

"There's that," Wyler said. "But no. I take your barbs out of respect for my sister. She asked me to give you the job and I did, and you've never let me down. But don't think you can't be replaced. Everyone can be replaced."

"Don't remind me of her," Nick said.

"Why not? We honor the dead by remembering them. You loved her. It's not your fault she got consumption and died."

"Don't remind me, I said."

Wyler moved to a window that overlooked the street. "Witherspoon tells me you'll be up and around in a few days. The only reason he made you stay in bed was all the blood you lost."

"That damned kid," Nick said.

"Yes, that damned kid." Sheriff Wyler leaned against the wall and folded his arms. "That damned, deadly, beautiful kid."

"What the hell are you talking about?" Nick shook his head. "You and your fine clothes and fancy talk. What are you trying to prove? That you're more than you are?"

"Nicholas, Nicholas, Nicholas."

"Don't call me that. I've told you before. It's just Nick."

"Nicholas P. Fulsome. Raised on a farm but you hated farm life. Spent most of your childhood hunting. Took up with my sister and needed a job, so I pinned a badge on you. That's your life in a nutshell."

"What did you say all that for?"

"Because I have a favor to ask. A very important favor. It involves our deadly young friend."

"He's no friend of mine."

"Nor the Harkeys," Wyler said. "He killed old Ezriah and that crazy witch woman. He killed Rabon and Woot and Scooter Harkey. He killed Lincoln Harkey and Lincoln's two brothers, George and Jefferson. He killed Festus Harkey. He killed Flannery, the townsman in your posse. And he shot you. Hard to believe he's only sixteen. The rate he is going, he will be the champion killer of all time before he is through."

"He's better than his years," Nick said.

"That boy is a match and he's lit the tinder."

"You're talking about the feud between the Harkeys and the Shannons."

"Three Harkeys were killed right out there in the street. Two Shannons died, too."

"All because of that kid."

"Word is that it started when Scarlet Shannon was raped. She's Buck Shannon's girl, or was. Makes her the kid's sister."

"Why was?" Nick asked.

"Because she's dead. So is her mother, Erna. We found their graves out to their place after the fire."

"You're losing me."

"Their cabin burned to the ground. From what we can tell it was set on purpose. No idea who. Buck Shannon is missing along with his brothers, Granger and Fox. It's a mess I am trying to untangle."

"What's the favor you mentioned?"

Sheriff Wyler walked to the bed. "Before I get to that, I need you to understand. The Shannon-Harkey feud was one of the worst ever. The killing never stopped. I'd been in office barely six months when Jed Shannon and Ezriah agreed to a truce. For twenty years this county has been peaceful. Now, thanks to the rape and this killer of a kid, all hell has busted loose. I won't have it. Not in Madison County, I won't." Wyler took off his hat. He had a full head of hair well oiled and cropped around the ears. "The feud has started up again and we have to stop it before it gets as bad as before. There's only one way to do that. The Harkeys want this kid's head on a platter and we're going to give it to them."

"We are?"

"They blame him for everything that's happened."

"What about the rape?"

"Most Harkeys think it's a lie the Shannons made up to excuse what the kid did. We bring him in, we make the Harkeys happy. I might be able to sit down with both sides and arrange a new truce."

"The Shannons will go for that?"

"The kid's grandfather, Jed, never liked the killing, and he should be easy to convince." Wyler paused. "If I can find him. He's disappeared, too."

Nick sat up and propped the pillow at the small of his back. "I'm still waiting to hear that favor."

Sheriff Wyler put his hat on. "I want you to go after him. I want you to track this Chace Shannon to the ends of the earth, if need be, but get him for me. Dead if you have to but alive would be better so we can put him on trial. Just so you bring him back. I've promised to get him one way or the other. It will show the Harkeys I'm a man of my word and they'll be easier to persuade to accept a new truce."

"You have this all thought out," Nick said.

"I do the best I can, Nicholas. I took an oath to uphold the law. I know people poke fun at me because of my size but no one can poke fun at me over the job I do."

"No," Nick agreed. "You're a good lawman."

"So, will you do it? It could take weeks, even months. Will you hunt down Chace Shannon for me?"

"Not just for you," Nick Fulsome said, and touched his shoulder.

*   *   *

Cassie pounded and pounded but it did no good. Barnaby didn't open the door; he didn't answer her shouts. She thought that maybe his wife would come if she shouted loud enough but no one did. Fighting down her fear, she sat with her legs crossed and her chin in her hands. She wished Chace was there. He would know what to do.

Cassie tried to make sense of it. The man had shut her in. Why? Plainly, he was up to no good. But what? She had admitted she didn't have money so it couldn't be that. It had to be the other thing—the thing her ma had warned her about when she was little, the thing that bad men did to women who didn't want to do it. The thing that had happened to Scarlet. *Rape.* The word echoed ugly in her brain. Cassie knew about "it." She'd been raised on a farm, after all. Cats did "it." Cows did "it." Horses did "it." People did "it." And this Barnaby must have been planing to do "it" with her.

Cassie shuddered with loathing. She was beginning to understand how Scarlet must have felt. Just thinking about Barnaby doing it to her was terrible.

Rising, Cassie groped the shelves. She needed a weapon. Some of the cans were heavy but she wanted something better. Her questing fingers brushed a long wooden handle. She ran her hand down it and discovered it was a broom. It wasn't much but it was better than nothing. She jabbed a few times at an imaginary foe.

Folded blankets were on a middle shelf. Cassie took one down and unfolded it and placed it at her feet. Next to it she placed a heavy can. She sat with the broom across her lap and said to herself, "Come and get me."

No one did. The minutes crawled into hours. Cassie's

head drooped. She felt herself falling asleep. Jerking her head up, she shook it to clear the cobwebs. Again and again she did the same but at last she succumbed.

A noise woke her. Cassie raised her head and listened but whatever it had been wasn't repeated. Light at the bottom of the door told her it was daylight.

She stiffly rose and rubbed her leg where the circulation had been cut off. She began pounding and hollering. Her hands hurt but she kept at it. Just when she couldn't take the pain anymore and was about to stop, the door shook to a blow on the other side.

"Stop that, damn you. I could hear you out front."

"Let me out, Mr. Barnaby," Cassie said. "Let me be on my way and I promise I won't tell anyone."

"You're damn right you won't because I won't let you."

"What is it you want?"

"You're pretty, girl, as pretty as he was handsome, and I like the pretty ones. Now be quiet in there and I'll fix you breakfast."

"As handsome as who was, Mr. Barnaby? Who are you talking about?"

"The boy who was here before you. He wasn't interested but you'll serve fine in his stead."

Cassie's heart beat faster. He must be talking about Chace. "When was the boy here? Did he say his name?" Barnaby didn't answer. She pounded on the door and raised her voice but it was no use. He had gone off. She should have been upset but she wasn't. She was elated. She was close on Chace's trail. If only she could get out, they could be together before the day was done.

Breakfast, Barnaby had said.

Cassie leaned the broom against the wall near the

door and put the heavy can next to it. She gripped the blanket in both hands and shook it a few times.

Everything depended on how quick she could be. She wasn't Chace but she wasn't a turtle, either. It might work.

The wait was forever. At last there came a thump on the door and Barnaby said, "I've brought you eggs and sausage. Step back from the door and keep your hands where I can see them."

"I won't try anything," Cassie lied.

"You better not. If you make me mad, you'll suffer."

The door started to open. Cassie was to one side, the blanket in front of her. Light crawled in, and two hands appeared holding a tray.

"Where are you, girl?"

Cassie sprang and flung the blanket. Barnaby recoiled, still holding the tray, and the blanket fell over his head and one shoulder. He cursed and dropped the tray and grabbed it. By then she had the can in one hand and the broom in the other. She smashed the can against his head and he cried out and staggered back.

She hit him again, but he moved and the can only grazed him. She was watching his hands and not his feet and she didn't see the kick that caught her across the shin and nearly upended her. She let go of the can, held the broom in both hands, handle out, and speared it at his gut and his chest and his groin. She was hurting him but not enough. He tore the blanket off and his eyes were terrible to behold. Spittle was dribbling from his mouth. With a growl he threw the blanket at her. Cassie dodged. Suddenly he had hold of the handle and was seeking to wrest it from her grasp. She let go and ran. She had always been fast and she was out into the main room and made it to the front door and yanked. She had forgotten the bolt. She clawed at it and arms encircled her from behind. She was lifted bodily and thrown at the floor. She hit and rolled and came up in a crouch, her heart hammering in her chest.

Barnaby looked the madman. His head was bleeding and he was breathing in loud gasps. Fingers hooked, he spread his thick arms. "For that you'll pay, you little bitch. God, how you'll pay."

Cassie darted to a chair. She had it up before he could reach her and brought it down. A leg splintered. He cuffed her, backhand, and she fell against a table. He lunged for her throat but she skipped away.

"You won't get past me, girl," Barnaby vowed.

Cassie circled and he circled with her. She tried to go right and he blocked her. She tried to get around him on the left but he was there. He laughed, as if he was enjoying himself. She didn't laugh. She was in deadly earnest. She would kill him if she could if that was what it took.

Unexpectedly, Barnaby straightened. "That was your brother, wasn't it? The other one last night? The handsome boy?"

"Chace," Cassie said.

"Was that his name? He never said. You look enough alike that he could be you and you could be him."

"We're twins."

"You don't say."

"I'm a girl."

"And he's a boy. Yes. And sheep aren't goats and goats aren't sheep but I have both in a pen out back."

"What does that even mean?" Cassie wanted to keep him talking. He was bound to let down his guard and she could slip past him to the door.

"I'll show you soon enough." Barnaby chuckled. "It's rare I get someone like you all by herself. Or your brother, for that matter. Usually they are with families and friends."

"You've done this before?"

Barnaby wiped his sleeve across his mouth. "I couldn't hardly sleep for thinking of you."

"You're a pig."

"More like a boar," Barnaby said, and grinned. Without warning he leaped at her.

Cassie threw herself back but his right hand snared her wrist. Pain exploded up her arm. She tugged but he was much too strong. She drove her knee at the junction of his legs but he turned, blunting the force. An ankle hooked her behind her leg and the next moment she was on her back and he was on top of her, straddling her. She bucked and he leered.

"Yes. That's it. I like it when they fight."

He reached for her dress.

Cassie screamed.

20

Jedediah Shannon drew rein and took out his flask. He was getting low but he didn't care. He gulped a few times and closed his eyes and leaned on his saddle horn. "God," he said. Shaking himself, he slid the flask into his pocket, raised the reins, and gigged his mule. It was a young mule and tended to be contrary, but that was his fault and not the mule's. Mules needed more training than horses and he had neglected the training for his drinking. He had neglected a lot of things for his drinking. His family, for one. He had stayed up in his cabin and let the rest of the world go to hell while he tried to drown himself so he could join his wife in the hereafter.

God, Jed missed her. Some folks would scoff. Some men would say he was being plumb silly. He didn't care. He'd loved Mary with all he was, and when she died it was all he could do to keep going. It was as if a part of him had been cut out and cast away. The best part. The part that made life worth living.

Jed tossed his head and tried to concentrate on the road. The ink of night still held sway but dawn would break soon. He should stop and rest. He should make a fire and put coffee on to clear his head and eat something. But he wouldn't.

For the first time in a long while he had a purpose and he would by God follow it through. He was going to find the twins. They were all he had left in the world, all that mattered.

That in itself showed Jed he wasn't the man he used to be. Was a time, the whole clan mattered. Was a time, he genuinely cared. Was a time, before Mary died, when that was important.

The bitterness returned, and Jed swore. He supposed he shouldn't blame them. But damn it, only nine Shannons had shown up, besides his boys and their families, for Mary's burying. Nine, out of a hundred and eleven, counting all the young'uns. Sure, he had made it a point to tell everyone that he wanted to be alone with his grief. Sure, it was harvest time, and a lot of the men couldn't interrupt the harvest to take a week or more to come. It had rankled, though. It rankled and festered to where Jed became bitter. To where he realized that being the patriarch didn't mean the clan cared for you as much as you cared for the clan.

Jed licked his lips and thought about taking out the flask. Some days he couldn't stop drinking for more than five minutes. Who could blame him now? He justified it. Three of his sons, dead. A daughter-in-law and granddaughter, dead. The twins missing.

Jed had barely felt anything over the Shannons killed in the fight in Wareagle. They were kin but so what? Did they ever come visit? Did they ever show they gave a damn?

Jed shook his head in disgust. Not at them, at himself. He had become a lonely, spiteful fool. Make that a lonely, spiteful drunk. He was everything that at one time he'd looked down his nose on. It was life that did it. Life that wore a person down. Life that kicked a person in the teeth again and again. Now life had kicked him in the gut, too, and he was more bitter than ever. What was the point of there being people you cared for if life came along and took them from you? It wasn't fair. It wasn't right.

"God," he said again.

Jed was sore and stiff from all the riding. He hadn't done this much in years. But he refused to stop. He had to find Chace and Cassie. They had always been dear to him, those two. He'd been there when they came into the world and he had held them in his arms and marveled at how beautiful they were. Some people said babies were ugly. Not him. Babies had a beauty that went beyond looks, and the twins had been the most beautiful of all.

Back then, he had paid more visits to Buck than he ordinarily would just to see them. He'd watched them grow and loved them more and they loved him in return. At night in his cabin when he lay alone with an empty flask on the floor, he would think of them and grow warm inside.

Now they were in trouble. Chace, anyhow. That boy puzzled Jed sometimes.

Chace had changed since the stable incident. Before, the boy was always smiling and carefree. After, Chace went deep inside himself and stayed there. It had troubled Jed but there was nothing he could do. He'd promised Cassie not to talk about it, not to even mention she had confided in him.

Cassie. Sweet, wonderful Cassie. Jed adored that girl. She'd never lost the purity she'd had as a baby. To him she was as good a person as anyone could be and he loved her more than he had ever loved anyone except Mary. Including his sons. That might be awful but there it was.

The sky behind him brightened. He sensed it before he twisted in the saddle and saw a splash of pink that heralded the new day. The forest around him had begun to stir to life. He continued to the west. He was sure that was the direction the twins had gone.

Another mile, and Jed stopped and took out the flask. He sniffed, then drank, and was appalled when the last drop dribbled down his throat. Shifting, he opened his saddlebags. He only had one bottle left and it was almost empty.

He chugged what there was and threw the bottle into the brush.

"Damn."

Jed needed whiskey. He tried to recollect how far ahead the next town was, and couldn't. His mind was too befuddled. It got that way after he drank a lot, but befuddled was good. When he was well in his cups he didn't think as much about Mary.

Jed pocketed the flask and jabbed his mule. "Get along, Tiberius." He'd always like that name. He'd heard it as a kid somewhere and it stuck in his head.

Actually this mule was his third Tiberius, but he wasn't about to call it Tiberius the Third. Folks would laugh.

He was winding along a wooded road. He spied a building and figured it to be a house but as he got closer he saw a hitch rail and a mule and a sign that had the word TAVERN. He chuckled and smacked his lips and said, "Glory be. Thank you, Lord." He reined to the rail and alighted and stretched to get a kink out of his back.

About to go in, he noticed the mule. It was familiar. No two were alike and he had seen this one before but in his befuddled state he couldn't remember where. It hit him at the same instant a shrill scream came from inside.

Jed was up the steps and to the door in a rush. He flung himself against it and hurt his shoulder. The door was bolted or barred. He went to kick it but had a better idea. Holding the Sharps in front of his face, he hurled himself at the window. The crash of glass brought pain and then he was rolling on the floor. He came to his knees and beheld Cassie on her back with a man straddling her. He jerked the Sharps up and thumbed back the hammer.

"No!" the man bleated, throwing out his hands.

Jed shot him in the face.

Blood spattered Cassie and drops got in her eyes. Blinking, she saw a gory hole where Barnaby's nose had been. His heavy weight fell against her and she pushed the body and slid out from under. She had heard the breaking of glass and turned to see who her rescuer was. "Grandpa!"

Jed was unable to speak for the lump in his throat.

"Oh, Grandpa." Flooded with joy, Cassie threw her arms around him and put her cheek to his chest. "It was awful. That man wanted to . . ." She couldn't bring herself to say it but she told about how the man had tricked her into the closet and kept her there all night.

Jed coughed and patted her. "It's all right," he said softly. "I'm here." He struggled to collect his wits. It had all happened so fast. "You're lucky I came along when I did."

Tears filled Cassie's eyes but she refused to cry. Crying would be weak and she had to be strong. "I'm so happy to see you."

The lump returned, and Jed trembled.

"Are you all right, Grandpa?"

"Fine, girl." Jed sounded hoarse. He cleared his throat and said again, "Fine, girl. How about you?"

Cassie drew back and dabbed at her eyes. She had important news to share. She didn't glace at Barnaby; she refused to look at him ever again. "Chace was here sometime last night. The man you shot told me."

"Did he say where Chace was going?"

"No. But I can find him. I feel him, in here." Cassie touched a finger to her chest over her heart. "It's like one of those magnets, pulling me to him."

Jed stood and helped her to her feet. His head was strumming like an out-of-tune banjo. The danger to Cassie, the whiskey, the lack of sleep, were taking a toll. He needed to think clearly. "Excuse me a moment." He went to the bar and around to the shelves. His mouth watered; there were so many kinds and brands: whiskey, brandy, bourbon, Scotch, rye, rum, and more. His favorite brand was Cutter, and by God, there were three bottles. He took all three outside and put them in his saddlebags.

Cassie followed. She didn't want him out of her sight. She saw what he was doing, but she asked, "What are you doing?"

"I don't want to run dry. It could be days before we catch up to Chace," Jed said. Or it could be weeks.

"Isn't that stealing?"

"The son of a bitch in there—" Jed stopped. "Pardon me, missy. That scum in there won't miss it. You ask me, he owes us." The notion took root. Jed went back in and around the counter again. At one end was a drawer. He opened it and whistled.

"What did you find, Grandpa?"

Jed laid out the bills and coins. The total came to twenty-two dollars and fourteen cents.

"It's a fortune," Cassie marveled. The most money she ever saw at one time was twenty dollars, the day her cousin's calf won over to the county fair.

"It's a start." Jed stuffed the money in his pocket.

"We're stealing that, too?"

"For what he did to you we should take the whole tavern."

"Do we bury him?"

Jed glanced out the shattered window. Someone could show up any minute. They'd ask a lot of questions and maybe send for the law. "We have to hurry," he said. "Go from room to room and look for more money." He started around the counter and had another troubling thought. "Is anyone else staying here?"

"Not that I know of. If there were, you'd think they'd have heard me yelling and pounding last night and come to see what the ruckus was about."

"Good. Then hurry."

Cassie reluctantly went down the hall to the first door. A guest room, she reckoned, with a bed and table and chair and washbasin and chamber pot. She went to the next room and it was exactly the same. The one after, though, must be Barnaby's; it had a rug and a chest of drawers and the bed was twice the size of the others. At the foot of a bed was a trunk. Cassie tried to open it but it was locked. She rummaged through the chest of drawers and found nothing except clothes. In the closet were two coats and a pair of scuffed boots. She went back to the chest.

"Anything?" Jed asked from the doorway. He had checked the other rooms without success.

"Just this," Cassie said, and gave the trunk a kick. "It's locked."

"I have an idea." Jed went to the body and rolled it over. The second pocket yielded keys. He rose to go back and looked out the front door. Beyond was the road, aglow in the new dawn. Bending, he slid his hands under Barnaby's arms and dragged him behind the counter, leaving a smear of scarlet.

Cassie had waited by the trunk. "I bet it's clothes. He doesn't have hardly any in there." She nodded at the closet.

"Could be," Jed allowed. There were four keys on the ring. The third brought a click and the lock opened. He removed it from the hasp and set it on the floor.

"Hurry," Cassie urged. "Someone is bound to stop sooner or later and I want to be gone."

So did Jed. He raised the lid.

"God in heaven!" Cassie breathed.

Inside the chest were the remains of a young girl. Wisps of red hair poked from under a yellow bonnet and hung over empty eye sockets and withered skin. A matching yellow dress clung to her stick figure. Brown shoes were on her feet, or, rather, on the bones of her feet. Her teeth were bared in an eternal lipless smile.

Jed's skin crawled as if with ants. "Why on earth would a man keep a thing like this?"

"Was it his daughter, you think?" Cassie asked. She couldn't bear to look at it but she couldn't tear her eyes away, either.

"There's no telling." Jed shut the lid and replaced the lock and snapped it shut.

"Maybe it was just some traveler like me," Cassie said in horror at the prospect. "Maybe I'd have wound up in there."

"Let's not think about that." Jed stood. He had lost interest in searching for more money. "Go down and wait with the mules. I have something to do."

"What?"

"Shoo," Jed said, and gently pushed her out.

Cassie was reluctant to leave him, and said so.

"You need to keep watch and give a holler if anyone comes. Or would you rather your grandpa wound up behind bars?"

"For shooting that awful man? You had to. You were protecting me."

"You know that and I know that but the law might not see it that way. They don't like it when folks blow other folks' faces off." Jed hustled her along the hall and across to the front door. "Please, girl. Do it for me."

Cassie stood by the hitch rail, a bundle of nerves. She couldn't stop thinking of Barnaby, of his hands on her, of her terror. Sounds from inside suggested her grandfather was moving about, but doing what, she couldn't imagine. She closed her eyes and tiredly rubbed them and when she opened them she saw a rider, a man in homespun on a big-boned horse that looked better fit for a plow than a saddle. The man wore a straw hat and had a bushy beard. She started to turn to run inside and warn her grandpa but it might seem suspicious, her darting off. She patted Bessie, her dread rising the closer the man came. She took it for granted he would stop. When he went by and smiled and touched his hat brim, she was relieved. She smiled in return.

It was five full minutes before Jed hustled outside.

"A man came by," Cassie said. "I was scared to death."

Jed glanced both ways. "Where did he get to? He didn't stop?"

"No."

"Climb on your mule. We want to be gone before the smoke rises."

"What smoke?" Cassie asked, and had her question answered by a spurt of flame. "Grandpa, what have you done?"

"I piled blankets on him so he'll be burned to a cinder," Jed said. "With any luck they won't ever guess he was shot." He stepped into the stirrups and reined Tiberius to the road.

Cassie was quick to follow on Bessie. "Wait until Ma hears about this. She'll tar and feather us."

Jed had forgotten about Erna and Scarlet. "Ride like the wind, girl," he said. He would tell her later.

"We're acting like criminals," Cassie complained. "What if the law gets after us, too?"

God, Jed hoped not. That was the last thing they needed.

21

Galveston, Texas, was on an island in Galveston Bay. The only way to reach it was by ferry or boat or over a railroad bridge but that didn't hamper its growth. Its location accounted for the boom; Galveston was one of the biggest cotton ports in the South. Ships constantly came and went. The population was pushing thirty thousand and people were everywhere, going every which way.

Chace stood on the ferry landing with Enoch's reins in his hand and said, "It's downright beautiful."

Buildings of every size and description pressed against one another in a riot of construction. Some reared several stories or more into the air. The Beach Hotel, near where Chace stood, had enough rooms to accommodate every last person in Wareagle, and then some.

Chace wandered the busy streets, taking in the feast of sights, sounds, and smells: ladies in elegant dresses, men in expensive suits, fancy carriages drawn by fine horses, barbershops, and shoeshine boys. A whirl of activity that never ended, day or night. There were an opera house and a cathedral and businesses galore. There were saloons and gambling dens.

"I've died and gone to heaven," Chace told Enoch. He passed a restaurant and the aroma of coffee and food made his mouth water. He passed a saloon, and his nose tingled to the odor of liquor and tobacco smoke.

A small girl popped into his path, a ragamuffin in scruffy pants and a boy's shirt two sizes too big. "Have an apple, mister?" She held a wooden box filled with ripe reds and yellows. "Only two cents."

"If I had it, I would," Chace said.

"You new to town?" She had sandy hair cropped boyishly short and a pixie face smudged with dirt.

"Just off the ferry."

"You remind me of my brother. He had corn hair, too. He got hit by a wagon and his head was crushed. I cried so much, my eyes hurt." She showed rows of nice white teeth. "I'm Tallulah."

"Chace."

"You're awful easy on the eyes."

"You're awful young to notice." Chace led Enoch around her and acquired a second shadow. "You want something?"

"Will you be looking for work?"

Chace regarded the stream of human traffic in both directions and the buildings that lined the street. "I reckon I will. I have to eat. Why did you ask?"

"Might be I can help. Tunk is always looking for new hawkers. You're young enough yet—he might let you work for him."

"Who is this Tunk?"

"He runs the streets. The hawkers, that is. You can't hawk if you don't hawk for Tunk. But he lets you keep ten cents on every dollar you make."

"That much, huh?"

Tallulah didn't look happy about it. "Anyone complains, he has them beat up."

"What do your folks think, you working for a man like that?"

"He ain't no man. He's not much older than you. And I don't have any folks. My pa left when I was a baby and my ma took sick and died last year. There's just me now. I lived on the street a whole month before Tunk took me in. A bad month, that was. I about starved."

"How old are you?"

"Twelve. How old are you?"

"Wouldn't you like to keep more of your money?"

Tallulah looked at him. "Why wish for what you can't have? Tunk makes the rules, not me."

Chace spied a water trough. As Enoch dipped his muzzle, Chace wet his hand and cooled his brow and his neck. Tallulah watched him, quiet and intent.

"How many hawkers does this Tunk have working for him?"

"Altogether?" Tallulah puckered her mouth. "Gosh. I never counted. But we work the whole city. I'd say forty or better."

"And all of them pay him the same as you?"

"They do or they have their bones broke." Tallulah's green eyes showed puzzlement. "Why are you asking so many questions? Do you want me to take you to him so you can ask to hawk?"

"My ma would call you an omen," Chace said.

"You don't make sense. Is that yes or no?"

"When can we go see him?"

"Not now," Tallulah said. "Tunk moves around a lot,

checking on us hawkers. He's never in one place for long except at night when we all meet in the Roost, an old pirate building. You can talk to him then."

"Pirate building?"

"You sure don't know much about Galveston, do you? It got its start by a pirate. Lafitte, I think he was called. The army or somebody drove him off a long time ago but some of his old buildings are left. The Roost is one of them. No one ever goes there but us." Tallulah glanced down the street. "I better get to hawking. If Tunk finds me talking to you, he'll get mad. Meet me out back of the Texas Star Flour Mill about sunset."

"Where is it?" Chace asked as she hurried away.

"Ask anyone. They can tell you." Tallulah smiled and waved and then raised her voice to shout, "Apples! Fresh apples here!"

Chace patted Enoch and ambled on. He spent fifteen minutes crisscrossing streets. A carriage came at him and he moved aside. He was standing close to a board-walk when perfume wreathed him and he turned to find a large woman in a red dress and a gay hat with an os-trich feather. She was studying him and twirling a pink parasol.

"How do you do, ma'am?"

"My, aren't you polite?" She had a deep, musical voice that did not fit her bulk.

"My ma's doing."

The woman had great puffy cheeks and full puffy lips and was wide enough to be mistaken for a buckboard. Her lively green eyes danced with amusement as she scru-tinized Chace.

"I'm Madame Bovary. Could be you've heard of me."

"Could be I haven't."

Madame Bovary laughed. "That will teach me to be more humble. I run the best house in Galveston. Folks come from hundreds of miles inland to pay my place a visit. A night with my girls is a night in paradise, they say."

"Is that a fact?"

"I can tell you're not impressed. At your age I wouldn't have been, either." Madame Bovary came over and patted Enoch. "Nice mule you've got here."

"You know mules?"

"Mules and men," Madame Bovary said, and chuckled. "Mules I learned on the farm. Men I learned when we got thrown off the farm by the bank and I had to help make ends meet." Some of the amusement faded from her eyes. "That was years ago. Now I'm successful and rich and can do as I please and it pleases me to invite you to tea."

"Ma'am?"

"Are you hard of hearing? I'd like to sit you down and have a talk. Maybe offer you a job at my establishment." She reached over and caressed his hair. "You're about the most beautiful boy I ever did see."

"What kind of job?"

"I'll explain when we talk. How about four? It's two now. That gives me a couple of hours to complete my errands and do a little shopping. Just knock on the front door and Sam will admit you." Madame Bovary twirled her parasol and moved off.

"Wait," Chace said. "How do I find your place?"

"Austin Street. Can't miss it. Look for the biggest house."

"What do you make of that?" Chace said to Enoch. He

roamed on, leading rather than riding, and came across a stable. Inside, it was cool and still and smelled of hay and horses. An old man was stabbing hay with a pitchfork and feeding it to a stallion in a stall. Chace went down the aisle and said, "I'd like to put up my mule."

The old man had skin like leather and gray-and-white grizzle on his bony chin. He went on pitching. "Pick a stall or there's the corral out back."

"I don't have any money."

The old man leaned on the pitchfork and regarded Chace. "This is a paying proposition."

"I figured it would be."

"I let folks board their animals for free, I starve."

"I'll pay you soon as I can. I've just struck town," Chace said. "I'm not afraid of hard work and I might have prospects. A lady named Bovary has offered me one, but I ain't sure yet as I'll take it."

"Bovary, you say? *Madame* Bovary?"

"That's what she called herself."

The old man displayed tobacco-stained teeth. "They say she likes them young. And you want me to board your mule on her offer?"

"I said I would pay you."

The old man turned to Enoch. "Your animal is in luck. Do you want to know why?" He went on before Chace could ask. "Because you've been honest. I can't tell you how many try to skip out without paying me. I'll put up your animal and you can pay me when you can pay me."

"I'm obliged."

"One thing," the old man said, and nodded at the Spencer. "You might want to leave that with me, as well."

"What for?"

"You seen many folks parading around with rifles in their hands? No, you have not. Galveston has ordinances about firearms and the law here is prickly about having those ordinances broken. You want to go on toting it, be my guest. But don't say you weren't warned if they throw you in jail."

"Come to think of it," Chace said, "I didn't see any guns at all. Not even pistols."

"Told you. Galveston likes to think it is civilized. People have to hide their weapons."

"That's not right."

"A gun makes those in power uneasy. They don't like to be reminded that those they lord it over can rise against them."

"I never thought of it like that."

"Take the last stall on the left," the old man said. "I'll see that your mule is watered and fed." He turned back to the pile of hay. "I'm Clarence, by the way."

"His name is Enoch."

"What?"

"Enoch," Chace said. "My mule."

The old man said a strange thing. He stared at Chace and declared, "This city will eat you alive, boy."

After the shade of the stable, the sun was harsh and glaring. Chace took the warning to heart and pulled his buckskin shirt out so it was over his belt and hid his Arkansas toothpick. He continued exploring. Galveston was a bounty of marvels: the first streetlamps he had ever seen, the first fire wagon, the first streetcar, the first building with a giant clock. When he saw the time, he turned to a man walking past. "Pardon me. Can you tell me where to find Austin Street?"

The man wore a suit and bowler and smelled of lilac water. He sniffed and said, "Bumpkin," and walked on.

The second man reeked of sweat and had runny eyes and merely shook his head.

The third man had a dignified air and walked with a thumb hooked in his vest over a gold watch chain. He regarded Chace as Chace might regard a new kind of critter. "Austin Street, you say?"

"A lady named Madame Bovary has invited me to tea."

The man's eyes crinkled. "I can see why. Sure, son. I'll give you directions." He winked. "But you have to promise to never let my wife know I know where it is or she'll peel my hide."

Madame Bovary's "house" turned out to be a mansion set back from the road along a gravel drive lined with roses. Chace went up the marble steps and rapped with a brass knocker.

A black man in a brown uniform opened the door. He had gray at the temples and was clean shaven.

"You must be Sam," Chace said.

"And you must be the young gentleman madame told me to expect." Sam stepped aside and motioned.

"I am in the lap of luxury," Chace declared.

Plush carpet covered the floor. The walls were paneled and adorned with paintings of men and women in stages of undress or entirely bare and often entangled. In a recess stood a statue of a man and a woman, both naked, their hands where in public they would get arrested.

Chace stopped and stared. "I didn't know they had such a thing."

"It is madame's stock-in-trade, you might say," Sam said.

"You must love your work."

Sam smiled. "I care for madame. She's as fine a lady as ever lived. She bought me and freed me long before Mr. Lincoln came along."

A spacious room had been painted bright pink. Along the walls were velvet couches on which several women reclined or were sitting and talking. All were young and wore exquisite clothes.

Sam said, "It's early yet or there would be more of madame's girls." He moved on.

Chace noticed one of the women look at him and laugh. She had a heart-shaped face and red curls and lips as full as ripe cherries. He smiled and she gave him a scornful look. "Who's that one?"

"That would be Sasha," Sam said. "She tends to look down her nose at those who don't meet her standards."

A sitting room had three walls all of glass. Flowers were everywhere. In the center was a gilded table with four chairs and in one of the chairs was Madame Bovary. She had changed into a blue dress and wore a necklace studded with sparkling diamonds. "You came," she said happily, and bid him have a seat. "That will be all, Sam."

"Yes, madame."

The chair had cushions so that sitting on it was like sitting on a bed. Chace bounced a few times, and grinned.

Madame Bovary hung on his every movement. "Man and boy rolled into one. It will be a shame when you change."

"Ma'am?"

"Boys don't stay boys forever. They become men and lose a part of them they can never replace."

"I'll never lose me," Chace said.

A silver teakettle rested on a stand. Beside it were two china cups and saucers with floral designs and a golden bell. Madame Bovary filled both cups and sipped hers and sighed with contentment. "I do so love rosemary tea. It's good for the digestion, you know."

"My ma likes tea but I'm partial to milk myself."

"If you had tits you might think different."

"Ma'am?"

"I refuse to drink anything that comes from inside something else." Madame Bovary patted his hand. "But I didn't ask you here to talk teats. I asked you here because I like you and it would delight me greatly if you would like me. What do you say, handsome boy? Care to put yourself in my hands?"

Chace took a swallow of tea, and grimaced. "I'm listening."

"How would you like to be my greeter? I'll pay you two hundred dollars. Plus you can eat in the kitchen if you like."

"Two hundred?" Chace said. "My pa never made that much in a year in his whole life."

Madame Bovary chortled. "No, delightful one. Two hundred dollars a *month*. If you stay a year you will earn two thousand four hundred dollars."

Chace stared.

"Is something the matter?"

"Two thousand four hundred dollars?"

"My compliments. Your ears work." Bovary picked up her teacup and delicately sipped. "I'll give you the first month in advance so you can get rid of those smelly animal hides you're wearing and buy acceptable clothes. Have your hair trimmed while you're at it. You have beautiful hair but it will look even more beautiful if it is less shaggy."

"Two thousand four hundred dollars."

"Honestly," Bovary said, and put down her cup. "Be dazzled if you must, but it's less than I pay Sam. Of course, he does a lot more for me than be my greeter."

"What is that, exactly? A greeter?" Chace asked. "What would my job be?"

"You will work from six in the evening until six in the morning six days a week. You will wear a suit and polished shoes. When my customers come, you will admit them and show them to the parlor where my girls wait."

"That's all?"

"That's what greeters do. They greet people. What else did you expect?" Madame Bovary indulged in more tea. "Believe me when I say there are some who would kill to have a job like yours. Not only will you make a comfortable income, but you'll meet some of the most important people in Galveston. Hell, in all of Texas. So who knows? It could open doors for you."

Chace drained his cup in a swallow. "Damn, I hate tea."

Madame Bovary laughed. "Do we have an agreement? Or do you need time to think about it?"

"I ain't stupid," Chace said.

Her eyes twinkling, Bovary said, "I'll take that as a yes. And now, if you don't mind, I'd very much like to know what my weakness has led me to hire. Who are you, Chace Shannon? Tell me a little about yourself."

"What you see is who I am."

"That's no answer." Bovary reached across the table

and gently placed her hand on his. "Please. I would very much like to be more than your employer. I would very much like to be friends."

"That's all?"

"Oh, dear boy," Madame Bovary said. "You must learn tact. But trust me when I say I would never do anything to hurt you. Now, about yourself, if you please."

Chace stood. He walked to the glass wall at the back. Beyond was a magnificent rose garden. "You're powerful fond of roses."

"That I am. They're beautiful and fragrant and a joy to touch. Just like my girls. Now stop stalling and tell me."

Chace turned and looked at her. "This is hard for me. I don't like to talk about myself."

"A lot of people don't. I'm not asking for your life's story. I just want to know who you are."

"What was that about a weakness?" Chace asked.

"You're stalling again but I'll tell you anyway." Bovary motioned. "Look around you. All you see are beautiful things. My house, this room, my garden, my girls. Beauty everywhere—wouldn't you agree?"

"It's as close to heaven as I've come across."

Bovary laughed, then grew solemn. "The world outside isn't like my private world. Too often it's an ugly place, filled with ugly people. I saw enough of that when I was your age. I saw too much, in fact. So now that I can, I surround myself with beauty. I don't permit a shred of ugly in my life if I can help it."

"What does that have to do with me?"

"Have you looked in a mirror lately?" Madame Bovary responded. "You're beautiful, Chace. Perhaps the handsomest boy I've ever known. When I first set eyes on you, you made my heart flutter, and my heart hasn't fluttered like that in a *long* time." She straightened. "Now, for the last time, enough about me. What about you? Your sweet looks aside, for all I know I've hired a killer." She laughed merrily.

"You have," Chace said.

Madame Bovary laughed some more but then she stopped and her gaze grew troubled. "You're serious?"

"It's only fair you know."

"I sure can pick them." Madame Bovary sighed and raised her cup and set it down again. "How bad is it? Did you kill a rival for a girl's affections? Did you rob someone and have to defend yourself? What?"

"I did it because they killed my pa and my uncles and raped my sister."

"My God. Where in heaven's name are you from?"

"It's best if no one knows."

"How many lives did you take? Will you tell me that much at least?"

"More than you have fingers and thumbs. I shot a deputy, too, but I think he might have lived."

Bovary picked up the bell and rang it. Almost immediately Sam entered and bowed. "Whiskey, Sam, a bottle of my personal stock."

"As you wish, madame." He departed.

"I didn't expect anything like this," Madame Bovary said.

Chace came to the table. "I understand. I don't want to cause a gracious lady like you trouble. I'll go, and no hard feelings."

"No, no." Madame Bovary clasped his hand. "What do you take me for, thinking that I would throw you out?" She shook her head. "Sit down, please."

Chace sat and pushed the teacup away.

"I don't care what you've done," Madame Bovary said. "The past is the past. I've done unsavory things in my own life. I imagine you killed all those people because you felt you had to. You didn't really want to or like doing it."

"I liked it a lot," Chace said.

"You can't like *killing*."

"You like roses."

"But, Chace—" she began, and stopped. Shaking her head, she said, "You're confusing the hell out of me. How can you like taking another's life? It's just not right."

"Says who? Normal people? Normal is for sheep. Normal is for those who are afraid to stand up for themselves. My family has been feuding with another family for hundreds of years. We kill them like we swat flies. Or used to, until my grandpa went and made a truce. Which was the worst thing he could have done."

"Why?"

"You can't turn an enemy into a friend by shaking his hand. The only way to stop an enemy from being an enemy is to plant him."

Bovary looked up as Sam entered. He brought over a bottle and a glass and opened the bottle and set it on the table.

"Will there be anything else, madame?"

"No, Sam. I'm not to be disturbed. Tell Sasha to look after the girls until I'm through here."

"Yes, madame."

"Sasha is only a few years older than you," Bovary informed Chace. "I picked her off the street like I did you." She poured the glass half full and chugged it down. "God, I needed that." She coughed. "Now, then. My offer still holds. But I need to know. Is the law hard on your trail? Will they show up on my doorstep someday? I'd like to hear all you're willing to share."

"So long as this is the only time," Chace said, and told her about his sister and the aftermath. "I think I got plumb away but I can't give you my word that I did."

"Galveston is a long way from Arkansas and you say no one knows you're here." Madame Bovary nodded. "The law could scour the state of Texas for ten years and not find you." She smiled. "I'll take the chance. The job is still yours if you want it."

"Why are you being so kind to me?"

"I thought I explained. I like you."

"Why really?" Chace pressed her. "And don't tell me it's because I'm handsome or pretty. I've had my fill of those lately."

Madame Bovary refilled her glass. She turned the glass around and around with her fingertips, then said, "You're handsome and you're polite. Isn't that enough?"

"No."

"I mentioned Sasha. You and she aren't the first. I make it a point to help people your age. No one gave me a hand when I could barely keep my stomach full, and I remember what that was like."

"A heart of gold."

"Think what you will. Can I count on you? Sam is getting long in the tooth but won't admit it. You'd be doing me a favor."

"You're a nice lady," Chace said. "You have yourself a greeter."

Madame Bovary clapped in delight. "Excellent. Come with me, then. I must attend to your transformation."

"My what?"

"Your change." Rising, she clasped his hand in both of hers and ushered him out of the room and along the hall to the pink room with the velvet couches. The moment she entered, the other women all stood. "You can relax, my sweets," she said. "It isn't a client. I have an errand for Sasha."

"For me?" said the redhead with cherry lips. She wore a dress that clung to her in such a way that it appeared she wasn't wearing a dress at all. She fixed her emerald eyes on Chace. "Does it involve the country boy here?"

"Sasha," Madame Bovary said sternly. "I've taught you better. I want you to take him shopping. New clothes. A visit to the barber. He starts work tonight at six and —"

"Tomorrow," Chace said.

"I beg your pardon?"

"I have somewhere to be tonight. I promised someone I'd meet them at sundown."

Sasha poked a red fingernail at him. "When Madame Bovary wants you to do something, you do it."

"Now, now," Bovary chided her. "Tomorrow night is perfectly fine. But it's still hours until sunset. Plenty of time for you to help him pick new clothes."

"*Must* I?"

Chace said, "When Madame Bovary wants you to do something, you do it."

Bovary laughed. Sasha didn't; her face became the same color as her hair and her nose flared.

"He has you there, my dear," Madame Bovary said, "and yes, you must. Rickman the tailor is a regular of yours, isn't he? Ask him as a personal favor to me. Tell him to have Chace's suit ready by tomorrow at five.

That will give Chace time to pick it up before he goes on duty."

"Very well," Sasha said coldly. She turned her back on Chace and made for the hall. "Follow me, country boy. If I must, I must, but I don't have to like it."

Madame Bovary winked. "Don't take it personal. She's a sweetheart once you get to know her."

Chace caught up and passed Sasha. He opened the front door and she marched past as if he didn't exist. Again he overtook her and said, "Are you always this friendly?"

Sasha wheeled on him and jabbed him in the chest. "Listen, if I don't get back by six, its costs me money. My clients won't wait around. They'll go with another girl and I lose out."

"Clients?" Chace said. "Is that what they call men who want to get up your petticoats?"

"It's a living," Sasha said, and descended the marble steps to the gravel drive. She raised an arm, and around a corner of the mansion clattered a carriage driven by a man in a uniform.

"Wait," Chace said.

Sasha did no such thing. She moved to meet the carriage. The driver brought it to a stop and jumped down to open the door and lower the step. She climbed in and sat in the rear seat.

Chace pulled himself in and was about to sit in the same seat, but she shook her head and nodded at the front seat.

"Over there. I don't care to sit next to you, thank you very much."

Chace perched with his elbows on his knees. He

nearly slid off when the carriage lurched into motion, and she chuckled at his expense.

"Quite the man of the world, aren't you?"

"I've never ridden in one of these before."

"Never ever? What do you ride around in at home?"

"We have a buckboard but mostly I ride mules."

"How fitting," Sasha said.

"What have I done that you hate me so much?"

The carriage came to the end of the drive and wheeled into the street. The drum of the hooves and the clatter of the wheels were muffled by the curtains over the windows.

"Hate you?" Sasha said. "Don't flatter yourself that I think that highly of you. To me you're a nuisance, another of Gretchen's strays that she thinks she has to save."

"Who?"

"Madame Bovary, you lunkhead. That's her first name." Sasha folded her arms. "Look, just don't talk and we'll get along better. I'll do as she wants and you can be on your way."

"I'd like to say one thing," Chace said.

"If you insist. But it better be important."

"I like it how your eyes light with fire when you're mad."

22

Waves lapped the shore and a full moon hung over the bay that pirate ships once sailed. The Roost, they called it. Long neglected, the roof had sagged and collapsed in parts. The walls were peeled and cracked. The main door was on the ground, its hinges rusted through.

From the top of a nearby sand dune Chace watched furtive figures slip inside. "Friends of yours?"

"I told you," Tallulah said. "All the hawkers meet here regular. Tunk's orders."

"And you all have to do as Tunk says," Chace said.

"I don't know why you say it like that. We ask him nice, he may let you hawk. Isn't that what you want, to make money?"

"I've been thinking it would be smart to make a very lot of money," Chace said.

"Come on."

Tallulah slogged down the dune. They reached the building at the same time as a group of hawkers. Some were about as old as Chace; some were a lot younger. A boy of five or six carried a shoeshine case he could barely lift. A girl had a can with pencils.

Dust covered the floor and the walls. Tracks in the dust led into the bowels, down dilapidated stairs to a huge room that once might have been a warehouse for pirate booty. Dozens of hawkers were washed pale in the light of lanterns, all of them scruffy and dirty and with the nervous aspect of wild animals. They faced a raised platform littered with broken crates and other debris.

Chace stood quiet, his hands clasped behind his back. His buckskins received more than a few stares.

Tallulah was excited. "This is the best part of my day," she said so only he heard. "I like getting together with the rest."

"You have friends here?"

"We're mostly friendly," she said, and bobbed her head at the murmuring assembly. "They're the closest I have to a family."

Four boys climbed to the platform. They were the oldest and the biggest, and the best dressed. Their clothes weren't dirty. Their hair was combed. The very biggest had a swagger about him and looked out over the hawkers like a wolf sizing up sheep. Two of the four had large leather pouches slantwise across their chests.

The biggest stepped to the near side of the platform and held up his arms for silence. He had a shock of brown hair and a pointy chin and deep-set brown eyes that gleamed in the lantern light.

"That's Tunk," Tallulah whispered.

"Is everyone here?" Tunk called out, and someone in the group hollered that they were. "Good. I've got something important to say." He paused. "I'm not happy. I'm not happy at all."

"Uh-oh," Tallulah whispered.

Tunk pointed at a girl of ten in a torn dress. "Come

up here, Violet," he commanded. She obeyed, her head bowed, her fingers tight in her dress. She didn't speak. Tunk walked around her and then pointed at her and shouted, "Take a good look. I gave her the south wharf. There's good money to be made there. The last hawker brought me ten dollars a day, easy." He bent over Violet, who only came as high as his waist. "How much you got for me tonight?"

Violet answered so quietly no one could hear.

"Six dollars?" Tunk said loudly. "Six measly dollars. That's about all you ever bring. Makes me wonder." He straightened and faced his minions. "Makes me wonder why she does so poorly when others have done so much better. Makes me see I made a mistake." He spun and slapped her so hard she tottered. "The wharf is no longer yours. I'll give it to someone who works harder."

"I do the best I can," Violet whimpered.

"Ah." Tunk faced them all, his smile venomous. "How many times do I have to keep saying this? I make it as clear as I can." He raised his voice. "None of you has a home. None of you has anyone. I take you under my wing. I give you work. I give you a roof over your head at night. Ain't that right? And what do I ask in return? That you hawk hard and give me my share. That's all."

Some of the hawkers hung their heads. Others looked crestfallen.

"I'm the one gets you the apples and oranges," Tunk went on. "I'm the one gets you what you need to hawk. Do you think it grows on trees? I have to buy all that. I have to spend money for you to make money." He shouted in anger. "If you don't want to hawk, you don't have to. But if you do, you, by God, will give me my due!" He smacked his left palm with his right fist. "You hear me? I do all I can for you. I expect you to do all you can for me."

Many of the hawkers nervously shifted and fidgeted.

Tunk stopped railing. He lowered his arms and smiled as a kindly father might. "I shouldn't get so mad. But after all I do for you, you can't blame me. Are you with me or not?"

A few of the street kids replied that they were.

"I can't hear you," Tunk said. "I asked if you were with me or not? Yes or no?"

A chorus of "Yes" was raised to the rafters. Tunk wasn't satisfied and had them shout it again and yet again. Then he raised his arms and yelled, "I have a treat tonight. I got some bread from a bakery. Lots of loaves, so there will be some for everybody. As soon as the collection is over, we'll pass the bread out."

The two boys with leather pouches came down and stood in front of the platform. That was the signal for the hawkers to form into two lines. Each handed over the money he or she had hawked that day, and the boys put the money in the pouches. Tallulah's turn came. The boy with the pouch glanced at Chace.

"Who's this? He's not one of us."

"He'd like to be," Tallulah said. "I was hoping we could talk to Tunk. Can you ask him for me, Zeke?"

"Once we're done collecting," the boy said.

Tallulah went to the side of the platform. "You heard him," she said, smiling. "Tomorrow you'll be hawking, I bet."

"Tunk and his friends ever do any hawking?"

"They don't have the time. They have to find stuff for us to sell. Some days they work ten hours at it."

"Who told you that?"

"Tunk."

"He ever say how much money he makes from all this?"

"No, and I wouldn't ask. It's none of my buiness."

"Tunk tell you that, too?"

Tallulah cocked her head. "You just don't stop with the questions. Don't you want work?"

"I want it straight in my head," Chace said.

"Well, don't go pestering Tunk about anything. He doesn't like to be pestered."

"You gave them all the money you made today, didn't you?"

"No one holds out on Tunk. He gets madder about that than about anything. Hold out, and he has you beat."

"When do you get your share?"

"Saturday. Tunk brings sweets and pies for us to buy, too. It's the best night of the week."

"The Lord giveth and the Lord taketh away," Chace said.

"Was that the Bible?"

"Something my ma likes to say a lot."

"You're lucky to have a ma," Tallulah said. "You had any sense, you'd be home with her instead of here."

Chace reached behind him and ran his hand over the back of his shirt along his waist. "I have a cramp."

Tunk was sitting with his legs over the platform and was talking to one of the boys who had arrived with him. When the collection pouches were brought, he hefted each, and grinned. Zeke bent toward him and said something in his ear and pointed at Tallulah and Chace. Tunk glanced around and nodded. Zeke came partway over, then beckoned.

"Here's your chance," Tallulah said. "Be as nice as you can be. He'll let you join us. I know he will."

Tunk hopped down from the platform and faced them. Up close, he stood head and shoulders above Chace and had pockmarks on his face. His smile was cold. He flicked his eyes down and up Chace and then he put his hands on Tallulah's shoulders. "Zeke tells me you sold all your apples today, little one. Good going."

Tallulah beamed proudly. "Thank you."

"Zeke also says you found someone you think will work out," Tunk said, and gave Chace his flick look. "What's your name, boy?"

"His name is Chace and he just got in town—" Tallulah started to answer, only to have Tunk put a hand over her mouth.

"I asked him, little one, not you." Tunk squared on Chace. "Cat got your tongue?"

"How long have you been running this outfit?"

"I ask the questions, not you. You want to be a hawker, you'd best remember that."

"I don't aim to *be* a hawker," Chace said. "I aim to *run* them."

"What?" both Tunk and Tallulah said together. Zeke and the other two boys turned.

"I'm taking over," Chace said.

Tunk frowned at Tallulah. "What's this? What are you up to?"

"It's not me," she said plaintively.

"It's me," Chace said. "Since you are hard of hearing, I'll say it one more time. I'm in charge now. Your three friends can stay on or they can go with you, but if they stay I'll make it worth their while."

"Chace, please," Tallulah said.

A flush was spreading up Tunk's neck. "You son of a bitch. Think you can walk in and push me aside? You hear him, boys?" He laughed in contempt.

"I heard him," Zeke replied. "Worth our while, he said."

Chace nodded. "Whatever he's paying you, I'll give you twice as much. But I'll expect you to earn it."

"Earn it how?" one of the other boys asked.

"You do the same work you have been doing. Things go on as before except you take orders from me and only me."

"Twice as much money?" the third boy said. "That's twenty dollars a month."

"Zeke?" Tunk said. "Floyd? You work for me, not him. Get that through your heads."

"Make room," Chace said, and moved to the right so there was space between Tunk and him.

Some of the hawkers had caught on that trouble was brewing and were pressing forward.

Tunk slid a hand under his shirt. "You think you can take over. I've got news for you." His hand reappeared holding a double-edged dagger. "Either you get the hell out or I gut you like a fish and throw you in the bay. I've done it before. Lots of times."

"Big talk," Chace said, and drew the Arkansas toothpick.

Exclamations broke out, cries of alarm, and questions, and the hawkers jostled to see better.

"Leave while you can," Chace said. He glanced at Zeke and Floyd but they did not seem disposed to take a hand.

Tunk said, "Go to hell!" and came in low and fast. He arced the dagger up and in. Chace sidestepped and slashed. Tunk yelped in pain and sprang away, his knuckles opened. Snarling, Tunk circled and feinted right and went left.

The toothpick met the dagger and metal rang. Chace sprang back and crouched.

Instantly Tunk was on him, stabbing, thrusting. Chace countered, dodged, slipped a cut at his jugular. Tunk didn't relent; he was a tiger of the streets and he had a long claw. The dagger nearly opened Chace's cheek. Chace retreated, swiveled, and caught Tunk across the upper arm. Tunk didn't bat an eye. Dagger and toothpick wove a glittering tapestry. Suddenly Tunk sprang and drove his foot into Chace's leg. Chace almost went down. Scrambling, he parried a try at his face. An elbow caught him on the jaw. Stars pinwheeled and Chace staggered and heard someone scream. Tallulah, it sounded like. Chace fought the weakness, planted his legs, and refused to be budged. Tunk overextended and Chace shoved him. Tunk went stumbling. Chace streaked in, blocked a desperate stab, and drove the toothpick to the hilt between Tunk's ribs.

There were more screams. Several of the boys started forward but stopped.

Tunk was buckling. The whites of his eyes showed and he tottered against the platform. Clinging to the edge, he spat, "Bastard," and pitched onto his face and was still.

In the sudden quiet, the fall of a pin would have sounded like thunder.

Chace turned to Zeke and Floyd. "Am I going to have trouble with either of you?"

"Not for twice as much money you're not," Zeke replied.

"No one much liked Tunk, anyhow," Floyd said.

Chace climbed onto the platform. He gazed out over the anxious faces and gestured at the body. "You have a new leader. Anyone who objects say so now."

No one did.

"The thing to know is this. Nothing changes except one thing. You hawk like you have been doing, but instead of getting ten cents of every dollar you make, from here on out you keep half."

"Half?" a boy echoed.

"Did we hear that right?" From a girl with a scarred face.

"Your ears work fine," Chace said. "Half is fair, so half it will be. You've been taken advantage of long enough."

They looked at one another and it slowly sank in. A small boy in rags let out a yip and others whopped and hollered and a girl about Chace's age came to the front and pumped her arms and shouted, "Let's hear it for our new leader!"

The rafters pealed with the tumult.

Chace Shannon held the dripping toothpick aloft, and grinned.

23

There were three of them on swift horses. They swept out of the Arkansas mountains and south along the road to Texas. All had shocks of black hair and bushy brows and hard faces similar enough to hint that they were brothers. Wherever they stopped they asked the same question. Sometimes they got the answer they wanted.

The three passed through Fort Smith. They passed through settlements and hamlets clear to Dallas. In Dallas they were delayed. It was too big; there were too many people. They asked around and they asked around and no one had seen their quarry. Then they came to a stable on the south end and the stableman had seen a boy answering the description they gave. Better still, the boy had asked the stableman how far it was to Galveston.

The three thanked him and walked out and the middle brother said, "What in hell is he going to Galveston for?"

"Could be he wants to get out of the country," said the oldest brother.

"Could be he's taking a ship."

"Could be," agreed the youngest. "Or maybe he aims to lie low for a spell and go home when he thinks the law and us have stopped looking."

The middle brother swore. "The law might stop but I never will. Not as long as I draw breath."

"Randy and me feel the same, Newton," said the oldest. "He has to pay for what he's done. He has to bleed and suffer."

Randy nodded, hate in his eye. "I like that suffering part, Linsey. He's got to suffer a *lot*."

The next place they came across word was a hamlet called Delvin. It had a population of thirty-two, and one saloon. The brothers claimed a corner table and plunked their rifles down and Linsey said when the bartender came over, "We'd like a bottle of the cheapest bug juice you've got."

To them, raised on shine, it went down silken and exploded like a bomb. They drank half the bottle and Linsey got up and went over to the bar. "Got a question to ask you, mister."

The bartender was pouring rum into a stein. "Ask all you want but I can't promise to answer."

"You sound prickly," Linsey observed.

"I don't spout to hear myself talk." The bartender slid a stein down the bar. "Let's hear it."

"We're looking for a boy. He has hair like spun gold and blue eyes. Wears buckskins. He'd've been riding a mule."

"I don't look at the hitch rail much," the bartender said. "But there was a boy that matches that. I remember him on account of he was so young and I didn't think I should serve him but he convinced me."

"How?"

"He laid a Spencer on the bar and asked if I was bulletproof. Never pointed it at me but I got the idea he wasn't to be trifled with, even as young as he was."

"That sounds like him," Linsey said grimly.

"If you don't mind my asking," the bartender said, "why are you after him?"

"He killed kin of ours up to Arkansas," Linsey said. "He's a Shannon and we're Harkeys."

"What do you aim to do when you catch up to him?"

Linsey snorted. "What else? We're going to kill the son of a bitch."

The brass knocker rapped and Chace smoothed his new waistcoat and opened the door and gave a bow. "How do you do? Welcome to Madame Bovary's. If you will follow me, sir, I'll show you to the parlor."

A portly middle-aged man with rings on his fingers was leaning on a cane. "Who have we here?" he asked. "Where's Sam?"

"I wouldn't hardly know," Chace said. "I'm the new greeter. You want to follow me or not?"

A cloud of perfume enveloped them and Madame Bovary said, "Chace! That's no way to greet Councilman Patterson." She smiled and bowed and took the councilman's arm. "Permit me to escort you."

Chace shut the door and stood with his back to the wall and his hands folded at his waist. Across from him was a mirror for those who, as Madame Bovary had explained, "needed to put themselves together before they go off to hearth and home." He stared at his checkered pants and high boots. His hair had been trimmed shorter than it had ever been and parted clear from the front of his head to the nape of his neck. "I'm plumb gorgeous," he said.

"That you are." Madame Bovary swept upon him and stood with her hands on her wide hips. "My clients all say you're the best-looking boy they ever saw. But your manners need work."

"I'm being polite as I can be."

"It's not your manners; it's your tone," Madame Bovary clarified. "You've got to be polite *and* friendly."

"Hell," Chace said.

Madame Bovary took his hand and gently squeezed. "You're doing fine. Another month and you'll be as good as Sam." She hesitated and looked down the hall and stepped so close they practically brushed bosom and chest. "I've got a minute and I'd like to ask a question."

"Ask away. You hired me."

"It's not about this," she said. "It's about the kids who keep showing up. There was one at four in the morning last night. I heard crying and looked out my window and you were talking to a little girl. What was that about?"

"It's personal," Chace said.

Madame Bovary's lips pinched together. "Not when it's on my time. I'd like to know—"

The rap of the knocker stopped her. Chace smiled and opened the door, and Madame Bovary gave a slight start.

"Sergeant Rutter. This is a surprise. To what do I owe the honor?"

The man she addressed was tall and lanky. He wore an ill-fitting suit that bulged at the right hip. His face had sharp angles of chin and cheek and he sported a bristly mustache. On his vest was a badge. "I didn't come to see you, Gretchen," the lawman said, and focused his icy eyes on Chace. "I came to see your doorman."

Madame Bovary appeared flustered. "May I ask why?"

"You know better." Sergeant Rutter hooked a finger at Chace. "Come with me, boy." Wheeling, he stalked off.

Chace went to follow but Madame Bovary grabbed his arm.

"Do you have any idea who that man is?"

"The law, I take it."

Bovary glanced out the door and lowered her voice. "There are good police and there are bad ones, and he's the worst there is. Why would he pay you a visit? What in God's name are you involved in?" She clutched at her throat. "Wait a minute. Could it be about Arkansas?"

"Only one way to find out." Chace walked down the steps to the drive where Rutter was waiting. "Yes, sir?"

"Polite little killer, aren't you?"

"Sir?"

"Don't play me for a fool. Eight nights ago you were in a knife fight with Tunk Grundy. You killed him and had his body thrown in the bay. I could arrest you here and now and you'd spend the rest of your days in prison. But I won't."

"Awful kind of you."

Sergeant Rutter's eyes narrowed. "If I thought you were poking fun at me, I'd clamp you in these." He opened his jacket so that Chace could see the handcuffs attached to his belt, and a short-barreled revolver in a holster. "You don't want to rile me. Ask anyone."

"If you're not here to arrest me, then what?" Chace asked.

"We have business to discuss, you and me."

"We do?"

Rutter studied Chace as if trying to peer inside him. "He didn't tell you, did he?"

"Sir?"

"Tunk, boy. He didn't tell you about our arrangement before you went and stuck your blade in him."

"We didn't do a lot of talking," Chace said.

Rutter sighed and ran a finger along his mustache. "Figures. All right, I'll explain. Just this once. Pay attention, because if you don't hold up your end and I have to come back, I won't do any talking at all." He gazed about them, apparently to ensure that no one was close by. "In this city you need a permit to sell on the street. The little rats you are running don't have them. I could close the whole operation down. But why go to all that bother when the easy thing to do is look the other way? So long as they behave and don't outright cheat and steal, no real harm is done. Follow me so far?"

"Yes, sir."

"Good. Because for me to continue looking the other way, I get a piece of the pie. Three hundred dollars a month, each and every month. Miss a payment and I shut you down."

"Three hundred?"

"Don't sound so shocked. Your little legion brings in seven, eight hundred a month."

"So you're saying you want close to half."

"I want three hundred," Rutter said. "How much they make is up to them and you. Tunk made damn sure they didn't slack and I'd suggest you do the same." He tapped his badge. "Remember. I have the power of the law behind me. I can do whatever I like."

"You reckon that badge protects you?"

"Damn right it does. You buck me, you buck the whole police force." Rutter smoothed his mustache once more. "Any questions?"

"When do you get the money?"

"Once a month. Tunk was supposed to pay me two days ago. When he didn't show, I started to ask around and found out about you."

"I work most nights until daybreak," Chace said. "How about tomorrow afternoon? Do I come to where you work?"

"Are you crazy?" Rutter bent and jabbed him with a finger. "Listen, boy. This is between you and me. No one else is to ever know. Tell anyone, anyone at all, I'll cut your damn tongue out and make you eat it. Do you understand?"

"So none of the other police knows about this?"

"Didn't you hear a word I just said? No. And it's to stay that way."

"Good," Chace said. "Where do I meet you, then?"

"You don't have to come in person. You can send one of your rats. Put the money in an envelope or wrap it in newspaper like Tunk used to do."

"I'd rather handle this myself."

"Fine. Meet me under the wharf near Harvest Fisheries at one o'clock. Know where that is?"

"I'll find it," Chace said.

Sergeant Rutter nodded. "I like you, boy. You're being reasonable. Keep being reasonable and you and me will get along fine. Stop being reasonable and ..." He opened his jacket and patted the cuffs and the revolver. "Take my meaning?"

"Yes, sir."

Chace watched Rutter stroll down the drive. He turned and went back in and no sooner did he open the door than Madame Bovary flowed down the hall, wringing her hands.

"What did he want?"

"That's between him and me."

"Damn it all," Madame Bovary said. "It can't be good. He has his hand in everything. He even tried to wring money from me but I have important friends in government." She cocked her head. "What possible business can you have with him?"

Chace put a hand on her arm. "I'd tell you if I could. You've been nicer to me than just about anyone ever. But if I told you and he found out, he'd be mad. And as you just said, he's no saint. I wouldn't want him to hurt you."

Madame Bovary gripped his chin and peered tenderly into his eyes. "You dear, sweet boy. If you're in trouble, I can help. I have connections."

"It's nothing I can't take care of," Chace said. "In fact, by tomorrow night I expect that him and me won't have any reason to ever meet again."

"He and I," Madame Bovary said.

"Pardon?"

"You're to work on how you talk, remember? I know you never had any formal schooling but people judge you by how you speak. Try to use proper English."

Chace grinned. "This greeting stuff is harder than I reckoned."

Madame Bovary chuckled and patted his cheek and walked off, saying over her plump shoulder, "I've grown quite fond of you, sweet boy. Please don't let anything happen to you."

"I'll try my best," Chace said. He stayed at the door,

admitting visitors, for another hour and a half. Then Sasha came down the hall, as ravishing as ever in a silk dress, her red lips quirked.

"Time for your break. Although why Gretchen doesn't make you work clean through is beyond me. It's only twelve hours."

"Where's Sam?"

"Running an errand for her, so she sent me." Sasha touched his waistcoat. "I have good taste in clothes, don't I?"

"If you weren't a bitch you would be perfect," Chace said. He went out and along the portico to the corner of the mansion and on around into the rose garden. He stopped under a willow and whispered, "Tallulah."

She came out of hiding. "Here I am."

"Get word to Zeke. I need a derringer. I need it by the time I'm done work at six in the morning."

Tallulah didn't pester him with questions. She nodded and was gone like a shot.

Chace stared down the drive in the direction Sergeant Rutter had gone.

"Three hundred dollars, my ass."

24

Cassie was nervous. She wrung her hands and mustered up the courage and pushed through the batwings. Her mother had always said that good girls never went into a saloon but it couldn't be helped. That early in the day, there were two men playing cards and a man mopping the floor and another man behind the bar. They were considerably surprised.

The man behind the bar had a beard and a huge gut and one eye that was always half shut.

Cassie walked over and smiled. "I'm looking for someone."

"Get your tush out of here."

"Mister?" Cassie said in confusion.

"You heard me. You can't be, what, fourteen? Girls your age ain't allowed in saloons. I could get arrested."

"I'm sorry. I didn't know. I'm not from Dallas."

"Shoo," the man said, and motioned with his fingers.

"I'm looking for my grandpa. He said he was coming here last night and he never showed up this morning."

"Didn't you just hear me?"

"Yes, I did. But I need to find him. The feeling is strong again and we have to go while it is."

The man's half-shut eye jiggled and his mouth ticked. "What in hell are you talking about?"

"We're looking for my brother," Cassie explained. "Sometimes I can feel him and other times I can't as much. We've been resting up while I've tried to feel him again and I think he went south."

"That made no kind of sense."

"Please," Cassie said. "Did you see my grandpa? We're at the hotel across the street and he saw this place out the window and came over to wet his whistle, as he put it. I'm afraid he might have done more than wet it."

"Old geezer in buckskins?" the barman said. "Sucks down the bug juice like nobody I ever saw?"

"That would be him, yes."

"I know right where he is."

The barman came around the bar and led her down a dark hallway to the back door, and out. A small area, more dirt than grass, was fenced in. Over against the fence was a double outhouse. The smell was atrocious. The barman walked to the far side of the outside, and pointed.

"This him?"

Cassie held her breath against the stink and moved so she could see. Her heart dropped. "What am I to do with you?" she softly asked.

"Like I said, your gramps can suck down the juice. Drank the first bottle in no time. Went slower with the other three. That much coffin varnish, it's a wonder he's still alive." The barman's voice turned kindly. "He passed out about two last night. I had to close and I couldn't leave him inside, so I dragged him out here. Took him for another lush." He nudged Jedediah with his boot. "Do this often, does he?"

"Never this bad."

"Want me to lug him to the hotel for you?" The barman smiled. "I'm not supposed to but I will."

"That's all right. I'd best handle it myself." Cassie sighed in disappointment. She had asked and asked for him to stop drinking but he'd kept sneaking sips when he thought she wouldn't notice and at night he had gone off to heed nature's call a few times, or so he claimed, and come back reeking of spirits.

"I could use a pitcher of cold water, though."

The barman grinned. "Be right back."

Cassie squatted and poked and said, "Grandpa?" Jedediah didn't move. She poked harder and he snorted and mumbled but didn't wake up. Exasperated, she leaned against the fence. All these years, she'd never suspected his secret. Her pa and her ma had hidden it from her, to spare her feelings, probably. "I need you sober," she said to the still form.

Presently the barman returned with a glass pitcher filled to the brim. "Want me to do it?"

"I'd rather," Cassie said. "It will serve him right."

"Here." The barman gave her the pitcher. "I'd love to watch but I have customers. Bring it to me when you're done."

"I will," Cassie promised. She waited until he was gone, then rolled Jedediah onto his back. His mouth fell open and he commenced to snore loud enough to be heard in Arkansas. "Dang you," she said, and upended the pitcher over his face. The water cascaded into his mouth and nose and pooled under his head.

Jed came out of a black well sputtering and breath-

ing water. He was bewildered out of his wits. The last he
remembered, he had bought his third or fourth bottle.
"What the hell?" he gurgled. Spitting and shaking his
head, he squinted in the bright glare of the midday sun.
A shadow fell across him. "What are you trying to do,
you son of a bitch? Drown me?"

"Grandpa," Cassie said sadly. "It's me."

Jed wiped at his eyes with his sleeve. "Cassie girl?"
he said, and raised his head. The effort cost him. Pain
exploded between his ears.

"You never came back."

"What time is it?" Jed gritted his teeth and rose onto
his elbows. He sniffed a few times. "Is that me?"

"You left me in the room all alone all night," Cassie
said.

"I'm sorry," Jed said. He was sincere. The last thing
in the world he ever wanted to do was hurt her feelings. "I got to drinking and got so sleepy I couldn't stay
awake."

"You got so drunk, you mean."

"I might have had a little more than I should," Jed
allowed. He slowly sat up. The pounding in his head and
the churning in his gut made him so queasy, he was half
afraid he would spew his insides.

Cassie said bluntly, "You need to stop drinking."

Jed smacked his lips and scratched himself. "I wish to
God I could. Honest I do. But I can't."

"All you have to do is tell yourself you won't and you
won't."

"It's not that simple." Jed shifted so his back was to
the outhouse. He looked down at his buckskins. "Thanks
for washing them for me. I like to at least once a year."

"I'm serious, Grandpa," Cassie said.

"So am I." Jed ran a hand through his wet hair. "When I first took to drinking regular, it was because I lost Mary. She was the world to me, girl. It tore me apart, her dying."

"So you've said many times."

"Hear me out," Jed said. "I'd never been a heavy drinker. Not like some. Always figured I could stop whenever I wanted. But something happened. I'd sit at the table and want a drink so bad, I'd break out in a sweat and shake something terrible. The more I drank, the worse it got. I was up to two to three bottles a day when I got word about Scarlet. Took a lot out of me having to sneak drinks when I could at your place."

"You worry me, Grandpa."

"I'm sorry. I don't mean to. I came to the saloon last night thinking I'd have a glass or two but once I started I couldn't stop." Jed grinned sheepishly and patted her head. "Will you forgive me?"

"Can you give me your word it won't ever happen again?"

"No."

"Oh, Grandpa." Cassie turned away. This, on top of everything else, was almost more than she could bear. "I thought you cared for me."

Jed heaved to his feet. A sudden attack of dizziness made his legs go weak. He braced himself against the outhouse or he would have fallen. When he was able to, he put his hands on her shoulders and turned her so she faced him.

"Cassie girl, I care for you more than you can imagine. You and your brother both. I'd do anything for you. But giving up drink just ain't in me. I need it as much as I need to breathe."

"What am I to do when I have to count on you?"

"Except for now, when have I let you down?" Jed countered. He held up his hand when she opened her mouth to reply. "I know. What's to keep me from doing it again? Nothing, I'm afraid. Sometimes the craving is so powerful I'm not myself. But I give you my word I'll do my best not to give in."

"I want more than that, Grandpa. When you feel the craving coming on, I want you to tell me and we'll keep you sober together."

"They say that miracles happen," Jed said.

Seagulls screeched and wheeled in the blue vault of clear sky. On the shore other gulls sought edibles washed in on the tide; crabs were a favorite. The pilings under the wharf were encrusted with the residue of countless tides and the water smelled strong of fish. Out on the bay a pelican was taking off.

Chace leaned against a piling with his hands in his pockets and whistled to himself.

The crunch of boots heralded Sergeant Rutter. He stopped a good ten feet away. "You're punctual. That's good. Tunk kept me waiting half the time."

"I wanted to get it over with," Chace said.

"Did you bring the money?"

Chace took a hand out of his waistcoat pocket and patted it. "Three hundred dollars, just like you wanted."

"Bring it here."

Chace nodded and walked over. He slid his hand into the pocket and brought it out again holding a pearl-handled derringer. He thumbed back the hammer.

"What the hell is this?" Rutter snapped.

"Three hundred dollars is too much."

"Don't give me that," Rutter said. "You make three times that in a month. You can spare it."

"I'm letting them keep more of their money," Chace informed him.

"Why in hell would you do that? They don't deserve it, the little grubs. And even so, you hand over the three hundred or I'll have every hawker rounded up and turned over to an orphanage. Just see if I don't."

"What I want to see is you taking your six-gun out and setting it down."

"Like hell I will."

Chace pointed the derringer at Rutter's forehead. "This is your one and only chance."

"You don't scare me," Rutter said. "No one shoots a policeman. Not if they know what's good for them."

"After you set down your six-shooter, you're to walk into the water until it is up to your neck."

Sergeant Rutter laughed. "This is what I get for being nice. I've changed my mind. I'm hauling you in for murdering Tunk. I have a witness who will testify against you. The judge is a friend of mine and it won't be hard to persuade him to throw away the key."

Chace kicked him in the knee. Rutter cried out and bent to clasp his hands to his leg and Chace kicked him in the throat. The lawman fell back against a piling and clawed for his revolver. Chace kicked him in the other knee. Swearing and gasping, Rutter went down. He got his revolver out and tried to take aim. Chace clubbed him in the side of the neck, not once but several times. Rutter's fingers went limp and the revolver dropped. Seething mad, Rutter swung his other arm, but Chace skipped back. Rutter snarled and cursed. In a rush, Chace was on him, hitting Rutter's throat and neck again and again. The lawman sagged and broke into convulsions. His eyes rolled up in his head. Chace went on hitting him in the same spot. When the convulsions stopped, so did he. He pressed his fingers to a vein.

"Is he still breathing?"

Chace whirled. "What are *you* doing here? I didn't say you were to follow me."

"You didn't say I couldn't," Tallulah said as she came out of the shadows. "I wouldn't have shown myself except you're about to have company." She pointed down the beach.

A middle-aged man and his dog were having fun playing fetch. The man would throw a piece of driftwood into the surf and the dog would run in after it and bring it back to be tossed anew.

"Get down," Chace warned.

The dog came out of the water and stopped and shook itself, spraying drops.

Laughing, the man patted it on the head. He tried to take the driftwood but the dog held on. Their mock tug-of-war brought them near the wharf. When the dog finally opened its jaws, the man threw the stick as far as he could away from the pilings and the dog lit out after it. The man, puffing, trailed after.

"What would you have done if he saw us?" Tallulah asked.

Chace didn't answer. He let down the hammer and pocketed the derringer, then took hold of Rutter's ankles and pulled. Without being asked, Tallulah helped. She couldn't do much, as small as she was, but she huffed and tugged until they were at the water's edge. There she collapsed and said, "For a skinny man he sure is heavy."

Chace checked the shore. He quickly went through

each pocket and gave her what he found. He unpinned the badge and gave that to her, too. Then he hurried under the wharf, gathering an armful of rocks, big and small. He made several trips. Kneeling, he stuffed the small ones in Rutter's pockets. The large rocks he put up Rutter's shirt in the front and rolled the body over and shoved more rocks up the shirt in the back. He tightened Rutter's belt, braced his feet, and pushed. It took some doing but after a minute the body was on the bottom in three feet of water.

Chace waded onto shore.

Tallulah was staring at him with a strange look in her eyes.

"What?" Chace asked.

"I heard what he said. You did that to keep him from taking our money, didn't you?"

"My reasons are my own," Chace said.

Tallulah's eyes sparkled. "Can I tell you something?"

"If you want."

"When I'm older I'm going to marry you."

25

Linsey, Newton, and Randy weren't happy. They had just got off the ferry and stood with the reins to their mounts in their hands staring at the bustling hive that was Galveston.

"Damn, it's big," Linsey said.

"Bigger than I reckoned," Newton said.

"Big enough it could take forever to find him," Randy threw in.

They left the landing and hiked along the street taking in the sights and sounds. In a while they came on a side street with a lot fewer people and Linsey went down it and stopped in front of a bakery. The aroma had all three sniffing.

Newton's stomach rumbled like thunder in the distance. "We ain't ate in a spell."

"We will in a minute," Linsey said. "First we've got to work this out. We have to do it smarter than we did in Dallas. I want to find him quick."

Randy said, "We all do. But how?"

"We could ask the law," Newton suggested. "Maybe

he's got into trouble and they'll know where we could find him."

"Oh, that's smart, sure enough," Linsey said. "They'd want to know why we're asking and we'll just up and tell them we're looking to bury the son of a bitch."

"We could lie."

Linsey shook his head. "We keep the law out of this. We find Chace Shannon, we turn him into maggot bait, and we head home." He rubbed his chin. "Think, you lunkheads. Where is he likely to be?"

"He'll need a place to stay so we could ask around at the hotels," Randy suggested.

"Unless he's staying at a boardinghouse," Newton said.

"He needs to eat, so we could try all the restaurants and such," Linsey proposed. "A city this size, there shouldn't be more than a couple of dozen. And he should stand out, wearing those buckskins we've been told he's partial to."

"If he's still wearing them," Newton said.

"We could go to all the whorehouses," Randy brought up. "He'd bound to need a woman."

"Unless he's taken up with one and is getting it for free," Newton said.

Linsey growled, "Keep shooting them down, why don't you? I'd like to hear your idea."

Just then a boy with dirty cheeks came up to them. A small wooden box hung from a strap over his shoulder. "Shine your boots for you."

"Get lost, runt," Randy said.

"Only two bits each," the boy persisted. "I'll shine them so good you can see yourself."

"That's stupid," Newton said. "Who wants to see themselves in their boots?"

"I'll shine all of you for two bits. How would that be?"

"Go away, consarn it," Linsey said, and swung his foot at the boy's backside. The boy skipped out of reach and made a face and hurried off.

"Little nuisance," Newton grumped.

"Now, where were we?" Randy said.

"We were trying to figure out who to ask about Chace Shannon," Linsey reminded him. "There has got to be someone."

A lonely stretch of prairie spread ahead and behind them. They'd only seen a few other travelers all day. At sunset they made camp beside a stand of trees that offered some shelter from the wind. Cassie gathered fallen branches and Jed kindled the fire. He had shot a rabbit that afternoon and Cassie skinned it and chopped some of the meat into pieces and impaled the pieces on sticks. Her hair kept falling into her face as she chopped and she brushed it back with her bloody fingers.

Jed held his spit to the flames. Presently the smell of the roast meat made his mouth water. "I sure am hungry. Thirsty, too."

"You touch that flask, I'll kick you," Cassie said. She was glad that for two days he had behaved. "I've put coffee on."

Jed would have dearly loved a drink. The craving had come over him. Not as strong yet as it would be but strong enough that a drink was all he could think of. He went to take another bite when the shadows in the trees moved and two men emerged. "Cassie girl," he whispered in warning, and lowered his hand to his Sharps.

Both wore clothes that had seen a lot of wear, along with floppy hats. One had a hat with a leather band; the other's hat was plain. Both had unkempt tangles of beards and cradled large-bore Ballard rifles in their brawny arms. "How do, friend?" said Plain Hat to Jed.

About to take a bite, Cassie froze. The men were big and scary looking. She didn't like how their eyes gleamed in the firelight, or how although the one had spoken to her grandpa, he was staring at her.

"We'd be obliged for a bite of supper," said the other.

"Have a seat, gents," Jed said, and placed the Sharps across his lap. "There's plenty enough for all of us. Cassie, why don't you cook some of that there rabbit for our guests?"

"Sure, Grandpa." Cassie pried a leg off the rabbit, and sliced. She avoided looking at the men.

"That your name, girl? Cassie?" said Hat with the Leather Band.

"That's a pretty name," said Plain Hat.

Jed sniffed. An odor clung to them strong. It made him think of a bear rug he once had, only different. "What's that smell?"

"Buff," said Plain Hat.

"You're hide hunters?" Jed guessed.

Plain Hat nodded. "Got our horses and pack animals in the trees. We're on our way to St. Louis."

"Not many buffs there," Jed said.

"Not many buffs anywhere, anymore," Plain Hat said. "Used to be millions and now there's a trickle."

A couple of the other man's front teeth were missing,

and when he grinned, it made him look like a simpleton. "We like to go to St. Louis for the ladies."

Cassie had made spits for them. Rising, she gave a spit to each.

"You're as pretty as your name," Plain Hat said.

"How old are you?" asked the one with the hat with the leather band.

"That's enough about my granddaughter," Jed said gruffly. He didn't like how they were admiring her.

"We thought maybe she was your wife," said Hat with the Leather Band.

"As young as she is?" Jed said.

Plain Hat licked his lips. "I like them young. Older ones nag too much. And they don't taste near as sweet."

Jed felt a flush of anger. He started to raise the Sharps, then saw that Hat with the Leather Band was pointing the Ballard rifle at him.

"I wouldn't," Plain Hat said.

"What is this?" Jed demanded, although he knew perfectly well what it was, and a finger of ice ran down his spine.

"It's a long way to St. Louis," Plain Hat said.

Jason Drake came every night to Madame Bovary's, without fail. He came at the same time, seven o'clock. He always chose Sasha, and he always stayed an hour and only an hour. He was a gambler, and it was said he was the best in Galveston, if not all of Texas. He always wore the same attire: a wide-brimmed black hat, a black frock coat, a white shirt with a black tie, black pantaloons, and black boots made of calf leather.

Chace opened the door and gave a slight bow as Madame Bovary insisted he do. "Mr. Drake," he said.

The gambler entered and paused. He always paused and examined himself in the mirror, and if need be, adjusted his attire. "Mr. Shannon." He always had an easy smile, too. He nodded and started down the hall.

"Mr. Drake," Chace said again.

Jason Drake stopped and turned. A certain wariness was in his poise and his gray eyes. "What is it?"

"I want to ask a favor."

"I only do favors for my friends."

"I'd like for you to take me under your wing."

Drake was puzzled. "Under my wing how?"

"I want to be a gambler like you."

"Do you, now?" Drake's easy smile returned. "You're too young, son. In a few years ask me again."

"How old do you have to be?" Chace asked. "I'm old enough to have been with a girl and had a taste of liquor. I'm old enough to have snuffed a wick or three. But I'm not old enough to play cards?"

Drake gave Chace a scrutiny. "Damned if I don't believe you about the wicks. But it takes a lot of practice to become good at my profession. I wouldn't have the time to teach you."

"I'm a fast learner."

"I'm sorry." Drake started to move on.

"What if I paid you?" Chace asked.

The gambler stopped. "I can always use stake money but I doubt you can afford me."

"Would two hundred dollars be enough to start and then two hundred a month thereafter?"

"That's a lot of money for someone your age. Fixing to rob banks and stagecoaches, are you?"

"How I get it is my business," Chace said. "But I *can* pay you. And it won't take a lot of your time. An hour a day, or every other day if that's too much. In a month I can be earning big money like you."

"It's not that simple," Drake said. "Cards take skill. Even then, luck trumps skill more than you would think. There are nights I earn big, yes. There are nights I lose big, too."

The brass knocker thumped the door. Chace admitted two townsmen, and when they were out of earshot said, "I can't do this all my life. Gambling strikes me as something I'd like. You work when you want. You don't have a boss saying what you should wear and how you should talk. If I get as good as you, I can dress nice like you do and afford a fancy lady every night."

Jason Drake smiled. "You've given it thought, I see. Did you hear me say it takes skill? You have to be quick with your hands and in your head. You live by your wits and your instincts and you never know when some hayseed is going to pull a pistol or a knife on you because he's lost all he has. It isn't like clerk work or law work or any kind of work you can think of. You are your own man, and sink or swim, it is up to you."

"So what are the bad parts?" Chace said.

"You remind me of someone," Drake said, and laughed.

"Who?"

"Me when I was your age."

"You're not much older," Chace said. "Ten years or thereabouts, according to Madame Bovary."

"Gretchen sure is fond of you," Drake remarked, and touched his hat brim. "I'll think it over and get back to you."

"If it will help, there's something else you get besides the money."

"What's that?"

"Me as your friend."

"You should sell patent medicine for a living," the gambler joked, and moved on to the parlor.

"That went well," Chace said to the mirror. For the next hour he worked the door for a stream of well-to-do clients. They were polite and pleasant but nearly always treated him with reserve. An older man with a face like a hatchet always pinched him on the cheek and said what a fine boy he was. Chace balled his fists and smiled.

At seven o'clock Jason Drake came back down the hall with his wide-brimmed black hat in his hand. In his curly brown hair, over his right ear, was a rose.

"My, oh my," Chace said.

"I have shot men for mocking me."

"A special girl gave me a flower once. It was a daisy she picked in a meadow. I wore it in my ear just like you." Chace opened the door. "Let me know when you've made up your mind."

Drake took the rose out and put it in an inside pocket. He stood in front of the mirror and put his hat on, tilting the brim so it hid his eyes. "Ever been to the Gem Saloon?"

"Not in it but I've seen it. Down by the water, not far from Harvest Fisheries."

"The corner of Avenue A and Twenty-first Street. I'm usually there by three in the afternoon. Meet me there tomorrow and I'll give you your first lesson."

"You won't regret this," Chace said.

"I hope not. But you have Sasha to thank, not me."

"Sasha?"

"I mentioned our talk to her and she said that she thinks you have what it takes."

"Are we talking about the same Sasha? The one I'm thinking of would like nothing better than to pound me with a rock."

Drake stepped to the doorway. "If you're serious about this, I'd suggest different clothes."

Chace looked down at himself. "What's wrong with these?"

"Nothing. For a doorman." Drake took the rose out of his pocket and sniffed it and stuck the stem in a button hole. Whistling to himself, he went off into the night.

A soft rustling brought Chace around. "He told me what you said. That was awful nice."

A green dress with no back and a low front accented Sasha's many charms. She smiled and pursed her ruby lips. "You are so dumb."

"Says you," Chace said.

Sasha touched the tip of a long painted fingernail to his chin and dug the nail into his skin. "I'm for anything that helps get rid of you."

"So that was why."

"Still think I'm nice?"

"Bitch," Chace said.

26

"Grandpa?" Cassie had just seen one of the buffalo hunters point a rifle at him.

"We can do this easy or we can do this hard, old man," Plain Hat said to Jed. "Take your hand off the Sharps, stand up, and turn around."

Jed considered resisting. But he would take a bullet, maybe more before he got off a shot. He slowly placed the Sharps on the ground and raised his hands over his head. Standing, he turned. "Happy now?"

"Very," Plain Hat said. He nodded at the other one, who came around and took the Sharps and tossed it in the grass.

"You shouldn't ought to have done that," Jed said.

Plain Hat laughed. "There's a lot we shouldn't have done but did. It's a wonder the law ain't after us."

"Grandpa?" Cassie said once more.

"Any last words you got to say to him, girl," the hunter with the leather band said, "now's the time to say them."

"Make it quick," Plain Hat said. "We've been roaming the prairie for weeks and I've got the itch bad."

Cassie gripped the handle to the coffeepot and took the top off. The water had reached a boil. "The only words I have to say," she said quietly, "is that this world isn't like I thought it was."

"How else would it be other than what it is?" Plain Hat snorted. "Leave it to a female to say something so silly."

Cassie looked at her grandfather. "Remember Chace and the drunk in the stable?"

Jed tensed his legs. "I will never forget it."

"What are you two talking about?" Plain Hat asked.

"This," Cassie said, and swung the pot at his face. The boiling water caught him full in the eyes and the nose and mouth and he shrieked and stumbled back. She went after him. He had dropped his rifle and covered his face with his hands but his chin was exposed and she hit him with the pot.

The other buffalo hunter pivoted toward her and jerked his rifle to his shoulder. Jed sprang, whipping his bowie from its sheath, and slammed into the hunter just as the rifle went off. The slug intended to end Cassie's life thudded into the ground instead, and Jed drove the bowie into the man's chest. Or tried to. The blade had penetrated barely an inch when the man roared and grabbed Jed's wrist in both hands and wrenched Jed's arm.

Cassie swung the pot again. The metal on bone made a dull *clong*. The man staggered but didn't go down. With a savage snarl he unleashed a backhand. His knuckles only grazed her head but it was enough to stagger her. He was furiously blinking his boiled eyes. The skin around them had been seared pink and was split and blistering.

"I can't see, Hank! God in heaven, I can't see!"

Hank had his hands full with Jed. They grappled fiercely, Jed striving to wrest free and Hank holding his wrist in a vise. A foot hooked Jed's leg and he went down with Hank on top. Intense heat spread across Jed's back and he realized they had fallen in the fire. He attempted to roll out of the flames but Hank slammed him down and grabbed him by the throat.

"Going to choke you dead, you old goat." He glanced at the other hunter.

"Watch out for the girl, Vern!"

Cassie smashed the coffeepot against Vern's knee. He yelped and clutched wildly for her and fell on both knees, which made him yelp louder. Cassie darted in and struck him on the cheek and the forehead. She was trying to batter him senseless but his head was proof against her pounding. She had raised the pot to bash him with all her might when thick fingers wrapped around her leg.

"I got you now," Vern crowed.

Jed was finding it hard to breathe. He bucked but Hank was a lot heavier and a lot stronger. The vise on his throat continued to tighten. He couldn't pull his knife arm loose. He was close to blacking out when he twisted his face and sank his teeth into Hank's arm. Hank howled and the pressure on Jed's throat let up enough that Jed sucked in a breath.

Cassie pulled frantically on her leg, to no effect. She slammed the pot against Vern's ear. Blood spurted but he held on and the next instant she was on her back and he had his other hand on her chest.

"Ever squished a bug, girl?"

To Cassie it felt as if the weight of the world bore down on her. She kicked and hit with the pot but he was immune to her blows. She heard a great roaring in her ears, as if all the blood in her body was being forced up into her head. She realized she might die and never see Chace again. She couldn't bear that. Vern's blistered eyes were just above her. Whether he could see or not, he could still feel pain, and letting go of the pot, she sank her fingernails into his sockets.

At Vern's scream, Hank looked over. Jed used the distraction; he tore his arm free and speared the bowie at Hank's throat. The big blade stroked in like a knife into butter and Hank's scream mingled with Vern's. Hank's changed to a roar of rage as he batted Jed's hand from the hilt, and with the bowie sticking from his neck, Hank proceeded to choke the life from him.

Blood poured from Vern's ravaged eyes. He threw himself back onto his hands and knees. Cassie pushed upright. Near her lay one of the buffalo guns. She scooped it up and brought the stock to her shoulder. It was the heaviest gun she ever held but she got it steady and thumbed back the hammer.

"Where are you, girl?" Vern roared.

"Right here," Cassie said. She gouged the muzzle into his face and squeezed the trigger. It was like a cannon going off. She was flung back and nearly lost her hold. Acrid gun smoke swirled into her nose and mouth and she coughed to clear them. Vern was on his back with his arm flung out, a hole where one of his boiled eyes had been.

Jed was losing consciousness; the world was fading to black. His lungs were fit to burst for their need for air, and his body was going numb. In a final act of defiance he gripped the bowie's hilt and twisted it like a corkscrew. Hank arched his back and his face went slack and his arms sagged. Breathing shallow, he pitched onto his side. It took all Jed had to get up on his knees. He yanked the blade out and bent over the buffalo hunter. Hank's mouth was opening and closing. "You mangy son of a bitch," Jed said, and stabbed him four more times.

Cassie was so weak, she could hardly stand. She teetered and put her arm across his shoulders and sagged against him, saying, "I am plumb tuckered out."

"You and me both, girl," Jed admitted. He wiped the bowie on Hank's britches. "What is it about you that draws these coyotes like flies?"

"Oh, Grandpa."

"From here on out we don't trust anyone," Jed vowed.

Cassie said, "Especially if they wear britches."

The Gem Saloon was as glamorous as a saloon could be: a chandelier sparkled like the stars, velvet covered the tables, the bar was mahogany, the spittoons were polished, and the floor was swept several times a day. Two bartenders were always on duty to meet the demand. Situated as it was near where the ferries and boats unloaded and boarded passengers, the Gem was the busiest saloon in Galveston.

Chace held the batwings apart until he spied Jason Drake, and entered. He crossed to the table and waited for the gambler to look up.

"Damn, son. What have you done?"

"Sir?"

"You look like me."

"You said to get new clothes." Chace was wearing a

black frock coat with a white shirt and string tie. He had on black pantaloons and black boots made from calf leather. To crown his new wardrobe, he had bought a wide-brimmed black hat,which he wore with the brim tilted low.

Drake chuckled and motioned for Chace to take a chair and said again, "Damn, son."

"I have a name," Chace said.

"Do you have a weapon?" Drake asked.

Chace patted his frock coat. "I have a pistol in my pocket."

"Is it an ordinary pocket?"

"What other kind of pocket is there?"

"A tailored pocket made of leather so you can slick your smoke wagon faster." The gambler sat back and thoughtfully drummed his long fingers on the table. "All right. First lesson. Our profession is not without its perils. I've had to shoot four men and stab two others. Not because I wanted to. Because they left me no choice." He glanced at the bar and raised an arm and held up two fingers and one of the bartenders nodded. "The problem is those who sit at our tables. Too often they are terrible at cards. They don't know how to play but they think they do. They bet too much on poor hands. They bluff when they shouldn't. They try to have a stone face so we can't read them but they are poor at it. So they lose, and if they lose a lot, they get mad. They say things they shouldn't. The same with the drunks but the drunks are worse. Drunks are always on the prod. When they lose, they jerk a pistol or a knife. Then there are our fellow cardsharps. They take losing as a personal slight and sometimes resent it so much that they pull on you, too."

Drake stopped and grinned. "Do you still want to be a gambler?"

"More than anything," Chace said.

The bartender brought over a tray with a bottle and two glasses. He set the bottle and a glass in front of Drake and a glass in front of Chace and left.

Drake waggled the bottle. "I'm treating you to a drink to see how you handle it. When we work we need a clear head. I never drink when I'm playing for stakes and I advise you to do the same."

Chace shrugged. "I'm not much of a drinker."

"Good. Stay that way. I've seen too many good gamblers brought low by red-eye. Their play suffers to where they lose more than they earn. It's a downhill slope that ends in ruin. The only thing that destroys more of our fraternity is women."

"My ma is as nice a lady as ever lived. Not all women are bad for men."

About to pour, Drake said, "Not all, no, I grant you. But they can cause no end of trouble. They want nice dresses and they want to eat at nice restaurants and stay at nice hotels and be pampered and waited on hand and foot, so they badger you to earn more, and yet they smile at every man they see and expect you to ..." He frowned and fell silent.

"What was her name?" Chace asked.

A slow smile spread across the gambler's face. "I was much younger, and stupid. Fortunately I came to my senses before she put me in the poorhouse."

"That explains Madame Bovary's."

Drake filled a finger's worth in his glass and the same in the other. "A man can't go without. It can be a distraction if it is all you are thinking of while you are in a game. I pay Sasha a visit to keep my head clear for cards."

"Anything else I should know?"

"Oh, hell. We've barely scratched the surface." Drake slid the glass across. "What I'm giving you are the basics. No drinking. No women. Always be armed. Which reminds me. Do you have any compunction against killing?"

"Any what?"

"Some men don't have it in them to kill even when their own lives are at risk. Can you if you have to?"

"I reckon it's safe for me to say it won't be a problem."

"Good." Drake sipped and set the glass down. He picked up the cards he had been playing solitaire with and shuffled them, his fingers moving so swiftly the shuffle was impossible to follow. He splayed the cards, riffled them, shaped them into a pile, and shuffled them again. "Can you do any of that?"

"No," Chace admitted.

"Then learn." Drake reached inside his frock coat and brought out a new deck and tossed it to Chace. "For you. Practice as much as you can. Not for in a game but to show the yokels you can."

"I don't understand."

"When you're playing for stakes you always deal slow so everyone can see. Otherwise some fools will accuse you of cheating. Deal from the top and pretend your hands are molasses."

"But those tricks you just did."

"They're for showing off. Do it before a game or between games. It impresses the hell out of the store clerk or butcher or bank president who has sat at your table. You dazzle them and they regard you as a professional. You deal square and they regard you as honest. And they'll keep coming back and keep losing their money but they won't resent it and they won't pull a hideout on you and try to blow your brains out."

"You put a lot of thought into this."

"Gambling isn't for dull-wits. A good gambler is thinking all the time. It's what separates him or her from the store clerks and separates them from their money."

Chace opened the deck. The cards were shiny and smooth. He hefted them and shuffled them fast and smoothly and set the deck down.

"Not bad," Drake said. "You've had some practice."

"These are the first cards I've ever held," Chace said. "Ma didn't take with gambling and such. She didn't allow them in her home."

"Shuffle them again."

Chace complied, and imitated the riffling trick the gambler had performed, although not as fast.

"A natural, by God," Drake declared. "You have the knack. Some don't. They try and try but the best they will ever be is fair. You keep at it and you could be one of the best."

"Folks say that you are."

"Here in Galveston, yes. I have bigger dreams. I want to work the riverboats. I want to gamble in places like St. Louis and New Orleans and Denver. That's where the real competition is. And that's where fortunes are made."

"You're in this to get rich? I thought you gamble because you like to play cards."

"I do, but I wouldn't mind having more money than I know what to do with."

"Me either."

Jason Drake chuckled. "Get good at our trade and hope Lady Luck favors us and you just might."

"And one other thing."

"What might that be?"

"I have to live long enough," Chace said.

27

Linsey, Newton, and Randy Harkey stood at the bar in the Dirty Molly.

Linsey was facing the mirror. His brothers were leaning on it with their elbows and watching the goings-on in the packed saloon.

Linsey chugged a swallow, smacked the empty glass down, and swore. "We're poor manhunters."

"We tracked him this far," Newton said. "I don't call that poor."

"He has to be somewhere," Randy said.

Linsey refilled his glass and raised it to his lips. He looked in the mirror, and stiffened. "Quick. Turn around."

"What?" Randy said.

"Do it," Linsey commanded, and when they had their backs to the room, he said, "We don't want him spotting us."

"Want who?" Newton asked.

"Look in the glass. Over yonder by the table near the door. Who is that talking to that gambler?"

"I'll be," Randy blurted. "It's that deputy works for Sheriff Wyler."

"Nick Fulsome," Linsey said. "Wyler's brother-in-law." A crafty gleam came into his dark eyes. "Now what do you suppose Deputy Fulsome is doing way down here in Galveston?"

"By God, I bet he's hunting Chace Shannon, the same as us," Newton said excitedly.

Linsey smiled and nodded.

"Should we go over and acquaint ourselves?" Randy asked. "Maybe we can hunt together."

"Use your damn head," Linsey growled. "He's the law. He's here to arrest the boy. We're here to kill him. Fulsome finds out we're here, he could make trouble for us. He might go to the local law and have them escort us out of town. Then where are we?"

"I didn't think of that," Randy said.

"What do we do?" Newton asked.

"We play it smart," Linsey said. "We let the law dog do the hunting for us. That badge of his will get him more answers than we get. So we take turns following him and sooner or later he'll lead us to the boy."

Newton chortled. "You sly fox."

"Why do you suppose he's talking to a gambler?" Randy wondered.

Linsey scratched his chin and gnawed his lower lip. "It just hit me. We should have been doing the same. Gamblers see a lot of the comings and goings. Same as the bartenders."

"Look out," Randy said. "He's coming this way."

They lowered their heads and watched in the mirror as the lawman roved among the tables. Fulsome stopped to talk to another gambler and after a while moved toward the batwings. He didn't come anywhere near the far end of the bar.

"Newton, you take the first turn," Linsey said. "It shouldn't be hard, as many people are out and about all the time. Stick with him until he turns in for the night, then come fetch us. You know where we'll be."

Newton nodded and drained his glass and hurried out after the deputy.

"Come on," Linsey said. He had already paid for the bottle and took it with them out to the hitch rail. He unwrapped the reins to Newton's mount, climbed on his own, and rode leisurely along street after street until they were at the south end of Galveston and the buildings gave way to brush and woodland. They rode into the woods to a clearing. In the middle were the charred embers of their previous fire. "Get it going," Linsey said with a nod. Sliding down, he sat on a log they used for a seat and put his chin in his hands.

Randy went into the trees and came out with an armful of broken limbs. He hunkered and began placing them over the embers. "What are you pondering, big brother?"

"How to go about the boy. Fulsome being here changes things."

"I don't see how."

"I get tired of telling you to use your head," Linsey said. "We want the boy dead but we don't want to end up behind bars for doing it."

"Oh." Randy snapped a long piece of limb in half. "You're saying we wait for the deputy to find him and pick him off with a rifle so the deputy don't see us."

"No. I have me a better idea. We're going to kill both of them."

Randy looked up. "Are you drunk?"

"Didn't you hear Newton a while ago? He called me a sly fox." Linsey chuckled. "With the feud started up again, it would help us Harkeys if the law was on our side and not the Shannons'."

"How will killing a deputy win the law to us?"

"Follow my trail, damn you," Linsey said. "Sheriff Wyler takes his job serious. He's always fair to folks. He treats us and the Shannons the same. He doesn't favor us over them or the other way around. We can change that."

"How?"

"It's simple. We kill the deputy and make it look like the boy was to blame." Linsey laughed. "What do you think of that?"

"I think Newton was right. You're sly as hell."

As had become his habit, Chace was at the Gem Saloon promptly at three. Some of the regulars nodded at him and he nodded back. His hands were in his pockets. He went to the same table as always.

Jason Drake was playing solitaire. He placed a red seven on a black eight. "You're grinning like the cat that ate the canary."

"I did it. Just like you said."

Drake set down the deck and studied Chace's frock coat. "You had a tailor take out the pocket and sew in a leather one so you can draw faster?"

"Not just one pocket." Chace grinned and his hands flashed. In each he held a Colt Lightning double-action, nickel-plated with ivory handles. He twirled them forward and did a reverse spin and slipped them back into the special leather pockets.

"Slick as can be," Drake complimented him. "But two? Gretchen must be paying you more than I thought. Ivory handles don't come cheap."

Chace pulled out his usual chair and sat.

"You're not going to tell me, are you?"

"Tell you what?"

"Where you get your money? Those clothes, the pistols, that palomino you bought. And don't forget this." Drake took a gold watch from a coat and opened it and listened to the musical chimes.

"I wanted to show how grateful I am," Chace said.

"You didn't have to. You're paying me, remember?" Drake closed the watch and slipped it back. "But I've got to admit, I've liked teaching you. You learn quick. It's rare I have to show you anything more than twice." He folded his hands. "You learn so quick, it's scary."

"What will it be today?"

"Today I'll do the learning and you'll do the teaching," Drake said. "We'll start with your past."

"No," Chace said. "I'm surprised you'd bring it up. I thought we were pards."

"We are," Drake said gently. "Which is why I have to warn you that a lawman from Arkansas is on your scent."

Chace glanced at the front door and scanned the room.

"Nervous all of a sudden?" Drake teased.

"Where's this lawman?"

"I wouldn't know where he is right this minute but he's been asking all over Galveston about you. I found out from a friend of mine, a member of our fraternity. The friend told him he'd never run into anyone answering your description. Then he came to find me."

"Damn," Chace said.

"Which is why I'd like to know about your past. How much trouble are you in? Enough to get you hung?"

"From the highest tree there is." Chace frowned and slid his chair back. "I'd best be going. The lawman finds us together, there could be gunplay. I don't want you involved."

"Stay where you are. What sort of friend do you take me for? Besides, I have a proposition for you. One you might like. It will get you away from the law and let you see new sights."

"I'm listening."

"I mentioned before that I'd like to work the Mississippi riverboats. How would you like to go with me? We could leave tomorrow. That deputy will never find you."

"That sounds a lot to me like running away."

"A tin star is a stacked deck with two legs and no gambler ever bucks a stacked deck."

"Call it what you want." Chace shook his head. "I can't."

"Be sensible."

"I have to be true to me," Chace said.

"Don't let pride get you killed."

"It's not that." Chace shifted his chair so he could see the front door and slid his right hand into the right pocket on his frock coat.

"Explain it to me, if you would," Drake requested.

Chace was slow answering. "A while ago I had a decision to make. My sister had been raped and my pa had gone missing and was likely killed. I could either go after those to blame or let it go."

"Forgive and forget, a parson would say."

"Parsons don't live in the real world. They live in their head. Some things you can't ever forget. As for turning the other cheek, what good does that do if it gets your throat slit?" Chace stared at the floor. "I was at a crossroads. I knew if I did as I should, my life as I knew it was over. Maybe a sensible person would have let it go but life is more than common sense. Life is feelings, too, and I had to be true to mine. I had to do to those who hurt my family as they had done to us."

"Most your age never have to make a hard decision like that," Drake observed.

"Life is what it is. So I did what I had to and then I had to run and now a lawman is after me. I can go on running but he might keep on looking and the running won't have gotten me anywhere." Chace looked at Drake. "A thing like this should be settled sooner rather than later."

"What are you going to do? Confront him?"

"I don't know yet," Chace said. "I have to think on it some."

"Whatever you decide I'll back your play."

Chace watched several men enter. "There's another reason I can't go. I can feel her inside me. Which means she's close."

"Feel who?"

"Promise not to laugh."

"You have yourself a woman?"

"A twin sister. Ever since I can remember there's been this feeling inside me whenever she's near. I don't know how to describe it except that I can feel her like I feel hot and cold and wet." Chace paused. "I love her more than anyone in this world. That was the hardest part about leaving home, going off without her. I should have guessed she'd come after me. We never could stand being apart. She couldn't stand it even more than me." His voice broke and he stopped. He coughed and said softly, "If we could be man and wife life would be perfect."

Jason Drake filled his glass and drank it down in two gulps. He filled it again and drank half. Then he said, "Well, now."

"I need to find this lawman before he finds me," Chace said. "That friend of yours happen to mention where the lawman is staying?"

"I doubt he knew. But it might be I can find out. I know a lot of people. I'll ask around."

"I'd be obliged. And who knows? Maybe next week or next month that riverboat notion will appeal to me."

"It's worth considering." Drake swirled the whiskey in his glass. "Those new pistols of yours. You any good with them?"

"I've practiced some east of town," Chace said. "I'm better with a rifle but I can hit a man in the guts if I have to."

"I know a gent who could teach you things. He knows revolvers like I know cards. His name is Wilson. Has a son about your age. Works as a butcher, of all things, and has the quickest hands in Galveston. He's been in five shooting affrays and shot seven men dead."

"Why ain't he in jail?" Chace asked, and then corrected himself with, "Why *isn't* he in jail?"

"He never starts it. It's always self-defense. He doesn't look like much so others think they can pick on him and he proves them wrong."

"Maybe when this is over I'll see him," Chace said, and stood. "Right now I have hunting to do." He took a step but stopped. "You don't mind if I pass on the lesson today?"

"How to tell marked cards can wait," Drake said with a smile.

Chace went out onto the boardwalk. Dust motes hung in the hot air. Staying close to the buildings, staring at every face, he walked to the next corner where Zeke was holding a tray and shouting, "Suspenders! Get your suspenders here!"

Chace came up behind him and said quietly, "I have a job for you."

Zeke turned so abruptly he nearly tripped over his own feet. "Boss! You shouldn't ought to sneak up on folks like that."

"How many times have I got to tell you? Call me Chace."

Zeke looked him up and down and said in genuine awe, "Damn. You're a fancier dresser than Tunk ever was. And you smell like lilac water. Must be that lady at the whorehouse, huh?"

"I have a job for you," Chace said. "A job for everyone."

Zeke turned serious. "Anything you want. Anything at all. Thanks to you letting us keep more of our money, I've got more than I ever had my whole life."

"Get the word out. There's a lawman in town asking about me. I don't know what he looks like but he'll likely be wearing a badge and not many wear the tin."

Zeke moved his jacket so the stag hilt of a knife was visible above his belt on his left hip. "Want us to take care of him for you?"

"No. This is personal. Fifty dollars to whoever finds him. Another fifty if he can be found by dark."

Zeke chuckled. "For that much you'll have a hundred eyes and ears looking everywhere. That law dog is as good as found."

28

Deputy Nick Fulsome was coming out of a general store when the little girl came up to him. He had just bought chewing tobacco and was biting off a chaw.

About to turn, he nearly collided with her and had to stop short. "Careful, girl. You're liable to be stepped on."

"Care for an apple, mister? Only two cents."

Nick shook his head. "Apples and tobacco don't mix. Should have caught me before I bit."

"You a lawman?" the girl asked, staring at his badge.

"Arkansas deputy sheriff," Nick informed her. "Here on official business." He went to go by but stopped. "Say, I just had a notion. What's your name, anyhow?"

"Tallulah," the girl said sweetly.

"You must get all over town selling your apples."

"I reckon I do at that."

"Could be you've seen the gent I'm searching for," Nick said. "He hails from the same part of the country I do. He's not much older than you. His name is Chace Shannon but he could be going by any old name."

Tallulah scrunched up her face in thought. "Chace, you say? That's awful familiar."

"It is?" Nick said hopefully. Squatting, he gripped her by the arms. "Think, girl, think. It's important to me."

"How important?"

Nick reached into his pocket and pulled out a handful of coins. He offered her a silver dollar. "It's worth this much."

"Add four more to that and it might help me remember better."

"So that's how it is? A face like an angel and the heart of an outlaw." Nick grinned and jingled the five dollars in his palm. As she reached for the coins he closed his hand. "Not so fast."

"What's wrong, mister?"

"I'm not stupid. You don't get the money until you've taken me to Chace Shannon. For all I know you don't really know him. You could skip off like a bunny and I'd be out hard-earned money." Nick scrutinized her. "How is it you know who he is?"

"Like you said, I get around," Tallulah answered. "I met him when he first came to town. He needed work, so I tried to help him, but he went and took over the Hawkers Guild, as some call it."

"You don't say."

Tallulah nodded. "We used to get together every night but he works nights, so now we get together every day at five."

Nick consulted his pocket watch. "It's four now. Could you take me to where he'll be? If I get there early I can lie in wait for him and take him by surprise."

"I'd be happy to, mister," Tallulah said. "I didn't like

what he did to Tunk and the changes he made. You arrest him and things can go back to how they were."

Nick smiled and stood. "My luck has changed, running into you. Lead the way, little one."

Tallulah turned and started off. "What did Chace do back in this place you come from that you're after him?"

"He killed people."

"Bad people or good people?"

"The law don't care, girl. He did it, and that's enough. He'll be put on trial and likely swing."

Tallulah was quiet after that. Ten minutes of walking brought them out of town and east over broken ground covered with scrub growth and islands of trees. That in turn gave way to a bayou. A path wound into its reaches.

Nick swatted at a few early mosquitoes, and swore. He saw a snake glide off and put his hand on his revolver. "Ain't you scared in a place like this? What if a gator popped out?"

"I'd run real quick," Tallulah said. She looked back at him and grinned. "They don't catch rabbits much."

"You've got grit. I'll give you that."

Tallulah slowed at a disturbance in the water and then moved on. "Watch out for the water moccasins. They bite without any warning. The rattlesnakes at least rattle."

"Give me my mountains," Nick said.

Beyond the bayou they crossed a series of dunes. From the top of the last Tallulah pointed at an old building. "That's the Roost. It used to belong to pirates. It's where we meet."

Nick scanned the beach. "I don't see anyone."

"It's early yet but we'd better hurry if you want to hide." Tallulah descended the dune, sand flying from her small feet.

A side door hung by the top hinge. Inside, the building was as silent as a tomb. After the bright glare of the sun, the dark was near total.

"Hold up," Nick said. "I can't hardly see."

"Your eyes get used to it," Tallulah said, but she stopped. "We wait too long, others might come."

"Damn it all."

"Here," Tallulah said, and clasped his hand. "I know the way with my eyes closed. I'll help you." She didn't wait for him to agree but moved along winding halls and across open spaces vague with deep shadows. Finally she stopped in front of a door.

"You can hide in this closet. When you hear voices, come out but be careful." Tallulah let go of his hand. "It's the best I can do."

"Thank you, girl. You've done right." Fulsome gave her the five dollars. He groped at the door and worked a wooden latch. "Now scoot. Whatever you do, don't let on to anyone."

Her teeth were white in the darkness. "Duck your head, mister. The ceiling is kind of low."

Nick ducked and stepped through and the unmistakable muzzle of a gun jabbed him in the face and others on the sides of his head. He froze and blurted, "What the hell?"

Lantern light flared, revealing a large room filled with boys and girls from six to sixteen. Half a dozen pistols and derringers and knives had been brandished. They were all grinning at the joke they had played. To the right and left stood two of the older boys, their cocked six-guns against Nick's temples. In front of Nick stood a figure in a wide-brimmed black hat and a frock coat holding an irory-handled Lightning. His grin was the widest of all.

"How do you do, Deputy?"

"Shannon," Nick said.

Chace relieved him of his revolver, then stepped back. "Keep him covered," he said, and slid the Lightning into a pocket. "Bet you didn't expect this."

"It was slick," Nick admitted.

"You wanted to see me and here I am."

"What now? You murder me and have your street rats bury me in the sand?"

"There's a notion." Chace chuckled and turned and the others parted to make way.

The older boy on Nick's right said, "Walk slow and keep your hands at your sides and you get to go on breathing. Were it up to me I'd kill you here and now but he says not to."

"What you're doing is against the law. You know that, don't you, boy?"

"The name is Zeke. And you know what you can do with your law. All that matters to us is us."

Across the room were a table and two chairs. Chace pulled one out and motioned for the deputy to take the other. Chace propped his feet up, took off his black hat and set it on the table, and laced his fingers behind his head.

Surrounded by urchins, two revolvers gouging him, Nick eased into the chair and placed his hands on the tabletop. Zeke and the other boy stepped back but didn't lower their weapons. "Well, then?"

Tallulah came and stood at Chace's side. He smiled

and stroked her hair and said, "Thank you, little one. You did right fine."

"It was easy. He's not very smart."

Nick surveyed the patchwork of faces. "Got yourself your own army, have you?"

"They're not *mine*," Chace said. "They're free as birds to stay or not. But they do sort of look up to me."

"I'll say," Zeke said to the deputy. "He's more to us than anyone ever and we won't let you take him or harm him."

His comment caused a stir of hostile murmuring. Resentful looks were cast Nick's way. One girl moved a knife across her throat as if slitting the deputy's throat.

"You are chock-full of surprises," Nick said.

"I could say the same of you coming this far to find me," Chace said. "Why couldn't you let it be?"

"Be serious, boy. You killed how many? And you expect the law to roll over and pretend it didn't happen?" Nick made a clucking sound. "Sheriff Wyler won't rest until you're caught. You kill me, there will be another after me. You kill him, the same. You have gone from a nobody to the most-wanted criminal in Madison County."

"I never thought of myself as a criminal," Chace said.

"Maybe you should start. When you break the law that's what you are. And you've broken it so many times, you can't ever set your life right again."

"You talk about right. Was it right that those who raped my sister should be fancy free? Was it right that those who killed my pa and his brothers didn't pay?"

"It was the law's to do, not up to you."

Chace scowled and started to come out of his chair but didn't. "That's your answer to everything. The law. Like we should bow and scrape to it and do whatever it says to do and our own feelings be damned."

"Good people make the laws to keep bad people like you in line," Nick said.

"That how you see it?"

"How else?"

"Laws are made by the high and mighty to keep the rest of us under their thumb. We can't do this or we can't do that even when what we want to do is right."

Nick went to fold his arms and Zeke pressed the revolver to his ear and he stopped. "Make all the excuses you want but killing ain't ever right. You have to answer for what you've done."

"What am I to do with you?" Chace said.

Just then a commotion broke out. A boy was shouting, "Let me through! Let me through!" An opening was made for him and he rushed to the table and said excitedly, "They were followed."

Both Chace and Deputy Nick said at the same time, "What?"

"I'm on lookout on the roof," the boy said to Chace. "I saw Tallulah bring this one over the dunes and a while after a man snuck up and is lying out there now, spying on the place."

Chace looked at Nick. "You don't say."

"It's not my doing," Nick said. "I'm alone."

"He's lying," Zeke said. "Let me spatter his brains and be done with him."

"Hold your temper," Chace said. "We kill a lawman and we'll have tin stars after us from now until forever."

He donned his hat and said to the boy who had brought the news, "Take us up there. Zeke, you and Floyd bring the deputy and watch him careful."

The route was precarious. It involved climbing a rafter that had collapsed and was propped against a back wall. Handholds had been carved but one slip and they would plummet forty feet. The boy on lookout warned them where the roof was weak and might collapse under their weight. Under his guidance they crawled to where a tilted slab hid them from view below and beyond. He peeked over it and said, "The man is still there."

Chace took off his hat. He slowly raised his head high enough to see over and then glared at Deputy Fulsome. "You son of a bitch."

"Why are you so mad all of a sudden?"

"If that's not a Harkey I'm a gosling. And where there is one there are bound to be more."

"You're seeing things," Nick said.

"Take a gander. But don't show yourself or we'll chuck you over the side."

Zeke and Floyd moved in close and jammed their six-guns against Nick. He looked, and went on looking, and then sat with his back to the slab and said, "Something ain't right here."

"That something is you."

"No," Nick said. "As God is my witness, I'm not working with the Harkeys. How he got on to me, I'll never know."

Chace stared at the deputy for so long, Nick fidgeted. Finally Chace said, "Damned if I don't believe you. But if that's so, either they latched onto you on their own or the gent you work for set you up as bait."

"Sheriff Wyler?"

"Think about it," Chace said. "He sends you after me. He lets the Harkeys in on it so they can follow you and when you find me they can make buzzard meat of me."

"The sheriff wouldn't do a thing like that."

"He sent you all this way," Chace said.

"I tell you Wyler treats everybody fair," Nick insisted. "He's a stickler for the law you think so little of."

"Whether he is or he isn't I have two problems. How to deal with those Harkeys and how to deal with you." Chace slid his hands into the pockets of his frock coat and drew both ivory-handled pistols and pointed them at the deputy.

"Any suggestions?"

"I say shoot him," Zeke urged.

"We'll throw his body in the sea and the tide will take it out," Floyd said.

"Let the fish eat him," said another boy.

"What to do, what to do," Chace said.

29

The room was small and smelled of odors Nick Fulsome would rather not have breathed. He paced and paced and paced some more, the lantern casting his shadow on the wall. By his watch over three hours had gone by when the bar outside grated and the door swung open.

"You can come out," Chace Shannon said.

Nick cautiously emerged. Tallulah was holding Chace's hand. A lot of the other hawkers were there, twenty or better, many armed. Enough that if Nick made a break, he wouldn't get two steps. "What's the idea of keeping me cooped up so long?"

"I had to decide," Chace replied.

"And have you?"

"Yes."

Nick put his back to the wall and bunched his fists. "What's it to be? A bullet to the brain? If so, you can start the dance now. I'll be damned if I'll go quietly."

"I thought I'd feed you and we'd shake hands and I'd send you on your way," Chace said.

"Was that a joke?"

"Honest." Chace crossed his heart with a finger. "Follow me." He walked down a hall to a flight of stairs and up them to a room that overlooked the dunes. The window had long since been broken out and a warm wind blew. "Your friend is still out there but he can't see us from where he is. Have a seat."

In the middle of the room a blanket had been spread and on it were a plate of food and a glass of water. The food consisted of beans and peaches and several slices of buttered bread.

Nick hunkered and drank half the glass in thirsty gulps. "I was thinking you might starve me to death."

"I'm not cruel."

"Is that so?" Nick drained the rest of the glass. "Tell that to Ezriah Harkey. They say you did things to him even a Comanche wouldn't do."

"He had to be persuaded to talk." Chace opened his frock coat and sat cross-legged. "I want you to take a message to Sheriff Wyler for me. Will you do that?"

"What message?"

Chace gestured. "Eat up. You must be hungry."

Nick picked up a spoon, and hesitated. "How do I know you didn't taint it somehow? Could be you aim to poison me."

Chace reached over and took a slice of bread and dipped it in the beans and then in the peaches. He bit and chewed and swallowed. "Feeling foolish yet?"

"You are a funny boy." Nick scooped up beans and ate with relish. With his mouth full he said, "And you haven't said the message."

"In return for me sending you back alive, Sheriff Wyler leaves me be."

About to spoon more beans, Nick laughed. "You've got gall."

"What?"

"It's uppity, you thinking you can tell the sheriff what to do." Nick shook his head. "He's the one wearing the badge." He folded a slice of bread and dipped it in the bean sauce. "You could help your cause another way, though."

"I'm listening," Chace said.

"Give yourself up and come back with me. I promise you can keep your hands free and your pistols until we get there. You turn yourself in, the judge might be more lenient."

"Life behind bars instead of a necktie social? That's your idea of lenient?"

"It's better than being on the run. And you'd be doing your clan the best favor you could."

"I must have overlooked that part."

Nick spooned peaches into his mouth and smiled in delight. "If there's anything I like more than peaches, I have yet to come across it." He motioned in the general direction of the dunes. "That Harkey out there is one of a hundred or better who want your blood spilled more than they want anything in this world."

"Tell me something I don't know."

"How about this?" Nick lowered the spoon. "So long as you're free, the Harkeys won't rest until they've found you and bucked you out in gore."

"I say again, tell me something I don't know."

"Have you thought about what it will cost the rest of the Shannons? You've ignited the feud again, boy. There's already been killings on the main street of Ware-agle and it won't stop there. It will be the old days all over again. The Harkeys will take out their anger at you on your kin. Bushwhacking. Raids in the nights. Cabins burned. Shannons go missing with no clue." Nick thrust the spoon at Chace. "Is that what you want?"

"I was hoping the Harkeys would blame me and leave the rest of my kin alone."

"You're hoping wrong. But if you come back and turn yourself in, the Harkeys won't have cause to keep the feud going. The killing will stop."

"I don't know," Chace said.

"I'm telling you it's for your own good."

A clatter from outside drew Chace to the window. A buckboard was approaching along the rutted track into town. Zeke was handling the teams. In the bed of the buckboard was a large crate. Chace turned and looked at Floyd. "It will be soon."

Floyd nodded.

Nick went on eating. He finished the beans and scooped up the last of the peaches and cleaned the plate with the slice of bread. Patting his stomach, he sat back and said, "That was damn decent of you, Shannon."

"You may not think so after I set you straight on a few things." Chace leaned against the wall. "To start, all that talk about the Harkeys is hogwash. I turn myself in, the feud will go on anyway. It's not just me they want dead. It's all the Shannons."

"It wouldn't hurt to try."

"That's like saying to a buck that it won't know if the hunter will shoot until it steps in front of the rifle. The Harkeys hate me and mine. I see now that it was wrong of me to run off. I need to get back and finish what I started."

Deputy Fulsome stood. "Like hell. Unless you kill me, I'm placing you under arrest. You're going back with me to stand trial. Will you come along peaceably?"

"Not today. Not tomorrow. Not ever." Chace turned. "Floyd, let's get it done."

"Get what done?" Nick asked.

Floyd stepped to the door and said, "Now." Other boys filed in, seven, eight, nine, ten of them, the biggest and oldest of the hawkers. At a nod from Chace they spread into a ring around the lawman.

"What is this?" Fulsome said. "What are you up to?"

"I have those Harkeys to take care of and I can't have you meddling. So I'm getting you out of Galveston." Chace grinned. "Will you come along peaceably?"

Nick glared at the boys who had surrounded him. "Go to hell and take the rest of these pups with you."

"I was thinking New Orleans." Chace nodded at the boys. "All of you at once."

"We should just shoot him," a large boy said.

"You'll do as I tell you, Harold."

"I agree with him," Floyd said.

Chace sighed. "Do I still run things or not?"

"You do."

"Then all together, if you please."

The boys swarmed Nick Fulsome. They piled on the deputy and grabbed at his arms and legs and attempted to wrestle him to the floor. For a few moments it appeared they would succeed; Nick acted surprised that they would dare try. Then he exploded into movement. He tore his right arm free of the two boys holding it and punched each in the face with two swift blows. Pivoting, he clubbed the boy holding his left arm and once his arms were free he beat at the others while kicking out with his legs. The next instant he was free and in a boxing stance, and when Harold came at him and sought to wrap his arms around his, Nick slammed several punches that knocked Harold back. Whirling, Nick blocked a swing by another boy and unleashed an uppercut that sent him tottering.

A path to the doorway was clear and Nick took a bound but before he could get any farther another boy tackled him and down they crashed. Nick lashed out with a boot to the face and was about to rise when four more piled on top of him. In a melee of fists and feet, Nick made it to his knees. He punched a boy in the gut. He slugged another. He heaved upright and turned to the doorway again only to have a pair of husky boys come at him from either side. They imitated his boxing stance and traded a flurry of hits that ended with the boys bloody and backing off and Nick sidling toward the door. Harold barred his way. Nick sought to batter him down by brute force but Harold was the biggest of all the boys and absorbed the punishment. Several others leaped to help him. Nick became a whirlwind.

The thud of punches was constant. A boy cried out and went down with a broken nose. Another gripped his knee and buckled. Nick was almost to the door.

That was when Chace unfolded and drew both Lightnings. He came up unnoticed and slipped behind the lawman and slammed the right-hand revolver against the back of Nick's head and then the left-hand revolver and the right and the left and Nick took a faltering step and collapsed, unconscious. Chace slid the pistols into his pockets. "Truss him," he commanded.

Rope and a gag were produced and presently Deputy Nick Fulsome was bound wrists and ankles and gagged tight.

Chace studied the ropes. "This ain't enough. When he comes to he'll raise a ruckus. We have to make it so he can't move. Bend his legs back and up and tie them to his arms." The boys jumped to comply and he added, "Don't bend them more than you have to. I don't want him hurt."

Zeke entered and took one look and said, "What hit you fellas? A hurricane?"

"He's a scrapper," Harold said, with a nod at Fulsome.

"Wish I'd have been here," Zeke said. "I love a good fight more than I love food."

When they were done Chace had them bring water and when a girl put a glass in his hand he poured it over the lawman's face.

Nick's eyes snapped open. He tried to speak but all that came out was muffled grunts. He tried to move and couldn't.

"You are hog-tied." Chace stated the obvious. "I have a few words to say and then we'll be on our way." He sat and rested his elbows on his knees and his chin in his hands. "You're the law and you do what you have to. I understand that. I even admire you a bit. You've been honest with me, so I'll be the same with you." He paused. "I thought that by running off I'd spare my ma and my sisters from having to . . ."

Nick raised his head and tried to talk again, his muffled sounds loud and urgent. He shook his head and bobbed it at Chace over and over.

"You have something to say?"

Nodding vigorously, Nick said the same thing half a dozen times. The gag made it hard to understand, but the word sounded like "Ma."

Chace said, "Take the gag off."

"But—" Floyd began.

"I want to hear. You can put it back on, after. Take it off. Now."

Reluctantly, Floyd pried and tugged. "There."

Nick coughed and ran his tongue over his lips. "Damn you," he said. "Damn all of you for doing this to me."

"Did you have something to say or was this a trick?" Chace asked.

Nick looked at him. "It hit me while you were talking. You haven't heard, have you?"

"Heard what?"

"I wish I didn't have to be the one to break it to you."

"Break what, damn it?"

"About your ma and your sister and your cabin."

The color drained from Chace's face. "You're saying something happened to them after I left?"

"The cabin was burned to the ground. The sheriff found two fresh graves and had the bodies dug up." Nick stopped. "I'm sorry, boy. One was your ma and the other was your sister."

"No," Chace said softly.

The assembled hawkers were stones. Tallulah started toward Chace but Zeke grabbed her arm and shook his head.

Chace coughed and said something.

"I didn't catch that," Nick said.

"Which sister was it the sheriff found?"

"Oh. The older one, Scarlet."

"How were they killed? Shot? Stabbed? What?"

"He didn't say and I didn't think to ask."

"What about Cassie?"

"There was no sign of your twin. We have no idea where she got to. The sheriff thought that maybe the

Harkeys got hold of her but if so they are keeping it a secret."

"And my grandpa?"

"There was no sign of him, either. Could be he went back to his place in the mountains. The sheriff was going to send someone to look for him about the time I left to come find you."

Chace walked to the window. He clasped his hands behind his back and stood staring out a good long while. Finally he turned. "I reckon I don't need to talk to the sky anymore."

"The sky?"

"Nothing," Chace said.

"Again, for what it's worth, I'm sorry."

"I appreciate that. I truly do." Chace laughed a strange sort of laugh.

"What's so funny?"

"You're not nearly as sorry as the Harkeys are going to be."

30

The *Memphis Belle* was a schooner. She was old but well kept by her owner and captain, who was twice as old and refused to give up sails when many of his salty breed turned to steam engines. A two-master, the *Memphis Belle* could cruise at eleven knots when the wind was right. She never lacked for cargo as her owner had a reputation for braving the worst of seas and always getting through.

The buckboard rattled to a stop at the dock and Chace jumped down from the seat. "Stay here," he said to Zeke and the boys in the bed. He crossed the dock to the gangplank and was about to go up it when a stern voice stopped him.

"That'll be far enough, lad."

Out of the shadow of the quarterdeck came a bulky man in a sea coat that was gray like his hair. He had on a seaman's cap and a pipe jutted from his slash of a mouth. He puffed a wreath of smoke.

"I'm looking for Captain Schumacher," Chace said.

"That would be me." Schumacher stopped at the

gangway and regarded the buckboard and the boys. "What is that you've got there?"

"A crate."

"I can see that." Schumacher took the pipe from his mouth and tapped the stem on the rail. "Would you be thinking I'm weak in the head?"

"No, sir," Chace said. "I've heard you are anything but. That you are a man of your word, and honest, to boot."

"Flattery, lad, never falls on deaf ears." Schumacher uttered a rumbling chuckle. "Now, then, since you're here on business, suppose you explain its nature."

"I've heard you're fixing to sail on the next tide."

"That we are," Schumacher confirmed. He gazed at the bay and at the shore. "In less than half an hour. All our cargo is on board and we're ready to lift sail."

"Have you room for one more crate?"

Schumacher came down the gangplank. As he did, sailors appeared at the rails, hard, sun-weathered men watching their captain and Chace and the boys with the sharp eyes of ospreys.

"That's a big one, lad."

"It's for the dog," Chace said.

Schumacher's bushy eyebrows met over his nose. "Did you just say you have a dog in there?"

"Yes, sir. I'm sending it to my aunt in New Orleans." Chace pointed at the crate. "You can see the air holes we made."

Schumacher moved to the bed. Floyd and Harold and the other boys clambered out the back and stood as meek as a church choir. Schumacher raked them with a hard look and said, "Haven't I seen some of you lads somewhere?"

Chace said quickly, "You might have if you get around town. They're friends of mine."

The captain leaned on the buckboard and put an eye to an air hole. "These are so tiny I can't see anything."

"There are enough of them the dog should breathe fine."

Schumacher thumped the crate twice with his fist and when nothing happened he thumped it again. "Awful quiet animal you've got in here, lad."

"I muzzled him," Chace said. "Otherwise he'd yap up a storm."

"Even so," Schumacher said.

"I was also worried about him getting sick so I had an animal doc give him something."

"A veterinarian?"

"Is that what they call them? The doc said Nick will mostly sleep the first couple of days."

"Is that the dog's name? Nick?" Schumacher gave the crate another thump. "Why didn't you use a cage?"

"I was told dogs had to be in crates when you ship them," Chace said. "Was I told wrong?"

"I suppose it doesn't matter."

"You'll take him, then?"

"So long as you understand that sending an animal on a ship is a risk. Any animal. Some don't take to it. I'll treat it the best I can but I refuse to be held to blame if it dies on the passage."

"I won't hold it against you." Chace pulled out a roll of bills. "How much do I owe you?"

"Thunderation, lad. Where does someone your age get that much money?"

"I work three jobs."

"Three?" Captain Schumacher repeated, and smiled

warmly. "I like that. It shows character. Too many young people today are too damn lazy." He tapped the crate. "Twenty dollars should do it."

"I'll pay forty for a favor," Chace said.

"What kind of favor?"

"When you're two days out will you open the crate and let Nick have some air and give him a little exercise?"

"I can have one of my crew do it," Schumacher offered. "And you don't need to pay extra."

"That's nice of you."

"I've owned a few dogs in my time."

Captain Schumacher put two fingers in his mouth and whistled and several sailors hustled down the gangplank. Schumacher only had to flick a finger and they slid the crate from the buckboard and carried it on their shoulders onto the ship.

Chace paid, and Schumacher held out his hand. A single shake, and the captain wheeled and stuck the pipe back in his mouth and strode back up the gangplank.

Zeke and Floyd and Harold stepped up to Chace.

"That was a neat trick," Zeke complimented him. "You're as fast between your ears as you are with your hands."

"I like that part about the dog," Harold said. "How do you think of things like that?"

Chace shrugged. "It just comes to me." He had all of them climb on the wagon. Zeke took the reins and they clattered up the street.

"What now?" Zeke asked.

"We take the buckboard back to Clarence. You go on about your hawking and I do what I have to do."

"We want to help," Zeke said.

"No."

"We owe you," Floyd said.

"No."

"You're being stubborn," Harold said.

"It's still no."

Zeke wouldn't let it drop. "There are three of them to your one. I've seen them. Mean-looking bastards, with bulges under their shirts and the vest the oldest wears. They go heeled."

"They're Harkeys," Chace said. "They'd never go anywhere unarmed, law or no law."

"We could lure them to the Roost," Harold said. "Do to them like we did to the deputy."

"For the last damn time, no, no, and no." Chace shifted in the seat. "You heard the deputy. My ma and my older sister are dead. My pa before them. This is for me to do and only me and I won't hear another word about it."

Fifteen minutes later the buckboard was at the stable and the boys reluctantly drifted off. Chace thanked Clarence and patted Enoch and headed for Madame Bovary's. As he was winding up the gravel to the mansion, a diminutive figure appeared from out of the rosebushes.

"What the blazes are you doing here?"

"Keeping an eye on you," Tallulah said.

"You're worse than fleas."

"Who?"

"All of you." Chace took her hand and led her into a path that wound through the roses. He only went a short way. "You're to go to the Roost and stay there."

"What about the Harkeys?"

"Wonderful."

"They are?"

Chace squatted and put his hands on her shoulders.

"Listen, little one. I can't have you around me now. I have something to do and it's dangerous."

"I care about you."

"And I care about you." Chace smiled and brushed her bangs from her eyes. "Will you do as I ask? Please?"

Tallulah hung her head. "I love you, Chace Shannon," she said softly.

"You're too little to even know what love is."

"I'm twelve, and I do so. Love is when another person is in your heart. Love is when you think of him all the time. Love is when you'd do anything for him, anything at all." She kissed him on the cheek. "I wish I was older. I wish I was your age. Then you'd see."

"I couldn't ever love you more than I love my twin."

"I wouldn't care," Tallulah said. "I'd take what you could give." She kissed him on the other cheek, spun, and raced off.

"Damn life, anyway," Chace said. He stood and returned to the drive and walked up it to the door. The hall was deserted. He went past the paintings and the statue to the pink parlor. It was deserted, too.

"You're early today."

Sasha had come from the other end of the hall. She wore a dress that pushed her cleavage toward the ceiling, and a vanilla scent clung to her hair.

"Where's Madame Bovary?"

"Good to see you, too, you rude lummox. She's where she usually is at this hour, in her glass room with her flowers."

Chace went to go around her but Sasha snatched his arm. "Let go," he said. "I'm in no mood for your silliness."

"Listen, you country—" Sasha got no further.

Chace pulled her to him and kissed her fiercely full on the mouth. He traced her lips with his tongue and cupped her bottom and pulled her against him. Sasha placed her hands on his chest as if to push him back but she didn't push. When he stepped back her cleavage was rising up and down. "I'm no boy."

"No," Sashsa said huskily. "You're a bumpkin who takes liberties."

Chace continued down the hall. At his knock he was bid to enter. Madame Bovary was at the table, sipping tea. She smiled benignly and beckoned.

"What a delightful surprise. It's been days since we last chatted. Come and take a seat."

"I reckon I'll stand." Chace took off his hat and ran a finger along the brim. "I have something important to say."

"Spit it out," Madame Bovary coaxed. "I'm your friend, aren't I? And friends can always talk to friends."

"Yes, you are," Chace acknowledged. "You took me under your wing and gave me a job and for that I'm thankful."

Madame Bovary's features betrayed alarm. "What's this? You sound like you're saying good-bye."

"Not exactly," Chace said. "But if something should happen to me and I don't show up, it has nothing to do with you."

"Now I really am worried. Won't you change your mind and sit a spell and tell me all about it?"

Chace moved to a glass wall that overlooked a grotto with a small pond fed by water cascading over rocks. "I'm too restless to sit. But I'll tell you this. Life is never how we think it is."

"How's that again, dear boy?"

"A year ago I thought I had the world figured out. There was my family and there was the rest of the world. I couldn't trust anyone but kin. Then I came here and met you, and a little girl, and Jason Drake, and I found out good folk are everywhere."

"How sweet of you to say."

"I won't ever say it again. I'm surprised I'm saying it now. I'm not one for wearing my emotions on my sleeve, as my ma used to say."

"Most men don't," Madame Bovary said. "To them it's a weakness, like being female."

Chace watched a hummingbird flit about a feeder. "My ma was strong inside. Stronger than my pa, the truth be known. But I didn't come to talk about her. I came to talk about my twin."

"You don't say," Madame Bovary said. "Twin brother or twin sister?"

"Sister. She's as close to me as my skin. I ran off and left her when I shouldn't have. It could be she'll show up looking for me, and if she does, and you don't hear from me again, I'd like for you to tell her something for me." Chace turned and moved to the table next to his benefactor. "Will you do that?"

"Need you even ask?" Madame Bovary patted his arm.

"Tell her . . ." Chace averted his face. "Tell her I'm sorry we were born brother and sister."

Madame Bovary recoiled. "What a terrible thing to say. I'll tell her no such thing."

"There's more," Chace said. "Tell her I'm sorry we weren't born cousins because cousins can do what we can't ever."

"Marry?" Madame Bovary said, and laughed. "Surely

you're not suggesting that she and you . . ." She swallowed, and said, "Oh my."

Chace bent and kissed her on the brow. He put his hat on and strode to the door.

"Wait. What was that about not hearing from you? What on earth is going on, Chace? What is this about?"

"Playing cards," Chace said.

"A game of poker? I've heard that Jason Drake is teaching you to play."

"I'm talking about life. We are the deck and life is the joker."

"I don't understand."

Chace opened the door. "I'm about to cut the cards. High card, I live. Low card, I don't." And with that he smiled and walked out.

31

The Dirty Molly had a fitting name; the building was streaked with grime. It was on the outskirts of Galveston in a part of town the churchgoing crowd avoided. The rail on the hitch in front was broken, so those who came to slake their thirst tied their mounts to the uprights.

Chace Shannon stood under the overhang of a haberdashery across the street and watched those who came and went. The Dirty Molly and saloons on either side were doing a brisk business. He adjusted his hat and smoothed his frock coat and stuck his hands in the pockets and moved into the street.

It was close to midnight. The streetlamps had been lit, but their glow barely reached the batwings.

Chace took in the bustle. Every table filled with poker players or those bucking the tiger or spinning the wheel of chance. The bar was lined from end to end. Women in saucy dresses moved among men who had drunk too much, enticing them to drink more. A thick cloud of cigar and pipe smoke hung thick in the air.

Pushing on the batwing, Chace went in. He stepped

to the right so his back was to the wall. No one paid any attention. He scanned the tables and the bar.

A dumpling of a woman with lips like cucumbers swayed up to him and winked. "See anything you like, youngster?" Her breath reeked of cheap liquor and her eyes were bloodshot.

"Go away."

She winked again. "That's no way to talk to a lady."

"Show me one and I won't."

"Here, now," the woman said. "I won't be insulted by no sprout. What are you, all of fifteen?"

"What I am," Chace said, "is someone you do not want to rile."

"Oh, really?" She tittered and shammed a scared expression. "Should I faint now or later?"

"Stupid is as stupid does."

The woman crooked a painted nail at him. "I'm warning you. I can have you tossed out on your ear if you're not careful."

Chace locked eyes with her. "Oh, really?" He imitated her sarcasm. "Start the dance and see what happens."

Her throat bobbed and she seemed less sure of herself. "I was only saying, is all. How about you treat me to a drink and we start over?"

"You ever been shot?"

"What? No. What kind of question is that to ask someone?"

"There is going to be shooting. You might want to make yourself scarce," Chace advised.

"No gun talk in the Dirty Molly, you hear?" the woman said, and moved toward the bar.

Chace went on scanning the press of people. He moved along the wall. A loud laugh drew his gaze to the far end of the bar. His face hardened and he started forward. When anyone got in his way he said, "Move." Some did. Some laughed or ignored him until he said, "Look at me." When they did, they moved. Men and women pointed at him, and whispered. He circled several tables until he was ten paces from the end of the bar. Checking over his shoulder, he drew both Lightnings and held them low against his frock coat. Then he yelled, loud and sharp, "Harkeys!"

The two men at the bar turned. Dumfounded, they stared.

The cardplayers and others between Chace and the pair hurriedly moved elsewhere. Quiet fell, save for the bartender, who called out to Chace, "Here, now. What do you think you're doing?"

"Stay out of this."

"I own this place, boy. You don't walk in here and tell me what to do."

"I just did." Chace moved his hands so the ivory-handled Colts were plain to see.

"Oh hell," the bartender said.

Chace took another couple of steps. "Cat got your tongues?"

"Why, it's him himself!" the younger of the pair blurted. "Look there, Newton! And dressed like a gambler!"

"I got eyes, Randy," Newton said.

"There are supposed to be three of you," Chace said. "Where did the other one get to?"

"That's for us to know," Newton said. He set down his glass and lowered his left arm. His right hand was on his hip near a bulge in his shirt.

"I'll find him," Chace predicted.

Newton glowered pure hate. "If'n he don't find you first, boy."

"How come he's wearing gambler clothes?" Randy asked his brother. "Have him tell us that."

"What difference does it make?" Newton snapped. "In a little bit those fancy duds of his will be filled with holes, and him still in them."

"You couldn't let it be," Chace told them.

"Let it be?" Newton practically shouted, and quivered with rage. "Boy, you killed pretty near a dozen of us. You killed the head of our clan and his missus. And you want us to let it be?"

"I left," Chace said. "You didn't have to come after me."

"It's the law of the feud, boy. Didn't your pa ever teach you anything?"

"You Harkeys killed him," Chace said. "Killed my ma and my older sister, too. And now here you are, come all this way to do the same to me."

"So long as there's a Harkey breathing, you'll never be free of it," Newton said. "We'll hound you to the gates of hell if we have to. And when you're dead we'll laugh and piss on your grave."

Randy inched his fingers toward the small of his back. "Piss on your grave," he said, and cackled.

"I should thank you," Chace said.

"For what, you Shannon scum?"

"For showing me the error of my ways. I thought that by leaving, you Harkeys would let my family be. I was wrong. The only way to be sure my kin are safe is if there are no more Harkeys." Chace squared his shoulders. "It's too bad all three of you ain't here."

"Linsey is off seeing someone about you," Randy said.

"Shut up," Newton growled. To Chace he said, "Two of us is enough. You're not Wild Bill Hickok. You can't shoot both of us before we shoot you."

"Did I mention how Ezriah Harkey begged me to put him out of his misery?" Chace said. "Begged and cried and whimpered just like the dog he was."

Randy said, "You son of a bitch." He stabbed his hand behind his back and brought out a Remington revolver.

Chace flashed the Lightnings up and out. He shot Randy in the chest; the younger Harkey was slammed against the bar. Newton had slipped a hand up under his shirt and he streaked a Smith & Wesson from concealment. They fired at the same instant. Chace's slug caught Newton in the shoulder and spun him half around. Newton's slug tore a furrow in Chace's arm.

Even as the thunder of their shots boomed, women screamed and men swore and everyone dived for cover or bolted for the front door.

Randy was straightening. Chace pivoted and shot him in the gut. Then Chace was one of those diving for the floor because Newton had let out a roar of fury and sprayed lead. Chace rolled behind a table. He pushed, upending it, and heard the thunk of a slug. Rearing up, he lost his hat to a shot that nearly took off his head. A shot from Randy, not Newton, still on his feet and still game. Chace fired and Randy was jarred onto his heels. Randy fired and the lead scoured the table. Chace banged off shots from both Lightnings. Newton was reloading. Chace snapped off a shot intended for Newton's heart but it drilled his side. With surprising agility, Newton swung to the top of the bar and leaped over. Chace dropped behind the table.

Screams and oaths continued to rise in panicked chorus. Over by the front door men were shoving and fighting to get out, never mind the women, many of whom had fled to a far corner and were huddled holding one another.

Chace crabbed to a different table, slid around it, and heaved erect. He caught Newton flat-footed, staring at the first table. Newton spun and fired but Chace was a heartbeat quicker. Newton was punched back, recovered, and extended his arm to take deliberate aim. Chace shot him in the neck and scarlet spurted. Chace shot him in the arm. Newton cursed luridly, his face as red as his blood, and took a step nearer, gripping the Smith & Wesson tight in both hands. Newton's revolver banged. He missed. Chace sent two shots as swift as thought. At the second blast, Newton reared onto the tips of his toes. A look of astonishment came over him and he melted to the floor.

Randy was on his knees. Tears of frustration streamed from his eyes as, blinking, he took aim. Chace crouched behind the table to reload, his fingers flying. He heard the shuffle of a foot and rose and banged a shot from his left Lightning.

Randy responded in kind. Chace shot again. Randy shot again. The air was thick with the acrid tang of gun smoke. Chace charged toward the bar. He pointed both pistols and as Randy sighted along the Remington's barrel, Chace shot him in the face. The Lightnings were double-action. Chace didn't need to thumb back the hammers. He squeezed the triggers, squeezed them again.

In the sudden stillness women mewed and sniffled and men swore, but quietly. The people bottlenecked at the door were riveted in morbid fascination.

Chace walked up to the Harkeys. He poked each. Neither moved. Neither appeared to be breathing. He poked them again.

"They're dead, boy," the bartender said. "You done shot the both of them to pieces."

Chace barely heard the words. His ears were ringing. He slowly lowered the Colts. "They're my enemies."

"Not anymore," the bartender said. "They are no one's enemies now."

"The Harkeys killed my ma."

"How's that?"

Chace looked up and opened his mouth to answer. From behind him, from the batwings, came the boom of a revolver. He was knocked forward, blood spurting from his right shoulder, and clutched at the bar. More screams and curses ripped the saloon as he turned. Framed in the doorway was the third Harkey, a smoking pistol in his hand.

"You killed them!" Linsey roared. Pushing people aside, he stormed forward. "You killed my brothers!"

Chace raised his right arm but it wouldn't rise high enough. He swept his left arm up as the Harkey took aim.

"For Newton and Randy," Linsey said.

Chace shot him in the groin. Linsey staggered, cursed, jerked his pistol up. Chace shot him again. Linsey sagged to his knees. Chace shot him a third time. Linsey let out a shriek and got off a shot that thudded against the bar. Chace raised his left-hand Lightning and emptied it in Linsey's brainpan.

No one else moved. No one scarcely breathed.

Chace hooked his elbow on the counter and tried to stand. His legs wobbled and he looked at the bartender and grinned. "My insides are molasses," he said and pitched to the floor.

The four-poster bed had a red canopy and an orange frill. The smell of perfume was so strong that when Chace opened his eyes, he sneezed. He gazed sleepily about him. At the foot of the bed stood Jason Drake, talking to Madame Bovary. Sasha was over by the mirror, brushing her hair. Tallulah watched in fascination. In a chair by the bed sat Cassie, her chin on her chest. At the window, peering out, was Jed.

"I reckon I'm seeing things," Chace said.

Cassie squealed and came out of the chair as if catapulted. She enfolded Chace in her arms and kissed both cheeks and his forehead and said, "You're alive! You're alive! You're alive!"

"He won't be if you hug him to death, child," Madame Bovary said, coming around. "Let the poor boy breathe."

Chace stared at a bandage on his shoulder. "Who do I have to thank for mending me?"

"Sasha ran and fetched a doctor after Mr. Drake brought you here," Madame Bovary said. "I paid the doc extra to keep hush about it."

"Sasha did?"

Sasha made a face and went on brushing.

"And it was Jason who brought me?" Chace said.

The gambler nodded. "You have the sprite to thank," he said, patting Tallulah on the head. "She followed you to the Dirty Molly and came to get me."

"But how did she know you and me are friends?"

Tallulah answered for herself. "I've been following you everywhere you go since about the first day we met."

"Why?"

Tallulah looked away.

"And you and Grandpa?" Chace said to Cassie. "Where in blazes did you come from?"

"Arkansas," Cassie said, and giggled. She placed her cheek on his chest. "I'm sorry it took so long but it was slow going. I had to go by my feelings."

Jed said, "She brought us here, sure enough. But we might never have found you except we went to all the stables. I figured you'd board Enoch and I was right. The old man there said as how you had a job at Madame Bovary's."

"And here they are," Madame Bovary said.

"I'll be switched." Chace placed his left hand on Cassie's head. "I've missed you more than I can say." He glanced at Drake. "What about the law? Are they after me for the three Harkeys?"

"All the witnesses said you were defending yourself." The gambler grinned. "Besides, I got you out before anyone wearing a badge showed up, and no one there knew who you were."

"I did it, then," Chace said.

"Now all you need is to decide what to do next," Drake said. "You can come with me and do some river-boat gambling."

"Or we can go back home," Cassie said.

"Even though there's nothing for us there," Jed re-marked.

Chace looked at his grandfather and then at his sister and finally at Tallulah, and smiled.

"Mississippi River, here we come."

"A writer in the tradition of Louis L'Amour and Zane Grey!"

—*Huntsville Times*

National Bestselling Author

RALPH COMPTON

**Available wherever books are sold or at
penguin.com**

GRITTY WESTERN ACTION FROM

USA Today BESTSELLING AUTHOR

RALPH
COTTON

FAST GUNS OUT OF TEXAS

KILLING TEXAS BOB

NIGHTFALL AT LITTLE ACES

AMBUSH AT SHADOW VALLEY

RIDE TO HELL'S GATE

GUNMEN OF THE DESERT SANDS

SHOWDOWN AT HOLE-IN-THE-WALL

RIDERS FROM LONG PINES

CROSSING FIRE RIVER

ESCAPE FROM FIRE RIVER

FIGHTING MEN

HANGING IN WILD WIND

Available wherever books are sold or at
penguin.com

S909

From
Frank Leslie

THE KILLERS OF CIMARRON
After outlaws steal a cache of gold and take a
young woman hostage, Colter Farrow is back on
the vengeance trail, determined to bring the woman
back alive—and send the killers of Cimarron
straight to hell.

THE GUNS OF SAPINERO
Colter Farrow was just a skinny cow-puncher when
the men came to Sapinero Valley and murdered his
best friend, whose past as a gunfighter had caught
up with him. Now, Cole must strap on his
Remington revolver, deliver some justice, and
make a reputation of his own.

THE KILLING BREED
Yakima Henry has been dealt more than his share of
trouble—even for a half-white, half-Indian in the
West. Now he's running a small Arizona horse ranch
with his longtime love, Faith, and thinks he may
have finally found his share of peace and prosperity.
But a man from both their pasts is coming—with
vengeance on his mind...

**Available wherever books are sold or at
penguin.com**

Charles G. West

"RARELY HAS AN AUTHOR PAINTED THE
GREAT AMERICAN WEST IN STROKES SO
BOLD, VIVID AND TRUE."
—RALPH COMPTON

The Blackfoot Trail

Mountain man Joe Fox reluctantly led a group of
settlers through the Rockies—and inadvertently into
the clutches of Max Starbeau. Max had traveled with
the party until he was able to commit theft and
murder—and kidnap Joe's girl.

Also Available

Storm in Paradise Valley
Shoot-out at Broken Bow
Lawless Prairie
Luke's Gold

Available wherever books are sold or at
penguin.com

S805

No other series packs this much heat!

THE TRAILSMAN

Follow the trail of Penguin's Action Westerns at
penguin.com/actionwesterns   S310

Penguin Group (USA) Online

What will you be reading tomorrow?

Tom Clancy, Patricia Cornwell, W.E.B. Griffin,
Nora Roberts, William Gibson, Robin Cook,
Brian Jacques, Catherine Coulter, Stephen King,
Dean Koontz, Ken Follett, Clive Cussler,
Eric Jerome Dickey, John Sandford,
Terry McMillan, Sue Monk Kidd, Amy Tan,
J. R. Ward, Laurell K. Hamilton,
Charlaine Harris, Christine Feehan...

You'll find them all at
penguin.com

*Read excerpts and newsletters,
find tour schedules and reading group guides,
and enter contests.*

Subscribe to Penguin Group (USA) newsletters
and get an exclusive inside look
at exciting new titles and the authors you love
long before everyone else does.

PENGUIN GROUP (USA)
us.penguingroup.com